DEADLY TIDE

WILLIAM NIKKEL

SUSPENSE PUBLISHING

DEADLY TIDE
By
William Nikkel

PAPERBACK EDITION
* * * * *
PUBLISHED BY:
Suspense Publishing

Cover Design: Shannon Raab
Cover Photographer: shutterstock.com/ Michael Rosskothen
Cover Photographer: Mix Pix Box

PUBLISHING HISTORY:
Suspense Publishing, Print and Digital Copy, August 2021

OTHER BOOKS BY WILLIAM NIKKEL

Jack Ferrell Series
GLIMMER OF GOLD
NIGHT MARCHERS
CAVE DWELLER
MURRIETTA GOLD
BLOOD GOLD
SHIPWRECK
SAILOR TAKE WARNING
SEA OF HEARTBREAK
HOSTILE WATERS

Max Traver Series
DEVIL WIND
DANCE WITH THE DEVIL

Novellas
TIBETAN GOLD

To the brave men of the USS Indianapolis.

ACKNOWLEDGMENTS

As always, a big thank you goes to my wife Karen for her invaluable input and contributions to the story—including putting up with me.

And of course, no novel would be read without a publisher bringing the story to light. Thanks to John and Shannon Raab and the dedicated people at Suspense Publishing for their insights and hard work.

And to my brother Ray for his colorful suggestions.

To my neighbor and first reader, Jim Jackson.

And I'd like to extend a special thank you to the brave men and women of the military, past and present, for all you sacrifice to keep the country safe.

PRAISE FOR *DEADLY TIDE*

"Gripping and scary, the best thriller of this kind I've read since *Jaws*. Nikkel is a born storyteller."
—No. 1 Bestselling Thriller Author, Peter James

"A compelling tale, layered with suspense, all unfolding within the intriguing ambiance of Hawaii. What more could a reader want?"
—Steve Berry, International Bestselling Author of *The Kaiser's Web*

"Using his talent for mystery and authenticity, William Nikkel has crafted a wild and thrilling story about the hidden dangers that lurk beneath the ocean waves. Let's hope this nerve-wracking tale remains nothing more than fiction!"
—Boyd Morrison, #1 *New York Times* Bestselling Author

"Submersibles, sharks, suspense—Nikkel delivers his most entertaining *Jack Ferrell Adventure* story yet! The research is steeped in authenticity, the dialogue sizzles. Think *Jaws* on steroids. Truly sensational!"
—K.J. Howe, International Bestselling Author of *SKYJACK*

"*Deadly Tide* is every bit as good, and in many ways better, than the very best of Clive Cussler's seagoing adventures. William Nikkel's latest effort to feature Jack Ferrell is his most ambitious and accomplished yet, staking his claim to a spot in the highest echelon of thriller writers. Readers looking for thrills and spills of the highest order will find plenty of both in this roaring, rollicking humdinger of a high-stakes tale."

—Jon Land, *USA Today* Bestselling Author

"Dr. Jack Ferrell often finds himself in hot water, but this time trouble lurks beneath the surface. William Nikkel's *Deadly Tide* is a pulse pounding thriller that delivers."

—Bruce Robert Coffin, Award-Winning Author of the *Detective Byron Mysteries*

"From deep in the Pacific Ocean to the shallow water off Waikiki Beach, *Deadly Tide* is an all-thrilling adventure with high-stakes danger. Fast paced and tautly written, it will leave you never wanting to swim in the ocean again."

—Gary Braver, bestselling author of *Tunnel Vision* and, with Tess Gerritsen, *Choose Me*

"Jack Ferrell, an intriguing cross between Travis McGee and James Bond, rocks *Deadly Tide*, the tenth novel in William Nikkel's popular adventure series. While Ferrell doesn't seek danger, it always finds him. In this case, it comes in the form of deadly sharks. Nikkel expertly ramps up the level of suspense from the first page to the last. It's a page-turner, a stay-awake-all-night thriller, a shark adventure that sends shivers up your spine. I couldn't put it down. I highly recommend *Deadly Tide* for readers who enjoy mysteries, thrillers, and adventures."

—Jo-Ann Carson

DEADLY TIDE

A *JACK FERRELL ADVENTURE*

WILLIAM NIKKEL

CHAPTER 1

PRESENT DAY
The floor of the Philippine Sea

Three inches of titanium steel separated Jack Ferrell from certain death three and a half miles beneath the surface of the ocean.

His only portal into this silent world of perpetual darkness came from a cone of light extending ninety meters into the black abyss. The sphere of titanium he and the two-man crew huddled inside of provided the only protection from the immense pressure at this extreme depth. Mounted on the front of the deep-submergence vehicle, or DSV, two manipulator arms, resembling the front legs of a praying mantis, hung secured out of the way of his viewing port.

He placed his full confidence in the Navy's most advanced manned deep-ocean research submersible and checked his watch. *Alvin* had been descending for an hour and a half. The bottom had to be coming up soon.

Commander Carl Richards who piloted the DSV said to Jack, "Relax, we're almost there."

Jack averted his gaze from the port in front of him. "You noticed me glance at my watch?"

Richards continued to study his instruments. "You know what they say about a watched pot. You're better off enjoying the view and forgetting about the time. That's my job."

Jack refocused his attention, squinting into the abyss. "I'm anxious to see her but I'm far from bored. This is one trip I never dreamed I'd be making, and wouldn't be now if Admiral Casey hadn't made it possible."

"You're indeed lucky," Richards said. "Extremely lucky. The *USS Indianapolis* is designated a war grave. No one is allowed to explore or salvage the wreckage except the military. In fact, the exact location of her is classified a secret."

"How deep are we?"

"Passing eighteen thousand feet." Richards spoke into his mic, a status report to the support vessel *Atlantis IV* hovering on the surface, as much as in response to Jack's question. "The ship should be coming into view any minute."

Jack peered into the gloom at the farthest reach of *Alvin*'s LED light array and watched the *USS Indianapolis* materialize out of the darkness a section at a time. The wreckage was too large for the lights to illuminate all of the debris at one time.

He took a deep breath in response to the cruiser's remains unveiled before him. "Unbelievable."

"I thought the same thing the first time I saw her. As you can see, many of the ship's guns are still in place."

Twin barrels aimed skyward appeared in the gloom as though prepared for battle. Jack pointed, the tip of his finger tapping the glass he peered through. "Those are the forty-millimeter antiaircraft guns, aren't they?"

"Still loaded and ready to rock and roll, though I doubt they'll fire." Richards chuckled at his apparent attempt at humor. "I'll take you over the eight-inch gun turret mounted on the stern. The two forward turrets broke off, along with a large portion of the bow, before the ship sank. They lay a mile and a half east of this location."

Jack shook his head in disbelief at the twisted armor plating. "It's incredible she remained afloat as long as she did when you see the amount of damage those torpedoes did to her hull."

"You know the story?" The question came from Ed Ramsey, the engineer seated at the porthole on the opposite side of Commander Richards.

Jack kept his face pressed to the viewing port; his gaze glued to the surreal scene unfolding before his eyes. "Everyone who has watched the movie *Jaws* knows the story. Though Quint failed to point out that, in addition to shark attacks, many of the men who went into the water succumbed to injuries they suffered in the explosions aboard ship, as well as drowning, dehydration, exposure, and salt poisoning from drinking sea water."

"I've read the official file on the Navy's findings, survivor accounts included," Richards said. "Delirium and hallucinations even caused sailors to kill themselves. Some stabbed and drowned shipmates who were believed to be the enemy. But the shark threat was real enough and that's what everyone remembers."

"Oceanic whitetips being the main culprits," Jack added. "Undoubtedly some tigers, too. But they would most certainly have fed on the corpses first."

He studied the dead ship and pictured the crew adrift in the sea; bunched together in tight groups spread out over a hundred miles of open ocean. He heard their screams pierce the night, imagined sailors without lifejackets, desperate to survive, stripping the dead of theirs. Everyone thirsty. Dorsal fins slicing the water. Each man praying, wondering if he would be taken next.

So many had.

He pinched his lids closed, but couldn't rid himself of the vision.

Nothing would take their faces away.

When he opened his eyes, more of the cruiser came into view. He leaned close to the glass and studied the wreckage. "Quint might have had a much different story if the sinking happened today. Due to the long-line commercial fishing industry and the shark fin trade in Asia, oceanic whitetips have all but vanished from these waters."

Ramsey said, "I understand that's why you're on this dive?"

"Partly," Jack said. "Some of my colleagues in the field consider me an authority on sharks. It's only fitting I get a first-hand look at the disaster that gave the creatures a bad name."

"The sharks gave themselves the bad name."

Jack couldn't entirely disagree with the man. Sharks were certainly savage killers.

He said, "That's one way of looking at it. But they were here millions of years before man stood upright and roamed the continents. We're the trespassers in their environment; they're only doing what they've evolved to do. That's to eat when a food source presents itself."

"Like a bunch of sailors thrashing around in the water."

Asking or telling? Jack wondered.

He said, "Oceanic whitetips are frequently seen in the Red Sea, off the Cayman Islands, and around Hawaii. But the sightings are usually lone individuals or very small schools called shivers. Cat Island in the Bahamas appears to be the last place on earth where large concentrations of the species can be found. Though ten years of tagging has shown far fewer inhabit those waters than researchers first thought. We all know it's impossible to rewind time and recapture what's been lost, but we have to try. The world believed the unspoiled seas of the 1950s teemed with an inexhaustible supply of fish, but now we can't comprehend that naïve idea."

The explanation garnered a grunt from Ramsey and nothing more.

It seemed the man's mind was made up.

Jack let it go.

Richards said, "We're coming up on the ship's bell."

A dozen feet ahead, the artifact lay visible in the pool of light illuminating the twisted metal.

He felt *Alvin* hover, and watched as the pilot maneuvered the right arm's pincers to almost the full length of the boom, grasp the bell, and pluck the object free of the wreckage with the care of a loving mother lifting her baby from its crib.

As deftly as the manipulator arm had seized the prize, it withdrew and deposited the artifact into a metal bin mounted on the DSV's outer skin.

"Egg is in the basket," Richards relayed into his mic. "Leaving the *Indy* and making a pass over the debris field."

Jack leaned back and rubbed the strain from his eyes. The entire operation was being viewed by the men and women crowded around the live digital feed displayed on monitors in the lab aboard the support vessel. A visual documentation of the dive from beginning to end.

The next best thing to being there.

Which made what he was doing all that more special. Nothing compared to cruising the bottom of the ocean eighteen-thousand feet down and watching it unfold before him.

A surrealistic adventure come true.

After a few seconds of quiet, Richards asked, "What do you think of her, Doctor Ferrell? Is the *Indy* everything you imagined?"

He struggled for the words to do justice to his overwhelming elation. Impossible to describe in the moment.

He met Commander Richards' gaze. "She's so much more."

A pathetic understatement, he realized.

He faced the viewing port. Nine hundred men went into the water. Four and a half days later, three hundred and sixteen men came out of the sea alive.

Quint had been technically correct.

Sharks took the rest.

CHAPTER 2

Waikiki Beach, Oahu, Hawaii

Fifteen-year-old Amy Watson straddled her surfboard riding up and down on the ocean swells rolling under her. Her long legs dangled freely beneath the surface of the clear water. Her waist-length brown hair, together with her long-sleeved rash guard, protected her from the worst of the mid-March sun.

Though early in the year, the daytime temperatures hovered in the low eighties. Had for several days. And with no wind and a near cloudless blue sky, the weather felt plenty hot. She reached down beside her and splashed water on her face and body until she was soaked.

She'd grown up a block from Laguna Beach and felt at ease in the water. Though she respected the dangers lurking in the depths, she had no real fear of them. In Southern California or here on Oahu; her home for the past three years. A line of surfers extended the length of the beach in both directions. Six floated astraddle boards no more than fifty feet away from her, including Alika, the cute seventeen-year-old boy she met on the beach an hour earlier.

She waved. "Alika."

The boy dropped to his stomach and paddled in her direction. Hair nearly as long as hers and shiny black, clung to his brown skin. He sat up, spun his board, and drifted another couple of feet.

He shook the water from his hair, spattering her in the process, and combed it back with his fingers. "What's up?"

She liked the way the drops rolled off his muscled shoulders and arms and down his flat stomach. And when she peered into his dark eyes, she lost herself in them in a way she hadn't with any of the other boys she had met.

Tingling with nervous excitement, she asked, "Would you like to go to an Easter costume party next weekend? My friend Kayla has invited a few friends over and I thought it would be fun if you came."

He matched her rhythm in the swells. "Do I have to wear a bunny suit?"

She laughed. "You can if you want. Kayla thought it would be fun to have everyone wear a costume. She's dressing up as a colored egg. I'll be a mermaid. It's not exactly an Easter costume, but…"

"That I'd like to see. I'll go dressed as a Hawaiian warrior. But only if you promise—"

A high-pitched scream cut him off. Alika turned toward the sound as she scanned the string of surfers in the group close to them.

Four were paddling for shore, arms flailing to catch a wave. Behind them, a yellow board rode up and over a swell, its rider gone.

Her mind was mired in confusion.

And apparently so was Alika's because he sat completely still, staring across the water.

Then the lone board began to move against the flow of the waves, towed by the ankle leash.

"Shark," Alika yelled.

His wild eyes met hers an instant before he dropped onto his stomach and began paddling toward shore.

His foot brushed her leg, turning her broadside into an oncoming wave that rolled her into the water. Separated from her surfboard, connected only by the leash Velcroed around her ankle, she sputtered to the surface. She could swim like a fish. That wasn't what worried her.

For the first time, she felt fear she hadn't believed possible.

Adrenaline shot through her body, urging her back onto her board. She reeled it in by the tether and grabbed hold, only to be bumped off.

At first, she thought she may have merely lost her grip in her frantic splashing to climb back on. She tried again and this time was jerked under water. There was no pain. Only a violent tug on her left leg.

She watched a dark shape glide away. Not huge, but big enough. Maybe six feet long.

Oh my God.

And then she saw a second shape.

This one even larger.

Much larger.

Pain and panic set in at the same time.

Her head and arms burst from the surface amid overwhelming desperation for survival. Gasping for air, she screamed and groped for her board, and this time pulled it under her. With no thought to the severity of her injuries, she paddled toward shore no more than fifty yards away.

A dorsal fin sliced the water in front of her.

Another broke the surface a second later.

Then…yet another.

She could see a line of white where the surge washed up onto the beach. She could see people standing on the sand, their eyes turned toward her, arms waving her ashore, fingers pointing. She could hear their yells.

Shock threatened to overtake her.

She didn't let it.

A wave rolled under her and she stayed with it. Flat on her stomach, she rode it toward shore.

Toward help.

CHAPTER 3

The Philippine Sea

Jack stood on the deck of *Atlantis IV* and stared at the surface of the Pacific. Behind him a team of technicians swarmed over *Alvin* checking and rechecking every component. Standard procedure after a dive the magnitude of the one he had made. For the past ten minutes, he tried to imagine the horrors of war that took place on these now tranquil waters. Three and a half miles beneath him lay a grim reminder.

And he'd gotten a close-up look at reality.

One he'd never forget.

"Have you seen any?"

Jack turned at the sound of Richards' voice. "What's that?"

"Sharks. Have you seen any?"

"Not a one. But then I haven't exactly been looking."

Richards pointed a stout cigar at the water. "Hard to imagine, isn't it—all those men cast adrift out there?"

Jack estimated Richards' age to be thirtysomething. His ruddy complexion and the fat stogie made *Alvin*'s pilot look older. He scanned the water. "No one can. Except those men who survived it."

Richards puffed and exhaled a blue cloud. "Ed kind of got under your skin, didn't he?"

"Maybe a little. I got the feeling he resented me being along on the dive."

"Or perhaps your connection with Admiral Casey."

"Whatever his problem is, it's no big deal."

"I'm glad to hear that. He can be a jerk at times, but he's a good man."

"I never thought otherwise."

Jack noticed a sailor he didn't know by name, approach. A determined stride. Strictly business. He gave him his full attention.

"Doctor Ferrell, sir." The sailor started to say more but Jack stopped him with a raised palm.

"I'm not a *sir*. Call me Jack."

"Yes, sir. Captain Conner needs to speak to you. She's on the bridge."

"Thank you. I'll be right there."

"I'll let the captain know." The sailor strode away with the same purposeful stride.

Richards pulled the cigar from his mouth and looked at Jack. "Better not keep the captain waiting."

"I don't plan to."

Jack climbed the stairs to the bridge and found Captain Cheryl Conner seated, staring through the windscreen. She turned her piercing gray eyes at his approach. He didn't waste his time saluting or standing at attention. He wasn't military.

"You asked to see me, Captain?"

Her attention on him, she said, "We received a message from the director of the NOAA office on Oahu."

"Megan O'Connell?"

"Your boss requested you return immediately. Arrangements have been made to have a seaplane pick you up and fly you to Manila where you'll catch a commercial flight back to Oahu."

"I assume the director has a ticket waiting for me?"

Conner handed him a sheet of paper. "Here's your itinerary."

Jack looked it over and checked his watch. "How long do I have before the plane gets here?"

"A couple hours."

"I don't understand the urgency. Did she mention what was so important?"

"No. Only that she needs you back there right away."

He thought it odd that his boss chose to keep him guessing, but figured she had her reasons for not passing along more information.

"Thank you, Captain. I'll be ready."

He stepped from the bridge, unable to imagine what was so vitally important it had O'Connell chomping at the bit. He didn't like having to leave *Atlantis IV* so soon, but he knew his duty and he felt he owed her. She had been more than understanding when she allowed him time away from his obligations to NOAA so he could sail the islands with Cherise Venetta. Time they used to heal the spirit. To get to know each other and themselves.

And afterward.

Admiral Casey and a new alliance. Cherise, who accepted his deep feelings for her and hers for him, while at the same time recognizing each other's need for independence. A boat to replace the one he'd lost…a renewed focus.

Much had changed for him in the past six months.

All of it good.

A new lease on life.

That's how he viewed it.

Though the romantic relationship had settled into one of random lust-filled rendezvous, he and Cherise had an understanding.

One they were both comfortable with.

And now this. The rare opportunity to see the *USS Indianapolis* up close and pay his respects to the men who went down with the ship; not to mention, those who perished in the sea; as well as those who lived.

All of them heroes.

When they left the island of Tinian, their mission complete, they had no idea what awaited them.

Any more than he did.

CHAPTER 4

Waikiki Beach, Oahu, Hawaii

From the helm of his twenty-eight-foot boat, Devlin Maxwell studied the beach through a pair of binoculars pressed to his eyes. On shore, a couple of hundred yards away, sirens wailed. Bystanders scrambled toward the water, caught up in the human desire to get a close-up look at what was going on.

He smiled at the panic that ensued; the lure of morbid curiosity strong among the spectators crowding the shoreline. He knew the beach would be packed with tourists and locals alike during Easter break. The young surfers behaved as though they were invincible. A few probably believed they were.

Especially when in a group of their peers.

He scowled at their youthful stupidity and continued to watch the mayhem play out on the beach. Not in horror and not out of compassion for the injured.

What drew him to the scene was a warm sense of satisfaction that the renewed impetus for state legislation to protect sharks of all species in Hawaiian waters would meet defeat, as people's love for sharks turned to blood lust.

Each and every do-gooder on the islands—even the staunchest shark-lover—would have no choice but to succumb to public fear and a demand to have the predators killed.

Two years earlier, he would never have dreamed of exacting revenge on anything or anybody. He had a home and a family. But that was before a shark killed his son Aaron, barely sixteen-years-old, and a surfer like most kids his age.

Like these kids.

His only son didn't have to die. The surfers on boards close to him could have saved his life. Instead, they fled to shore in fear and he was left behind.

Alone. Injured.

Defenseless against the shark.

The M.E. determined Aaron had drowned before the shark fed on him. Some consolation, though he would never have drowned if the shark hadn't attacked in the first place.

"We're sorry," the experts said. "The attack was a freak accident of nature."

With those words, his son's death became nothing more than a statistic in their records.

No family pictures of him on their desks. No fond memories of the child growing up. Only a few strokes on a keyboard, and even *that* would be lost in the obscurity of time.

But he would not let his son's death go unavenged.

Now the parents of these kids would feel the anguish and relive the nightmare over and over the way he had suffered…and suffered still.

On that day, he lost more than his son.

His only child.

He lost his wife Mayuko as well. Unable to live with the horror of knowing their son had been torn to pieces until there was little left of him to bury, she eventually took her own life to free herself of the pain. Leaving him to bear the loss alone.

My wife. My child.

All that was important in my life.

Dead.

Coworkers tried to help—nice men and women he had gotten to know at Manoa Electronics where he worked for the past twelve years. A few even looked the other way when he used company time and materials to work on his project.

Initially, he hadn't set out to exact revenge. Only to use his knowledge in electronics to make sure a death like Aaron's wasn't repeated.

But the pain festered.

An open wound that refused to heal.

The device attracting the sharks that attacked the two young surfers had been the result of a failed attempt to build an electronic shark repellant more effective than those already on the market. A foolproof way to protect divers and swimmers…surfers like his son. But that changed when he saw the water around his device swarm with sharks, frenzied by the desire to feed.

The way they were now.

The way they would again and again for as long as he controlled them.

That first failed attempt, it turned out, had been an epiphany. Only then did he begin to understand the pain of his son's death could never be soothed until the people of Oahu were made to understand his anguish. And the shark that ripped his son to pieces—all sharks—were killed.

Especially, Deep Blue.

A fifty-year-old, pregnant, twenty-foot-long great white that for the past year had invaded the water off the coast of Oahu. Two and a half tons of killing machine. The largest living shark on record. Everyone agreed she was a marvel of evolution. But how could people honestly believe this creature was anything more than a monster fish with one focus? Eating anything that would fit in her huge mouth.

Man or boy.

My boy.

What other people felt, whether pro or con, was of no importance to his quest. He would not rest until he had harpooned the massive shark to death.

Only then would he finally be at peace.

CHAPTER 5

24 HOURS LATER

NOAA Headquarters, Ford Island, Oahu, Hawaii

Jack never expected his boss's call to report back to Oahu. But then he hadn't been surprised by it, either. Trouble, it seemed, always had a way of seeking him out.

He had his Uber driver drop him off on Ford Island next to a sign that read National Oceanic Atmospheric Administration Pacific Islands Fisheries Science Center. Freshly painted since the last time he was here.

A nice addition.

Exhausted from nearly fourteen hours in the air and wound tight by caffeine and anticipation, he walked into Megan O'Connell's office and dropped his duffle bag on the floor. Every time he saw her, it amazed him how she never seemed to age. Pushing fifty with styled, shoulder-length auburn hair without a single strand of gray, she stood tall, straight, fit, and strikingly pretty.

Good family genes and a no-excuses daily workout regimen that included a 5K run and an hour in the gym, he suspected, had everything to do with that. He knew her routine, because he had been foolish enough to join her on a couple of occasions and regretted doing so.

She rose from her chair and stepped around her desk to greet him. "It's good to see you, Jack. I'm glad you made it."

He stroked his chin, noting the need for a shower and a shave. The aloha shirt he wore on the plane hung creased and limp on his sweaty body. Apparently, she didn't mind.

"You had doubts?"

She let her smile slip and shook her head. "Sorry to have to pull you away from your research aboard the *Atlantis IV*. You know I wouldn't have brought you here if it wasn't important. Would you like some coffee before we get started?"

One more cup wouldn't hurt. "Sounds good. First, tell me what's going on."

She sighed. "Jack, I wish I knew. The distressing truth is we've had a series of shark attacks on several young surfers. Seven have occurred over the past three days that we know of. Yesterday afternoon, a seventeen-year-old boy was killed, and a fifteen-year-old girl was seriously injured. Two other teens sustained bites on Saturday, followed by three more on Sunday. Fortunately, their injuries were minor. When I learned of the attacks over the weekend, I attributed them to chance encounters. After what happened yesterday—the poor boy killed—I can't say that. Sharks don't behave this way. Something unusual is going on."

He felt he could speak freely in that he and Director O'Connell had always been comfortable in their professional relationship. It had been that way for the six plus years he'd worked for her.

"Why do you need me?" He couldn't help thinking to have been pulled away from his research in the middle of the Philippine Sea to get him here seemed a bit drastic. "There are experts at the aquarium who can sort this out for you."

"Save your breath, Jack. They're tied up on a research vessel returning from Antarctica. You were closer. And—don't let this go to your head—you're my first choice."

He arched a brow. "Not sure it's deserved, but I'm flattered."

She gave a mild chuckle. "I've always known you were easy."

He grinned and pointed at the carafe sitting on the table next to the wall. "Is that the coffee you mentioned?"

"Help yourself."

He filled a Styrofoam cup, and asked, "Where did these attacks take place?"

She reached behind her and lifted an e-tablet from her desktop. She tapped the screen and a map of Honolulu flared on the monitor mounted to the wall facing her desk. Seven red dots appeared in the waters off Waikiki.

He didn't need to be told what they represented. That the dots were red was telling enough.

He let her talk.

She stepped to the map and aimed a laser pointer. "All seven attacks occurred during daylight hours in clear weather and in shallow water within fifty yards of shore. So far, there have been no reports of shark attacks off any of the other beaches."

"How about the other islands?"

"Nothing in the last year. So far, it's only these seven."

"And these attacks occurred over the past three days? Nothing before?"

"Not that was reported. Any ideas?"

He wished there was an easy answer that would put her mind at ease, but it was too soon for him to say. There simply wasn't enough data. She knew as well as he did that despite their man-eater reputation in books and movies, sharks rarely attacked humans. Data showed they would rather feed on fish and fat-rich marine mammals like seals.

She had been correct to be concerned.

This isn't normal shark behavior.

He studied the screen, his thoughts moving at breakneck speed in the same direction as hers. "What can I say that you don't already know? Sharks are curious creatures by nature. When they see or hear or smell or detect movement that could be a food source, they investigate. That's usually the case when a shark attacks a human. They've also been known to attack when confused. One or both of those scenarios might be the case here. There are always sharks around. People just don't see them. If one saw or heard those surfers splashing in the water, it may have investigated, resulting in an accidental attack."

"So, in your opinion, you think these kids were bitten by accident?"

"I'm saying it's possible."

"What about the boy who was fed on?"

He turned and saw her staring at him. The sunlight streaming through the window lit up a tight expression that made her look older than her years. She sought answers he couldn't give her. That bothered him.

"It's still possible the initial attack was accidental," he said. "But sharks do what they've evolved to do. Their impulse to feed is powerful."

"Right, but you said it yourself; sharks would rather feed on fish and fat-rich marine mammals like seals. So, you understand why I brought you here?"

He turned to the screen. The red dots stared back at him in grim reminder, and he winced at the thought of what the teenager's body had looked like when pulled from the water. He let the vision sink in.

She'd been right to send for him.

He said, "I assure you, we're on the same page here. Something unusual *is* going on."

"I'm glad you agree. Unfortunately, those attacks are only part of the enigma we're faced with. Over the past week, numerous shark carcasses—many of them tigers in the six- to eight-foot range—have washed ashore." She used the laser pointer. "Waikiki, Ewa, Manakuli, Maili, Makaha. More than a dozen total, and that's just what people have reported."

"Killed for their fins?"

She laid the pointer on her desk. "That's what's confusing. A few appeared to have been fed on by other sharks, but otherwise they were in one piece. All we know for sure is they didn't die by natural causes. They were killed and left to drift in the tide. Speared, by the look of the injuries. It's almost as though someone declared open season on sharks."

He nodded at the obvious implication. "You think the seven attacks on the surfers and the rash of shark deaths are connected?"

"I know how you feel when it comes to coincidences. This is one time I have to agree. It's no fluke they coincide with each other."

A further complication to the issue.

He stroked his beard stubble. "Sort of a question of who's hunting who? And which occurred first. I'm sure Waikiki Beach has been closed to swimmers?"

"As of yesterday, but it's spring break. Kids are out of school and the beaches are crowded with tourists all wanting to get into the water. It'll be impossible to keep them out for long."

It was easy for him to imagine the disgruntled crowds of tourists gathered on the sand. He pictured the throngs of young people with their bulletproof attitudes urging the defiant ones to take their chances in the water.

He said, "All we can do is hope the lifeguards and police patrolling the beach are able to make people understand the danger."

"That's a given. But as you know, there are always fools who will refuse to heed the warning."

He considered the full ramifications of what she was saying. Viewers see those idiots in the movies. People hear about them in the news. Clearly, the situation would likely get far worse before it got better.

He said, "I take it there's no shortage of political pressure to resolve this mess and get the beach open?"

She nodded a slow show of exasperation. "I've received no less than two calls from the governor, himself. Immediately is not soon enough for him."

"Meaning I need to find out what's going on, and fast?"

"That's why you're here."

Indeed, he thought, which put him in the eye of the political shitstorm as well.

The bottom of the proverbial hill that crap rolls down.

"I'm sure the news is making the most out of this?"

"Every channel. But you know how stupid people can be."

He drew in a deep breath and let it out. A crisis like this would be all the catalyst the nutcases on the island would need to raise the alarm. Global warming. A message from God. Alien attack.

The list would be endless.

He gave the map on the monitor a final quick perusal. "Unless you have something more to tell me, there's no reason to stand here rehashing what's been said. Whatever is going on, it's going on out there." He pointed. "That's where I need to be. Any chance I can get a ride to my place?"

She smiled awkwardly and set the e-pad on her desk. "Of course. I'll have Kirby fly you home in the chopper."

"Service with a smile." Jack couldn't resist. "I like that. I'll meet him outside."

He picked up his bag and started to leave the office. Her hand on his arm stopped him. He saw her smile slip.

"Sorry there's nothing more in the way of information that I can pass on to you at the moment. Hopefully, that will change." Her grip tightened. "Keep me informed, Jack. I'm counting on you."

She didn't need to say what was really on her mind.

He knew.

"I won't let you down."

CHAPTER 6

Jack climbed out of the helicopter, ducked beneath the spinning rotors, and waved to the pilot. Kirby gave him a thumbs-up in response, increased power, and lifted off on a course back to Ford Island.

With the rising heat of late morning bearing down on him, he watched the departing chopper grow small in the sky. The craft safely on its way, he turned and walked toward the one-bedroom *ohana* located at the rear of Robert and Kazuko's house on Kaneohe Bay. Other than his boat, the cottage was his home. By choice. Not necessity.

He had met Robert years earlier when the two of them were parking cars at a hotel on West Maui—two young men with a past, like so many of the transplants on the island—before Robert and Kazuko were married.

A tumultuous time—Jack recalled that year with little regret—when he and Ellery Seaport were engaged to be married. The beautiful, manipulative daughter of the mega developer whose unscrupulous real estate schemes would have brought ruination to all the Hawaiian Islands. Back when he found the WWII West Point class ring belonging to William McIntyre.

The pivotal point in his life when he chose to pursue a career in marine biology.

The quest to return the ring to its rightful owner—with no small amount of urging from Robert—had saved him from a horrible mistake. He couldn't imagine the nightmare his life would have been had he married the insatiable Ellery.

Long after the ordeal was over, Robert and Kazuko stood by him. And what began as camaraderie between co-workers grew into a lifelong friendship. They had shared in his adventures, even faced death together. Over time, their cottage had become his home when on Oahu with an added secure dockage for his latest acquisition, *Pono II*—a boat he was particularly proud of. In addition to being a temporary home when his job called for it, the fifty-eight-foot power catamaran served as a floating lab.

He headed there now.

Robert strode toward him from the house. His friend's thick growth of wavy blond hair curled back in the onshore breeze blowing off the water. He wore a faded t-shirt, a pair of ratty cutoffs, and tennis shoes. His normal attire when he had nowhere to be.

The rotor noise faded in the distance, and Jack said, "I'm glad you're home. No doubt you're aware of the recent shark attacks."

"I put two and two together when you called from the Philippines. Seems like trouble always has a way of finding you."

"Don't I know it. My boss wants answers. The governor wants people on Oahu to be allowed back into the water, and I've been dropped into the middle of it all."

"What's the official word?"

"No more than what you've probably heard. Except Meg expects me to figure out why the sharks are behaving the way they are."

Robert walked with him. "This isn't the first shark attack off Oahu's beaches. But never seven in almost as many days. Not that I recall, anyway."

"Nor does anyone else."

Jack lifted his fist to his mouth and fought back a yawn. More than once he had gone without sleep for twenty-four hours straight. Demands of difficult situations. The nap he had on the eleven-hour flight from Manila did little to stave off the exhaustion threatening to drag him down now. In order to keep going, he had resorted to running on caffeine and adrenalin and likely would continue to until the crisis was resolved.

Robert said, "I assume you'll want to clean up. I'll get some coffee going while you shower and change."

"You read my mind."

Thirty minutes later, he joined Robert on the lanai at the rear of his house. Rebel lay sprawled with her rear legs stretched out behind her, front legs forward, chin flat on the deck, ears spread like bat wings. Making no effort to move, she looked up at him with the same sad, expectant eyes he had peered into the night he rescued her from the ocean and certain death.

At the time he had no way of knowing that would be the beginning of a deadly adventure in the lava tubes beneath Kauai and the answer to one of Hawaii's most puzzling enigmas: the legend of the *Menehune*.

He stooped and gave the basset hound a scruff behind the ears before pouring himself a cup of coffee from the pot sitting on the table.

"You look better, if nothing else," Robert said.

"If you say so."

Jack sagged into a chair. He understood the importance and the enormity of what his director expected of him. Though confident he'd sort out the problem, how he would accomplish that task was only a guess at this point. The answer might be a simple one: the cause could even sort itself out before he had a chance to do his workup. He could hope for one or the other, but for some reason neither seemed likely.

Nothing is ever that easy.

He straightened in his seat. "I'm going to take *Pono II* around to Waikiki. You interested in coming along?"

"Absolutely. I'm sure Kazuko would like to join us."

"Can she get off work? Everyone at the aquarium is probably going apeshit over this shark business."

"And getting nowhere," Robert pointed out. "Which is why her boss will be thrilled to have her join you."

Jack understood completely. "Should I extend the invitation or do you want to make the call?"

"I'll do it. You drink your coffee."

Robert scooped up his cell from the tabletop, and Jack tried to formulate some semblance of a plan. Until he knew more, the authorities had done the only thing they could do. Although, posting signs and telling everyone it wasn't safe to go into the water would only work for a day, maybe two. After that, swimmers would grow skeptical of the warnings and ignore the notices until someone else was attacked.

Or worse, killed.

Either of which would surely land the blame on NOAA's shoulders.

And mine.

That left him precious little time to eliminate natural factors that may be causing the sharks to behave uncharacteristically. Changes in water temperature, current flow, a disruption in the availability of food—any one or all of them could upset the ecological balance. Let it tip too far one way or the other, strange things happen.

Another possibility existed; one that could not be overlooked. That no upset in the ecological balance existed. That the sharks had simply behaved erratically because that's what they have been known to do for no reason anyone could predict. In that case, removing the lure of swimmers—thus, eliminating the temptation—might return the sharks' behavior to normal.

That would take time.

Hence the problem, and worry that gnawed at him. There would be no way to know for sure if the delicate balance they hoped to reestablish had been achieved unless people were allowed back into the water.

A gamble.

Cold dread settled over him.

If I'm wrong, what then?

Jack didn't want to think about the consequences.

For the victims or for him.

He noticed Robert disconnect his call, and asked, "What's the verdict?"

Robert slid his phone into his pants pocket. "Exactly as I thought. She jumped at the chance to go along. If traffic cooperates, she should be here in an hour."

"I'm glad to have her help. While we're waiting, I'll open up

Pono II and air her out."

"What's the plan?"

"I haven't exactly had time to come up with one."

"Okay. So what do we do?"

Jack shrugged. "For starters, we'll collect water samples at two or three locations along the way and again off Waikiki. When we compare them, we'll know if there is any significant difference. I'll also try to figure out how other fish are behaving. If something that should be found in the ocean isn't or vice versa. Or if the fish sharks normally feed on have moved out of the area for some reason."

"Feel like you've been dropped into a Benchley novel?"

"A little. Only we're not talking about one monster shark; we're talking about a lot of sharks. Small and large. The largest, quite possibly, being a tiger maybe twelve- to fourteen-feet long. One that size can't swallow a person whole, as Quint put it in Jaws, but it sure can rip someone to pieces in a hurry."

Robert sighed. "Like that poor kid yesterday."

Jack felt his gut roil.

He pursed his lips, and said, "Well, we won't let it happen again."

The vision that filled his head drew his gaze out to sea.

Not today, anyway.

CHAPTER 7

Jack manned *Pono II*'s topside controls, inspecting the readings on the gauges. Below decks, her twin diesels gurgled at idle, sputtering bubbles as small waves washed against the exhaust pipes. Acrid diesel fumes rose at the stern and were carried away by the breeze. He'd owned the fifty-eight-foot power catamaran less than a year. A replacement for his previous power cat *Pono* that now lay in burn-scarred pieces at the bottom of Ala Wai Boat Harbor on the other side of the island. He loved *Pono* from the day he bought her, but had to admit that *Pono II* was better equipped to satisfy his scientific needs.

Running his fingers over the throttle levers where the finish on the chrome had dulled since his last inspection, he made a mental note to put another coat of polish on the boat's brightwork. The salt air would be quick to do its dirty work if he didn't keep ahead of the corrosion that plagued every boat owner.

"Aloha, Captain. Permission to come aboard."

He turned at the sound of Kazuko's voice and peered down at her. She stood on the dock a few feet aft of the stern-boarding steps. Standing next to her was a young woman he had never met. He guessed her to be twenty-one or twenty-two—attractive from what he could see—long, straight black hair pulled into a ponytail extending below her shoulders, and a dark-bronze skin tone a shade darker than his own burnt-in tan from his years of working in the sun; one that suggested an island lineage mixed with Caucasian.

She reminded him of a younger version of Kazuko.

The women were dressed in Waikiki Aquarium t-shirts, khaki shorts, and canvas sneakers. And they both gazed up at him from beneath the brims of ball caps bearing the aquarium logo.

"What's with the captain bit?" His question brought a grin from Kazuko as though he bore the brunt of some inside joke he wasn't aware of.

Unusually playful, even for her.

"Just kidding with you," she said, and gestured toward the young lady next to her. "This is Kiana Parker. She's a UCSB marine science grad student assisting me with my dolphin research. I asked her to join us."

He descended the ladder and waved the women up. "I doubt the trip will be all that exciting, but you're both welcome aboard."

Kazuko motioned Kiana toward the boarding steps. At practically that same instant, Robert emerged from the salon asking, "What's all the talk about?"

Jack arched a brow. "Kazuko brought a friend along."

"The more the merrier, I always say." Robert turned a smile toward Kiana before redirecting his gaze toward Jack. "Lunch is stowed in the refrigerator, along with a supply of beer and bottled water. We can get underway whenever you're ready."

Kazuko addressed Jack, "Robert said you plan on running an analysis on the water in several locations between here and Waikiki."

"Among other things." He wanted to stay on track. "What do you and your colleagues at the aquarium have to say? Surely you haven't been sitting on your backsides doing nothing."

"Quite frankly, we're stumped."

"For now, you can add me to the list."

He removed his Ray-Bans, cleaned the lenses on his shirt, and slid his sunglasses back on. They were getting nothing done tied to the dock. His boss wanted results. She had placed her trust in him.

He'd not disappoint her.

"No reason to waste daylight. Robert, cast off the bow line, if you will." He looked at Kazuko. "Take care of the stern line."

Having resumed his position at the topside controls, he

maneuvered *Pono II* away from the dock and put her on a course for Waikiki that would take them around the south end of Oahu. The spring storms that passed over the island chain the week before had left behind a bright, blue sky and intense tropical sunshine.

It would be a hot one.

"We need to do something about this sun," Robert said when he joined Jack at the controls. "It'll bake us for sure."

Jack swiped the back of his hand across the sweat beaded on his forehead. "You aren't lying. We'd best raise the sunshade."

The two of them got it rigged and Jack switched off the autopilot and took control of the helm. He asked, "What are the women doing?"

"Kazuko is giving Kiana a tour of the boat. My guess is they'll be joining us soon enough."

"She's pretty, isn't she?"

"Kiana?" Robert smiled. "She's something, all right. More importantly, knowing Kazuko the way I do, the young lady is smart as well or she wouldn't be here."

"We'll have to trust Kazuko on that."

Robert frowned. "You talk like something's wrong. What gives? Ordinarily, you'd welcome the chance to have an attractive woman aboard."

"Normally." Jack flashed on the memory swirling inside his head. "Probably still would. Only we're talking sharks, here. This is no pleasure cruise."

"None of us are under the illusion it is."

Jack said nothing. A part of him regretted his comment.

"It's Kelly you're thinking about, isn't it?" Robert rolled his eyes. "I thought you let go of what happened to her."

"I've always felt there was something more I could have done."

"That's ancient news, ol' buddy. Let go of all that. It's time you stop beating yourself up over something that wasn't your fault. Believe me. Kazuko would never have invited Kiana along if there was cause for concern."

"I'm sure you're right." Only Jack didn't let go.

He stared into a gentle swell building out to sea as they cleared the bay and entered open water. Over the years, he had made his share of mistakes, and more. Stupid stuff when he looked back on it. He made no bones about it. Some choices had been costly.

Kiana was a stranger to him, and he had no reason to compare her to Kelly Ann Hutchens who had almost lost her leg to a shark attack years earlier. Still, he found himself doing exactly that.

He and Kelly—young grad students like Kiana—had been diving off Necker Island in the Northwestern Hawaiian Islands when they encountered an eight-foot tiger shark. At the time, they had been dating for a couple of months. And during those blissful days, they had spent a lot of time together in the ocean as a research team pursuing their individual scientific degrees. Shark sightings were common enough, but that dive was the first time they encountered a tiger of that size.

She panicked and almost paid for the mistake with her life.

He didn't anticipate encountering a shark on this trip, least of all one of any real size, but the unexpected had a way of happening. He hated to think Kiana would do something foolish at exactly the wrong moment.

He dismissed the thought.

His friend was correct about her, of course. He had no reason not to trust Kazuko's judgment and chalked his paranoia up to too little sleep and too much caffeine. Not the first time, nor would it be the last. He would bet money on that.

"I'm sure you're correct. She'll do fine."

"No worries, then?" Robert said.

"None."

And he hoped he was right.

He inhaled the salt air, enjoying the feel of the boat. *Pono II* was a lot of vessel and she had taken some getting used to. Every boat has its good and bad points, he knew from experience. *Pono II* had hers, but she quickly proved to be everything he'd expected her to be, and more.

He eased the throttles forward. Savoring the cool breeze that came with the increased speed, he watched the speedometer nudge fifteen knots and hold. That's where he left it. *Pono II* had a twenty-three-knot top speed and a seventeen-knot fast cruise, but he felt it best to not push the engines.

Even with a relatively flat sea.

Waikiki Beach remained closed to swimmers and, to the best of his knowledge, was being patrolled to keep people out of the water. No one would be going into the surf.

At least, not today.

CHAPTER 8

With the salty air in his face and the rumble of the twin diesels beneath him, Jack felt rejuvenated and happy to be at the helm of his boat. As soon as *Pono II* cleared the bay, he set a course for Waimanalo Beach, the first stop on his list of destinations for no reason other than it seemed like a good location to collect his first water sample. Even though it felt a whole lot like he was groping in the dark for answers, he was relieved to be taking a first step that, with luck, would provide at least some insight into the shark problem at Waikiki.

A beginning.

He quickly realized they weren't alone on the water. The beaches in Waikiki had been closed to swimmers, but not others around the island. Nor did the order include boats.

And that meant divers.

Cage dives offered by Oahu shark-adventure tour companies had risen in popularity over recent years. That would certainly be the case now, and maybe more so. The temptation to swim with a man-eater would surely be too strong for thrill-seekers to ignore.

There would be fishermen, too.

He turned the helm over to Robert and stepped aft. In the distance, beyond the foamy wakes kicked up by *Pono II*'s twin hulls, Kaneohe Bay slipped from sight. To starboard, Bellows Air Force Station came into view.

Formerly named Bellows Air Force Base, and Bellows Field before that, he recalled it had been one of the airfields targeted by the Japanese during their attack on Pearl Harbor on December 7, 1941. A war that ended in 1945, after atomic bombs were dropped on Hiroshima and Nagasaki.

Bombs assembled in part from components delivered by the sailors aboard the *USS Indianapolis.*

His mind held onto the vision of the ghost ship rusting on the bottom of the Philippine Sea. The *USS Indianapolis* sank in twelve minutes. Nine hundred men went into the water. Four and a half days later, three hundred and sixteen men came out of the sea alive.

The sharks took the rest.

"You need to hear this," Robert said.

Jack let go of the vision and turned to his friend who sat hunched over the VHF radio. "What's up?"

"It's hard to make out; signal keeps fading. Some woman's talking about turtles beaching themselves."

Jack joined Robert at the helm. "You're on channel sixteen?"

"Seventy-three. I was scanning the boat chatter when I picked her up. But the woman keeps cutting off her transmission. I don't think she's had much experience using a radio."

"Who's she talking to?"

"No one in particular, as far as I can tell. Sounded like she just kind of threw the information out there to whoever was listening."

"You tried to call her back?"

"I did. But I think she keeps switching channels on me."

"And all you heard her say was that turtles were beaching themselves?"

"She sounded concerned."

Jack resumed his seat and accepted the mic from Robert's hand. "No reason for her to be worried. Unless something is driving the turtles onto shore."

"Like a twelve-foot shark on the prowl."

Jack knew his friend referred to the behavior associated with turtles beaching themselves to protect against attack from large sharks. Most often tigers.

"That's what I'm thinking," he said. "And considering—"

He stopped talking and listened.

A woman's voice said over the radio, "There's six on shore now. Large ones…just lying there. I think they're dying because…"

Jack listened to silence for a moment. She was gone. He raised the microphone to his lips and pressed the transmit button. "This is Jack Ferrell aboard *Pono II*. I repeat, this is Jack Ferrell aboard *Pono II*. Woman calling about turtles in distress. What is your location?"

Nothing.

He switched to channel seventy-four and heard a man say, "Release the button on the mic when you finish talking. You're holding it down."

Frustration speaking.

A mic clicked and a woman said, "Two more just beached themselves. Something really strange is going on here."

The same woman.

He keyed his mic. "This is Jack Ferrell aboard *Pono II*. Again, this is Jack Ferrell aboard *Pono II*. What is your location? I repeat: What is your location?"

"Thank God," the woman said. "I didn't think anyone was listening to me. My name is Donna. I'm on a rental boat off the point at Hanauma Bay. My husband is in the water. Someone had to do something to help these poor turtles."

He heard the desperation in the woman's voice. There was no telling what she might try to do, and he didn't want her going into the water after her husband, if in fact, sharks caused the turtles to beach themselves. And there wasn't just Donna and her husband to worry about; Hanauma Bay was one of Oahu's premier tourist attractions.

He shoved the throttle levers forward.

The woman's voice boomed from the speaker before he could respond. "The turtles aren't acting right, I tell you. Something needs to be done."

Speaking into his mic, he said, "Donna, get your husband back on the boat. The turtles are in no danger. Trust me on this. Just leave them alone. They will find their way back into the water when they're ready. Are there people on the beach or in the water?"

"There are a lot of people on the beach and a few snorkelers."

"How about lifeguards?"

"There's one, but he's not doing anything to help the turtles."

"Is he getting the swimmers out of the water?"

"I can't tell."

Jack didn't know what to think. He keyed his mic. "Stay in your boat and we'll be there in a few minutes."

Robert said, "You think it's a big tiger?"

Jack hung the mic on its hook. "If it is, I'm thinking there's more than one."

Robert gave a slow nod. "As in what's happened off Waikiki?"

Jack held his speed at twenty knots. Pushing the engines, but he figured they could be there in fifteen minutes…hopefully less.

"We'll find out."

CHAPTER 9

Jack pointed the bow towards Palea Point. Struggling with a growing feeling he might arrive too late to help the woman's husband, he nudged the throttles forward to their stops, increasing the boat's speed an additional couple of knots—added strain on the twin diesels to gain a precious minute or two.

The situation warranted it.

Pono II sliced through the swells instead of riding up and over the waves. The sleek, twin-hull design helped to smooth the ride and kept her topside dry, except for an occasional salty spray that peppered the forward deck. Overhead, the sunshade fluttered in the warm breeze. Visitors to Oahu called it paradise.

Not today.

The hatchway next to Jack swung open, and he watched Kazuko emerge onto the deck, widen her stance, maintain her balance, and peer toward the open water ahead. Kiana stepped out and did the same.

The grad student turned her dark eyes on him a long moment before sliding on a pair of sunglasses suspended from a cord around her neck. Her gaze reminded him of a feral cat on the prowl.

What in the hell was that all about?

He smiled.

Kazuko asked, "You've sped up. Is something going on?"

Jack redirected his thoughts, and said, "We intercepted a frantic radio call from a woman named Donna who's on a boat at Hanauma Bay. She claimed turtles were beaching themselves. Apparently, her husband went into the water thinking they need help. We're headed there now."

She peered toward the bow. "Sharks?"

"We'll find out."

He glanced at his watch, silently counting the minutes. Kazuko shared his and Robert's opinion of why the turtles had beached themselves, adding a flare of urgency to the woman's call for assistance.

Especially with people's lives at stake.

Her husband's...

Kazuko asked, "Have there been distress calls from anyone else?"

"Not that we've heard. And no more from Donna." He suspected that meant her husband made it back aboard their boat safely.

At the very least, he hoped that was the case.

Kiana said, "I understand sea turtles often go ashore to sun themselves."

Jack nodded. "They do. They've also been known to beach themselves when evading danger. If a large tiger has moved into the bay to feed, there's little cause for concern as far as the turtles go. It happens. But if there are several sharks present, as has been reported off Waikiki, we'll have an opportunity to witness what's been going on, first-hand."

A stroke of luck, he thought, *providing no one is bit...or worse, killed.*

Palea Point came into view in the distance. Beyond that, the expanse of water off Diamondhead.

When they rounded the point, he saw a boat at the mouth of the volcanic crater that formed Hanauma Bay a quarter mile away. The craft looked to be a white center-console model with a walk-around deck favored by fisherman—a Grady-White, Mako or Boston Whaler possibly, in the twenty-five-foot range, powered by two large outboards. The vessel appeared to be drifting...or anchored in deep water outside the reef.

Only one person in view.

He set a course directly for the boat.

They were less than a minute away when the radio crackled with the woman's voice, anxious with hysteria. "Sharks. There are sharks everywhere. My husband.... Please help him."

Silence followed.

A second later Jack heard the woman's scream cross the water.

He held the throttles against their stops.

Robert stood and said, "I'm going below to get the first aid kit."

Kazuko gave him room to get past her and told Jack, "I'll be ready with the life ring."

"I'll help her," Kiana said.

Jack pulled back on the throttles when he neared the reef visible in shallow water. Any one of the jagged coral heads could take the bottom out of either one or both of *Pono II*'s twin hulls. He looked in the direction of the woman's frantic pointing and scanned the surface of the ocean, fearing he might have arrived too late.

He saw the triangular fins first. Three of them, a foot and a half or more in height, vectored in on a man swimming toward the boat.

Tigers.

Full grown adults. Twelve- or thirteen-footers—each of them fifteen-hundred pounds of killing machine.

Sharks don't feed on humans.

He told himself that. Partly because it was scientific fact; mostly because he desperately wanted it to be true. But apparently these oceangoing meat-eaters had entered the bay in search of a meal, drawn to the man by his thrashing.

Human or not, he was on the menu.

Jack couldn't understand why the woman's husband was still in the water. He had told her to get him back on the boat. Why hadn't she motored over to him? Did she even know how to operate their boat?

Kazuko stood on the foredeck ready with the life ring. Robert had positioned himself to the side of her; Kiana, too. Thirty yards away, on the smaller boat, the man's wife screamed at him to hurry.

Jack needed no urging.

The fins closed on her husband...then dropped below the surface.

He pictured the attack. The sharks would first circle the man, studying him by prodding their prey with their snouts. And when their sensors identified him as meat, they would strike with deadly efficiency.

Behavior accepted by experts in his field.

Not a guarantee.

He shoved the throttles forward.

Powered by the two 450 HP diesels, the props churned the water into froth. But the heavy boat responded slowly at first before picking up speed. He knew he could never get to the man in time, but he had to try, and take his chances with the coral.

Timing was critical now.

It would be close.

From high up at the topside controls, he saw the dark torpedo shapes cruising just below the surface of the water; one shark leading the other two.

Definitely tigers.

Next came the bump with the lead tiger's snout, which in turn caused the man to stop swimming and frantically tread water. The others swam past and arched into a turn.

"Punch the bastards in the head," he yelled. "Fight 'em."

It's your only chance, he thought.

But his words were lost in the engine noise.

And in the man's own terror.

He cringed, powerless to stop what would happen next. His gut wrenched in a knot of helplessness as he watched the sharks strike. First, one sank his jagged teeth into a leg, then the other two took a turn.

Next came a guttural cry of pain and horror from the victim.

Blood clouded the water as the sharks ripped flesh from the man's limbs.

Jack glanced at the depth gauge.

The bottom was rising fast.

He hauled back on the throttles, shifted into reverse, and shoved the throttle levers forward. The deck shuddered under the vibration of the spinning props digging into the water as the *Pono II* drifted to a stop.

They were close enough now.

He moved the throttle levers to idle and shifted to neutral.

"Throw the life ring."

Kazuko's hands were already moving.

She dropped the floatation device inches from the guy's flailing arms.

The man grabbed hold of the ring and Jack hurried below to help. Everything was happening…fast.

By the time he got there, the guy was lying flat on the blood-soaked deck. One leg had been bitten off below the knee; nearly half of the calf muscle had been torn from the other. Robert had his belt pulled tight around the stump. Kazuko had the fingers of one hand pressed to the femoral artery on the inner thigh of the opposite leg, and the palm of her other hand flat on the wound. Kiana knelt, cradling the man's head, apparently trying to keep him calm.

"Towels," Robert yelled.

Already on the move, Jack grabbed a stack of folded beach towels from a storage locker in the galley, hurried outside with them, and tossed the wad to Robert who had finished applying the tourniquet.

Robert held compresses to the torn flesh and exposed bone. Kazuko took half and applied them to the other leg while keeping pressure on the artery.

Kiana continued to do her best to keep the man from thrashing.

Jack said, "If you have this under control, I'll get the Coast Guard in the air."

"Go," Robert said without turning from his grim task of wrapping an additional towel around the severed limb.

Jack didn't hesitate. He made the call from the radio inside the salon. While he explained the situation, he stared through the window at a dozen dorsal fins cutting back and forth through the dissipating cloud of blood and shreds of tissue.

Trash cans of the sea.

The authorities would need to expand the beach closures, immediately.

CHAPTER 10

That evening, over conciliatory beers with his friends on their lanai, Jack contemplated what he'd do next. The sun had set on the opposite side of the island, cooling the evening hours. The delicate scent of yellow and orange hibiscus blossoms mixed with the citrus fragrance of flowering mock orange bushes filled the air. The water samples they collected revealed nothing to explain the sharks' unusual behavior. And after having experienced an attack first-hand, he was at a loss for an explanation.

Sharks don't feed on humans.

That had proved to not be the case in what they observed.

"A hell-of-a first day," Robert said from his chair.

Jack scoffed. "One I'd prefer not to repeat."

"I agree," said Kiana. To Kazuko, she added, "I'd love to stay and have another beer, but I'm afraid I need to go. I'll call an Uber to save you the trip."

"Nonsense," Kazuko said. "Stay here tonight. We have a guest room all made up. We can drive in to the aquarium together in the morning."

Jack turned his gaze on Kiana. Earlier, at Hanauma Bay, she'd reacted responsibly in doing what she could to help. He thought afterward he might have misjudged her. But in the back of his mind, he couldn't shake the feeling she was trouble.

Her gaze shifted in his direction. "Sure, why not. After what I witnessed today, I can definitely use another beer."

His cell phone vibrated on the table next to him drawing his attention away from the group. He glanced at the name on the screen; Megan O'Connell was returning his call.

"You're working late," he said when he tapped on.

"What did you expect?" Fatigue echoed in her voice.

He could imagine the political backlash she had weathered following the shark attack earlier in the day. "Are you okay?"

"I'm a little tired but fine."

Probably more than a little tired, but he didn't press. "I knew shit would hit the fan. How bad is it?"

"After what happened this afternoon, everyone in Honolulu from the top down is screaming for answers. All want something done to stop the shark attacks…and they want it done immediately. I've been in meetings all afternoon. I finished up with the governor less than an hour ago."

"How about the news media?'

"Sensationalizing it. Like they always do."

"What in hell does everybody expect?"

"The shark problem gone, of course. And they don't really care how it's done. The tourist economy on the island is suffering because of it. Hotel cancellations, a slump in room bookings—you can imagine."

"In other words, they want a miracle."

"The governor's desperate, as is the mayor. I'll put it to you this way: They don't give a damn what it takes."

He scoffed to himself.

They say that now.

"They're both smart people" he said. "Surely they know it's not realistic to expect us, or anyone else for that matter, to carry out a vendetta against sharks that are only doing what they've evolved to do? They're not evil creatures. They're beautiful, they're terrifying, and they're mysterious…a scientist's dream. Christ, they've remained virtually unchanged for a million and a half years." He tensed with frustration. "Thinking we can keep a shark from obeying its innate instincts is plain crazy."

"You're right, no argument there." Her tone calmed. "But we can try and figure out what's altered their normal pattern of behavior."

"We can…in time. That's what I'm working on. But for the moment, closing the beaches to water activities is a first step to ensuring the public's safety. Which is a priority above all else." He caught himself assuming. "The beaches *are* being kept closed, right?"

"Signs are being posted—they had no choice in that—but only Waikiki Beach and Hanauma Bay have twenty-four-hour police patrols. Otherwise, lifeguards at the more popular ones will do what they can to keep people out of the water during the day. Beyond that, there's simply not enough manpower to cover every beach on the island."

"And the Coast Guard?"

"They'll have helicopters and boats patrolling offshore as much as possible, within the constraints of their resources."

"Then we're doing everything we can for the moment." A thought struck him. One that made his cringe. "You don't think we're overreacting, do you?"

"You're kidding, right? Please tell me you're kidding."

He wished he hadn't asked. "Just making sure we're on the same page."

She sighed into her phone, and said, "If anyone could come up with another way to keep people from being bitten or killed, I'd do it. There isn't. Now, do what you need to do and don't worry about me."

"You know I can't *not* worry about you?"

"I'm sure you meant that in a nice way." She paused as though thinking. "Any ideas yet about what got this mess started?"

"That's the million-dollar question," he said. "Unfortunately, I haven't a clue. I can say that what I witnessed today definitely wasn't normal in the sense there was no reason for the sharks to act the way they did. They're patrolling for food in the water along our beaches all the time, but they *don't* intentionally hunt people. Today, for no apparent reason I can find, they swarmed into Hanauma Bay in a feeding frenzy that cost a man his legs. By the way, how is Mr. Edwards?"

"Thanks to your quick action, he's alive. He's in intensive care, but his doctors are optimistic he'll recover."

"The thanks go to Robert and Kazuko and Kiana. They're the ones who saved his life. I just drove the boat."

"You're always the modest one, Jack. Too much for your own good."

He grinned. "People are occasionally bitten here in the islands; we know that. But not like this. It's almost as though something drove the sharks to attack."

"You're not serious? That's science fiction mumbo jumbo."

"Ridiculous, I know. But that's how it seemed to me. From what I've been able to determine so far, there's no significant change in the water temperature or composition, and there doesn't appear to be a change in their food supply. Not a thing in their environment to account for their erratic behavior."

"Yet it's happening." A statement, but her tone conveyed a question.

The answer to the problem plaguing the beaches, he had a feeling, would not be found in the ocean. According to research papers he had read, sharks at aquariums were being trained to perform tasks. The method used was a combination of colored boards and sounds, similar to the way the Russian physiologist Pavlov trained dogs. If someone on the island had discovered a way to send the sharks around Oahu into an uncontrollable frenzy, with a single predatory focus to feed, they could do it someplace else.

Even more scary, so could terrorists.

"I'd like to speak with the girl who was attacked off Waikiki, if you can arrange it. And I also want to speak with Mrs. Edwards. Now that her husband is in the hospital recovering, she might remember something that will help."

"Perhaps it's time I call in other experts to give you a hand?"

"You're the boss. Call in as many specialists as you like if that's what you want to do. They might get here in a week or two. That is if they can break away from what they're doing at the moment." He fought a surge of irritation, exhaustion adding to his edginess. "Meg, I saw that man attacked. He almost died. Others have. I'll not let that happen to anyone else. I'm in this, alone or with an army, and I'll see it through to the end."

"Relax, Jack. I never had any intention of replacing you. Only getting you some help, which I'm still going to do. In the meantime, you're all I have and I'm relying on you to stop what's happening."

"Consider it done."

He clicked off, ready for another beer. A deep sigh was all he could muster.

Robert handed him a fresh Longboard Lager. "I take it things aren't going so well."

"You saw what happened. The guy had his legs bitten off. What do you think?"

"I'm referring to the powers that be."

Jack popped the cap and tossed it on the table. "The governor and mayor want miracles."

"And?"

"You can't always get what you want." He tipped the bottle and took a long gulp.

CHAPTER 11

Jack lay awake on his queen-size bed aboard *Pono II*. Kiana confused him. She had tossed suggestive glances in his direction all evening, and one that lingered way too long when he said goodnight to everyone.

Damn.

He'd thought she could be a problem, and it was something like this he had been afraid of. Young and pretty was a deadly combination.

And how she looked at him.

He realized his life teetered on the verge of becoming a whole lot more complicated. But only if he allowed it to.

And he didn't see that happening.

Not for a second.

He was in that moment of complete relaxation, a second before falling asleep, when he felt an almost imperceptible shift in the pitch of the boat. He sat up on his bed and waited. A dream? Or had someone stepped aboard?

He grabbed his .45 from the night table.

A couple of seconds later he heard a tentative knock on the galley door.

He slid his legs from under the sheet and pulled on his faded swimsuit. Armed with his Colt, he crept barefoot up the steps and moved silently across the floor to the bulkhead separating the salon from the galley.

He listened. This time he heard a female whisper, “Jack, are you awake?”

Her voice brought a sigh of regret.

I am now.

He lowered the gun, stepped through the galley and opened the door leading aft. Kiana stood, staring in at him. Her eyes told him what she had on her mind. The pole light on the dock behind her sent a warm glow through the doorway and gilded her dark hair.

“What are you doing here?”

She stepped inside. “My god, I’ve been an absolute emotional mess for the past hour. You think I could let the evening end without a kiss goodnight?”

He swept her body with his eyes. The thin t-shirt she had on made it impossible not to.

No way, young lady.

Suddenly, she stepped close, forcing him to take a step back with no intention of letting the situation progress further.

But he wasn’t fast enough.

Her arms encircled his neck. He placed his hands on her shoulders and eased her away from the one-sided embrace. “I’m flattered, but we won’t be doing this, Kiana.”

She pressed toward him. “We can. And we are. Hurry, kiss me.”

“No.” He held her at arm’s length. “For one, you’re at least half my age. Dammit, I’m old enough to be your father. Two, this is just wrong.”

She squirmed out of his grasp. “You can’t mean that.”

He did mean it. There was nothing tender or romantic about the moment. For reasons that made no sense to him, she had come in search of hot and heavy sex.

“This isn’t going to happen,” he said. “Now scoot on back to the house before Robert and Kazuko see you.”

Her expression was one of surprise. “If that’s what’s bothering you, we can do this some other time.”

He turned her around and gave her a gentle shove to get here going. “No more games. Now run along back to your bed where you belong.”

She smiled and hurried off toward the house.

He had no idea what brought her to his boat. Besides being old enough to be her father, there had been no encouragement on his part. The idea had been all hers. Why, he didn't know. But she clearly wasn't done playing her game.

That he knew.

Definitely trouble.

CHAPTER 12

At nine the following morning, the sun bright at his back, Jack climbed into his Jeep for a drive across the island. Forty-five minutes later, he walked into Queen's Medical Center in downtown Honolulu, a few blocks from Honolulu Harbor. The hospital and this part of town fostered a ton of memories; a handful of them good. One topped the list.

Cherise.

A woman more than his equal.

Much more.

He grinned at the thought, so looking forward to their next romantic rendezvous and the time they would spend together.

Just the two of them.

Familiar with the layout of the hospital from when Robert's appendix ruptured a year earlier, he walked straight to the stairs leading up to the Med-Surg unit located on the third floor. On the way, he peered into the gift shop where Anna Hastings worked back then. The place hadn't changed…except for fresh flowers and a new face.

A sideways glance inside as he passed by the display window had been all he could manage. Anna held a special place in his heart; she was one of the really good people in the world.

He took the steps two at a time in a hurry to talk to Amy Watson. She could very well be the key to the enigma, and he was anxious to find out. Pausing at the doorway to Room 312, he knocked on the open door and peeked inside.

The courageous teen lay on her back in bed, covered to her chest, her hands clasped in her lap. The head of the bed had been raised to a forty-five-degree angle. Bags of medication hung from an IV stand. Polyurethane lines fed the fluids into a peripheral venous catheter in her arm. The outline of two legs and two feet outstretched beneath the sheet and blanket were clearly visible. Her mother sat at her daughter's side, her back to the wall. Seeing the flowers and the stuffed animals, he felt as though he should have brought the girl a gift.

What does a stranger get a fifteen-year-old girl these days?

Safer to keep the interaction on a professional level, that had been his way of thinking. He took a step inside and stopped.

"Good morning," he said, looking from Amy to her mother. "My name is Jack Ferrell. I believe you spoke to my supervisor on the phone: Director O'Connell. I'd like to speak with your daughter, if she feels up to it."

The woman stood from her chair and stepped around the foot of the bed. She extended her hand. "Doctor Ferrell, I'm Stella Watson, Amy's mother. Ms. O'Connell sounded like a wonderful lady to work for."

Jack stepped to the middle of the room and gently clasped her hand in a polite shake. "She is at that. How is your daughter?"

Stella smiled but he could see sadness in her eyes. "I'll let her tell you. Keep in mind they have her on some pretty strong pain medication."

Amy's gaze followed him to her bedside. He slid a straight-backed chair over and sat looking at her—on her level, not down at her. He mustered what he hoped was a positive expression, and said, "My name is Jack Ferrell. I'm a marine biologist working for NOAA. You're a brave girl."

"I don't feel brave," she said.

"Perhaps not, but you are just the same. Not many people would have kept their cool and reacted the way you did."

"Honestly, I was scared to death." Her gaze dropped to her hands in her lap. "All I could think about was getting to shore."

"Rightfully so. And that *will* to survive saved your life. Have you ever seen a shark before—I mean, while you were surfing?"

"I guess I never really thought about it much. When I lived in Laguna Beach, my friends, me, we all knew they were out there. We even joked about it. But we never believed something like this"—she pointed at her leg—"would happen to any of us. I felt the same way even after I moved here."

"Why is that, do you think?"

She shrugged.

"Did you and your friends ever see *Jaws*?"

"On Amazon Prime, but we knew the shark was fake."

"You're right in more ways than one. Sharks—even big ones like the one in the movie—don't intentionally hunt people. Which is why I'm here. If you feel up to it, I'd like to ask you a few questions about what happened out there."

"You mean the sharks?"

"Did you notice anything unusual that may have drawn them in? Did anyone have an open cut that might have put blood into the water? It only takes a tiny amount to draw them in if they are close enough. Even"—he paused amid a prickle of concern that he might embarrass her—"menstrual bleeding."

Her gaze met his; in it, he saw resolve. The same inner strength that saved her life.

"I'm not on my period," she said. "The sharks just attacked."

He sat looking at her. How much could the girl tell him? How much did she want to remember? And how much was clouded by pain medication?

Questions that left him feeling like he was grasping at straws.

A thought struck him.

"What about boats?" he asked. "Were there any close by?"

She lay quiet, her eyes betraying deep thought. After a moment, "I remember seeing one when I paddled out, but I can't tell you anything more about it. I was more interested in talking to Alika… until he left me there alone."

"What do you mean he left you there?"

"He knocked me off my board and then paddled away. He was only interested in saving himself."

"An accident?"

She shrugged, her gaze back on her hands. "I guess."

He could tell she struggled to understand how a boy she liked could leave her to the sharks. Maybe that hurt more than the shark bite. Betrayal, under any circumstance, can leave you feeling gutted.

He understood that all too well.

"This boat," he said, taking her mind off the boy. "Was it small or large, can you remember that much?"

"My uncle in California had one about the same size. Dad told me it was thirty-feet long."

"Do you know the difference between a cabin cruiser and a center-console fishing boat?"

"The one I saw was a cabin cruiser. White, I think."

Jack sighed. He knew it had been a stretch on his part to entertain the notion the woman and her husband on the boat at Hanauma Bay were somehow connected with what happened at Waikiki.

But he had to explore every possibility.

Amy's eyes closed and remained that way for a full fifteen seconds. When she finally opened them, she said, "Did I tell you I have nightmares about this?"

He had no problem believing she did.

Mrs. Watson stepped close and laid her hand on his shoulder. A silent dismissal. He looked up and saw her shake her head from side to side.

He nodded.

To Amy, he said, "I'll let you rest. In time you might remember something that could help me figure out why those sharks attacked you and the other kids. If you do, tell your mother so she can pass the information on to me."

He stood, dug his business card from his wallet, and handed it to the girl's mother. "My cell number is on the bottom. If your daughter thinks of anything that might help, anything at all, please don't hesitate to call."

Amy's mother studied the card before bringing her gaze back up to Jack's. "Do you have any idea at all what caused my daughter to be bitten? She could have lost her leg."

Jack let the woman's question hang. He desperately wanted to tell her yes. But he couldn't lie.

Not to her. Not to her daughter.

"None, Mrs. Watson. But I promise you I'll find out."

CHAPTER 13

Devlin Maxwell stood on the porch of his house. Diamond Head, framed by a blue sky, loomed in the distance. The Pacific Ocean glistened like molten metal in the afternoon sun. The scent of plumeria perfumed the air. The first fragrant blossoms of the year hung on the tree his wife had picked them from when she fashioned her leis...back in a time when the home brimmed with happiness.

Now they simply fell and lay in waste on the ground.

He sipped from a glass of freshly poured guava juice, and cringed when it soured in his stomach. The pleasure he felt the day before had been replaced by remorse for what his life had deteriorated into.

Not what he expected.

He held his glass over the railing and dumped the juice onto the ground. When he started to turn to go back into the house, he noticed Matt Corvin drive up in his bright orange Dodge pickup. A new 4x4 with dark-tinted windows that shielded the occupants from view, and a custom lift kit with monstrous off-road tires that Devlin thought were ridiculous for driving on the road.

The visit was unexpected.

The driver's door on the far side of the truck opened and Devlin waited for the bulk of his coworker to emerge. He rarely had visitors, so he wondered what brought Matt to the house today of all days.

He glanced at his watch.

Early yet.

He said, "I'm surprised to see you here. Shouldn't you still be at work?"

"Shouldn't you?"

"I took the week off. What's your excuse?"

Matt lifted a six-pack of Budweiser from a paper sack he held in his left hand. "What's the matter? Can't a friend drop by for a visit?"

Friend?

Devlin didn't buy Matt's explanation. He had only been to the house one other time. And they had never once sat and drank beers together.

"Yeah. But why are you here?"

Matt slid the six-pack back into the bag. His gaze came up and held. "I think you know why. We need to talk."

Devlin scrunched his brow, confused. "What about?"

"Don't think for a minute you're fooling anyone, least of all me."

"What are you talking about?"

Matt climbed the four steps two at a time and peered down at Devlin. "For two years, everyone at work—me, most of all—listened to your sob story. I watched you build that device, remember? Several of us did. And it's not like we're just going to forget what you were up to. But when this shark business started, I told the others, no way. Not Devlin. He's not capable of something like that."

Devlin held Matt's gaze, but said nothing.

"That's why I'm here," Matt laid a friendly hand on Devlin's shoulder. "There's money to be made."

Devlin shrugged off Matt's touch.

So that's what this is all about.

He let the words digest. How could Matt possibly know?

"Just what is it you think I'm doing?"

Matt laughed. "You really want to play ignorant? Why you're doing what you're doing is not important. What matters is your device puts sharks into a feeding frenzy, and *that* can work to our mutual benefit."

It *was* important why, and Devlin wanted Matt to understand that. "Hawaii wants to protect those killers. I want the fuckers exterminated—every last one of them—for what they did to my family."

"I know what happened to your son. And I know what his death did to your wife. But I'm telling you, there are people willing to pay big bucks for your device. You need to think about that."

"Who? Terrorist organizations? ISIS? Al Qaeda?"

"So what if the money comes from a bunch of fucking rag-heads. As long as the camel jockeys pay up, that's all that matters."

Devlin didn't like Matt or the way he talked.

"I'm not interested."

Matt's expression hardened, betraying the extent of the anger festering inside him. He raised his hand chest-level and with his index finger he pointed and jabbed the air, forcing Devlin back a step. "You self-righteous bastard, I don't give a shit about your sick little vendetta to avenge your son and wife. I'm telling you I have to get my hands on some money. A lot of it. And I need the cash fast. Otherwise, some very bad people are going to make life extremely unpleasant for me and my wife and kids. Understand what I'm telling you? This is my chance to make the big bucks I need. You, too, if you go along with my plan."

"If I go along with your plan." Devlin tried not to allow himself to be shaken by Matt's outburst. "What kind of bullshit talk is that?"

"No bullshit about it. You think I've just been sitting on my ass doing nothing while you run around playing avenging father? I've made important contacts. There's a market for this kind of stuff, and if we work the deal right, way more than enough money to pull my ass out of the ringer."

Devlin huffed. "And make me rich?"

Matt's lips spread into a mean smile. "That's right."

Devlin couldn't help feeling a tinge of compassion for his coworker, but the sentiment was fleeting. His focus returned to his own situation. He'd done what he felt he had to do, and now people were screaming for a bounty on sharks—*all* sharks. The governor vowed a quick resolution to the problem. Sentiment among concerned residents on the island who swayed toward protecting sharks had changed their views practically overnight. One or two more incidents would put public outcry over the top, and his work would be finished. That would be the end of it.

For good.

He wanted to keep it that way. He wasn't about to allow himself to be bullied into Matt's scheme, regardless of how much money was at stake.

He would definitely have no part in a terrorist plot.

Ever.

He shook his head at Matt. "Your money problems are your own. Sell your house if you need cash." He pointed at the pickup. "Sell that fancy truck. Do whatever you have to do if you're that desperate, but leave me the hell alone."

"Everyone needs money." Matt's eyes narrowed and held on Devlin. "I'll wager you do, too."

Devlin had his mind made up. He straightened and met the bigger man's stare head on. "You're wasting your time, Matt. I don't care how much cash you or any of your terrorist friends offer me. I want no part of it."

Matt's stern expression transformed into a smug smile. He turned and calmly gazed toward Diamond Head. "Bold talk for a man facing years in prison."

His hole card.

"Blackmail." Devlin swallowed his rage. "That's where you're headed with this?"

Matt turned a piercing gaze on him. "I drove over here to get what I want. It's your choice if you play ball or not."

CHAPTER 14

Jack walked out of the hospital sad and totally pissed off. Not at the young girl lying upstairs in bed, but at the grim circumstances. Something had caused sharks around the island to behave uncharacteristically to the point of attacking humans for no apparent reason. The worst part, he had no idea what was behind it.

Amy Watson would keep her leg.

Charles Edwards wasn't so lucky.

But he was alive.

Others weren't.

Jack dug his phone from his pocket and placed a call to Megan O'Connell's office. Her assistant, Cindy Adams, answered.

"Cindy," he said the moment he recognized her voice, "I'm ready to talk to Mrs. Edwards. Can you arrange that for me?"

"I'm not sure Mr. Edwards is in any shape to talk to anyone."

"I don't want to talk to Mr. Edwards; I want to talk to his wife, Donna. And see if you can get a copy of the Coast Guard report on yesterday's attack."

"Did you talk to Amy Watson?"

"Amy's a sweet girl but she couldn't offer much in the way of helpful information. I'm hoping Mrs. Edwards will do better. By the way, where is Meg?"

"On the phone with Mayor Kobayashi. Seems like her aide calls every ten minutes wanting an update on what's being done to open the beaches."

He didn't envy his boss. Mayor Atsuko Kobayashi was a star in Oahu politics and, from what he heard, no pushover when it came to getting things done.

"Let Director O'Connell know I'm working on it."

That brought a heavy sigh from Cindy. "I don't need to tell you she's catching a lot of heat."

"No doubt. I hear the mayor is tough as coconut husk."

"That's one way of putting it."

"She'll just have to learn to be patient." He fought back a sigh of frustration. "This problem won't be resolved overnight."

"The director knows that and I'm sure Mayor Kobayashi does, too. Anyway, according to the meteorological report, a storm front is moving in. Perhaps a little wind and rain will keep the tourists from pawing at the sand in a nervous rush to get into the water, and take some of the heat off of you. At least we can hope. I'll call you back when I have an answer."

"Appreciate it. Take care." He tapped off and spent a couple of minutes standing idle while he collected his Jeep from the parking attendant out front. He still had a difficult time adjusting to the notion of valet service at a hospital.

A sign of the times, he guessed.

Amy had been surfing with a group of youngsters. Normal teenage behavior, and what you'd expect them to be doing on an unseasonably warm day during spring break. What he didn't understand was why Charles Edwards was in the water. Not a smart move, under the circumstances. Did he honestly think he could swim to shore and help the turtles? Or was he, in fact, somehow responsible for what happened?

Both good questions.

But shots in the dark.

He tried to remember if there were any other boats in the vicinity when he and his friends arrived on scene. One in the distance, to the best of his recollection. White, a common color, and too far away. Hopefully, Donna Edwards would be of help.

There was only one way to find out.

Talk to her.

He parked in the lot at the harbor and sat, waiting for the callback from Cindy. A dirty shell-of-a-man dressed in a ragged t-shirt that had once been white, and filthy pants, his skin tanned dark and leathery, pushed a junk-filled shopping cart into the meager shade of a coconut palm.

Over the past year, Jack had become painfully aware of the homeless problem on the island. He had read there were some seven thousand homeless people in Hawaii, five thousand of which live on Oahu.

An underestimation, in his opinion and, apparently, one without a solution.

The call he waited for came five minutes later.

He tapped on and answered, "Good news, I hope?"

A chuckle. "It depends on what you call good news."

Cindy was full of jokes today.

He said, "Must we?"

Another chuckle. "Mrs. Watson is on her way back to their hotel. They are staying at the Hilton Hawaiian Village Resort, and she said she'd meet you in front of the Starbucks in the Kalia Tower in twenty minutes."

"And the Coast Guard report?"

"They're emailing it to me. I'll forward it to you the moment I receive it."

"You're a princess. Thanks."

He disconnected the call. It seemed there was no place on the island that didn't harbor a memory, good or bad.

CHAPTER 15

Jack left his Jeep with the valet attendant at the porte-cochère and headed for the Starbucks. An easy walk in the shade of the building behind him.

He saw a visibly exhausted Donna Edwards peering down at a watch on her left wrist. A brand similar to his own Seiko dive watch—stainless steel, metal band, rotating timing bezel. Too large for her wrist.

Her husband's watch.

She brought her gaze up at his approach. Judging from her shaky smile, she recognized him.

He greeted her with a sincere one of his own. "I'm sorry to intrude on your day. I know you have a lot on your mind."

"You're not intruding, Mr. Ferrell," she said. "I owe you and your friends so much. Spending a few minutes talking with you is the least I can do."

"Still…." He took another tack. "How *is* your husband?"

Her left wrist came up and her gaze dropped as she fiddled with the watch. "Stable. The doctor says he's lucky to be alive."

Jack extended his hand and motioned toward the cushioned chairs positioned in a U-shape around a low table. "Why don't we sit? Can I get you a coffee?"

She shook her head. "Thank you, no. I've had too much as it is."

He could believe it. "That makes two of us."

They took seats across from each other and he leaned into her gaze, resting his elbows on his knees. "I'd like to talk about what happened yesterday, but only if you're comfortable discussing it. Believe me, I'll understand if you're not."

"I appreciate your concern. The woman who called from NOAA—your director, I believe that's what she told me—said you're trying to figure out why the sharks attacked my husband. If I can help, I'm glad to."

"Thank you. And please feel free to call me Jack."

That brought a hint of a smile.

He gave her a moment, then said, "To begin with, I'd like you to understand that contrary to popular belief, sharks don't normally behave like this. Truth be known, they don't really like human flesh. They prefer more fatty meat, like seals."

Her glassy eyes told him she had a difficult time believing his words.

Rightfully so.

He added, "Sharks are curious creatures by nature. When they see or hear or smell or detect movement that could be a food source, they investigate. That's usually the case when a shark attacks a human. They have also been known to attack when confused. I can't say for sure one or both of those scenarios caused the shark attack on your husband, or the other attacks that have happened over the last few days. It's my professional opinion, however, that stimuli beyond that of the ordinary is causing the sharks to behave unpredictably."

She fiddled with the watch. She looked away, and back at him, her eyes still glassy. "If sharks don't like the taste of human flesh, then why are so many people killed by sharks every year?"

He wished he could take her pain away.

Sadly, he couldn't.

He said, "I understand your anger, Mrs. Edwards. The truth is there were only a hundred and thirty reported cases of shark attacks last year. And out of those, only four were fatal."

She shook her head. "I'm afraid there is nothing you can say that will change my opinion of those man-eaters."

"Granted, Mrs. Edwards, they're terrifying to look at, but they're not evil creatures. And contrary to books and movies, they don't *hunt* humans. Keep in mind, there are always sharks around; people just don't see them. If one does attack, it's usually just a test bite. Then they go away."

She swiped a tear from her eye with her hand. "That was no test bite that almost killed Charles."

He held her gaze. "Exactly. Which is why I'm here talking to you."

Resolve showed. "Then ask your questions so I can go back to the hospital and be with my husband."

"I'm sorry if I sounded insensitive toward his injury. That wasn't my intention. I just wanted you to have an understanding of normal shark behavior. Sharks are getting a bad reputation here on Oahu, and I want to find out what's causing them to behave the way they are. A question that *has* bothered me is why your husband was in the water in the first place?"

"I guess that was my fault. I'm the one who suggested we rent a boat and take it around Diamond Head. Stupid. Just plain stupid. Of course, he was quick to agree. The irony of the situation is we both had this fascination to see a shark." A tear streaked her cheek and she let it fall. "It was those damned turtles beaching themselves the way they were."

"Turtles have a tendency to do that when a large shark is nearby. Most people don't know that, so don't blame yourself. It's not your fault."

She played with the watch and remained silent.

"I'm curious," he said. "Where did you rent the boat?"

"Through the concierge at the hotel. Does it really matter?"

"Not at all. It was just a thought."

She straightened in her seat and looked around, sniffled. "I wish we had never come here for our vacation. Another stupid idea of mine."

He had heard the anguish in her tone, saw it in her tears. He'd been in her shoes more than once. Nothing anyone could say or do would change what happened, nor would it take the self-guilt away.

Only time could do that...and maybe not even then.

"Think back on yesterday. Out there on the boat. You were

anchored outside the reef, yet you say your husband jumped into the water and started swimming toward the shore thinking he could save the turtles. Did you notice anyone else in the immediate vicinity…besides people on the beach, I mean?"

She seemed to focus. "There was another boat. A white one. Only it was leaving the bay when we got there."

He squinted, thinking back to the boat he'd seen from a long way off.

The same one?

He had to wonder.

"Can you tell me anything else about the boat you saw?"

"I wasn't really paying that much attention to it."

Maybe she had, more than she realized.

He decided to take the approach he took with Amy Watson. "Do you know the difference between a cabin cruiser and a center-console fishing boat, like the one you and your husband rented?"

"The boat was a cabin cruiser. I do remember that much. Not one of those big, fancy fishing boats with tall outriggers; smaller. And I only saw one person on board; a man. But I can't tell you anymore about him."

"Nobody else was on deck?"

"Not that I saw."

"How about motors? Did the boat have twin outboards like yours, or was it an inboard?"

"It must have been an inboard."

"Good. Now I'd like you to think really hard." He leaned closer in anticipation of the answer to his next question. "Did you see a name painted on the transom?"

Mrs. Edwards sat fingering the band on the loose-fitting watch. Her eyes took on the thousand-yard stare of a person immersed in thought, a vision forming in the deep recesses of her memory. After a slow five-count, her gaze came up and met his.

He held it.

Her head moved slowly from side to side. "*Sea…*something, I think. I just can't remember. Perhaps Charles remembers."

He sighed.

In time, maybe.

Only how long would that be?
He hoped to have the enigma solved by then.

CHAPTER 16

Jack stood and watched Mrs. Edwards walk away, taking her pain with her.

Sea Swirl? Sea Nymph? Sea God...?

The list of possibilities was endless.

She had promised to ask her husband, but it would likely be days before the man would be close to coherent enough to dredge the name of the boat from the drug-induced haze clouding his memory. Provided he had even taken notice of it.

A big 'if.'

Days—Jack couldn't help thinking—he didn't have.

He considered his next move.

When Amy Watson mentioned seeing a white cabin cruiser nearby, it seemed a bit of a reach considering the number of vessels in the water off Waikiki on any given day. Now the information could prove to be vitally important. Excuses aside, it had been a big mistake on his part to not pursue the idea further with the courageous fifteen-year-old and ask if she had noticed a name on the boat.

A loose end he needed to tie up.

He followed the pathway through the resort, past the pools, and paused at the Hula Bar where it accessed the beach. Amid a flood of memories from the year before, he walked out onto the sand. Duke Kahanamoku Lagoon to his right—separated from the Pacific

Ocean by a grass-covered sand berm—swarmed with people. Kids splashed in the shallow water along the shoreline; paddle boarders skimmed the surface; other visitors seeking the security of the man-made pond swam to the tiny island in the middle, free from concern of a shark attack.

Just another day in paradise.

In front of him, a spattering of people clad in skimpy bathing suits exposed their sprawled bodies to the tropical sun in search of the tan they would take home from their Hawaiian vacation. But gone from the beach was the crowd that regularly laid claim to the sand at this time of day.

He scanned the Fort DeRussy Boardwalk—the scene was the same all the way to Waikiki. Also missing from the picture was the perpetual line of surfers floating in the swells a hundred yards offshore.

Far from normal for spring break.

Fifty feet away, two young boys waded knee-deep into the rising tide, only to be ushered back to shore by a lifeguard. Farther down the beach, a teenage girl screeched while being chased into the surge by a boy her age. They, too, were ordered out by a shout and a wave delivered from a police officer.

Racehorses straining at the gate.

The beachgoers were obeying the 'No Swimming' signs, but for how long?

He needed a break in the case.

His phone trilled.

He fished the cell from his pants pocket and saw Cindy's name on the screen. The thought that shot through his mind was there had been another shark attack. Another death. He prayed that wasn't the case and tapped on.

"I hope you're calling with some good news."

"You're striking out, I take it?" she said.

"You didn't call to ask me how I'm doing. What's up?"

"Director O'Connell wants to see you." Her tone had turned business-like with the boss prowling the office. "And before you ask, no, I don't know what it's all about. But she doesn't sound happy."

I'm sure she isn't.

He shelved the thought and checked his watch. “It’s almost noon. I’ll hit lunch-hour traffic but I’m heading that way now.”

* * *

Forty-five minutes later, Jack climbed the steps at the entrance to NOAA headquarters on Ford Island and strode inside. He got a smile and a go-ahead wave from Cindy. The subtle fragrance of the hibiscus flower he’d picked from the bush outside cast a delicate scent in the air. He handed the blossom to the woman and walked into Director O’Connell’s office. She stood looking at the monitor on her wall, a mug of coffee in her hand. Not a good sign.

He dispensed with his usual repartee. “You wanted to see me?”

She turned from the screen. “I’ve been on the phone with Mayor Kobayashi several times this morning. She wants answers. Honestly, Jack, so do I.”

You’re not the only ones.

He said, “With all due respect, you and I had this conversation. As soon as I have answers, you’ll have them. Then you can pass the answers on to the mayor.”

“I’m afraid it’s not that simple.” She stepped to her desk and set down her coffee. “The attack yesterday has the powers that be calling for heads. This morning you talked to Amy Watson. Reporters won’t be far behind clamoring for an interview. Before they put their twist on what happened, I need to know if she was any help.”

He looked at the monitor and noticed a red dot had been added to Hanauma Bay. The impact of that glowing dot hit him harder than he expected. How many more would appear on the screen before the anomaly was over?

Even one more is too many.

“And Donna Edwards,” he said. “Don’t forget about her.”

O’Connell sighed. “Believe me, I haven’t. The Coast Guard reports determined the shark attacks in both cases to be accidental. Please tell me you have more to add.”

He’d read the reports on Amy Watson and Charles Edwards, and found the Coast Guard’s findings surprising. Not that they had a choice. Without concrete evidence of another cause, there was no way for them to rule otherwise.

His opinion about what happened at Hanauma Bay hadn't changed. "Pardon me if I'm out of line, but we could've done this over the phone."

Her gaze didn't waver. "I wanted to hear it from you, in person."

He knew better than to try the director's impatience, and realized his own frustration over the situation had gotten the better of him. "I wish there *was* more I could tell you to put yours and the mayor's minds at ease. But there is no straightforward answer to what's going on…at least not yet. Was the shark behavior uncharacteristic? In my opinion, yes it was. That's all I can say for now. Bottom line is the sharks attacked that man yesterday, and probably the other victims, for no apparent reason; a fact we were already aware of."

"Not good enough, Jack. Especially since you were there and witnessed the attack on Charles Edwards first hand."

He didn't appreciate O'Connell's accusation. "Are you insinuating I missed something out there?"

Her eyes held a moment. She sighed. "Only that we need answers."

"Which is what I was in the process of getting when you called me in." He took a deep breath to keep his frustration in check, and let it out. "I don't want to get your hopes up, but something did surface that I plan to follow up on as soon as I leave here. After I talk to Amy Watson again, I'll have a better idea if it leads to something."

She crossed her arms against her chest. "Talk to me."

"Mrs. Edwards remembered seeing a boat leave Hanauma Bay about the time they arrived. A white cabin cruiser…*Sea* something. She couldn't recall the entire name. Amy saw a similar boat nearby shortly before the sharks attacked her and her friends. I unfortunately didn't get an opportunity to ask if she noticed a name, but if she confirms Mrs. Edwards's recollection, we have a direction to go in."

He detected a hint of a smile. The first since he entered the room.

She said, "You have a phone. Call her."

CHAPTER 17

Jack lowered his cell and tapped off.

"*Sea Odyssey*," he said in response to his boss' expectant expression.

"She's sure?"

"Amy's a smart kid."

Megan O'Connell picked up the receiver on her desk phone. "Cindy, drop whatever it is you're doing and check the registry on a boat named *Sea Odyssey* and get back to me right away with the information. Top priority."

He managed to contain his anticipation until she returned the receiver to its cradle. Her attention back on him, he said, "That shouldn't take long."

She smiled. "At least you know what you'll be doing this afternoon."

Hopefully, it would bring an end to the shark problem.

Envisioning himself staring into the eyes of the person behind the attacks, seeing the evil lurking in the depths of their mind, he said, "You know you can trust me to get to the bottom of whatever is going on."

"I do. I also know you all too well. I only want you to check out the information, Jack. If it looks like this person is somehow involved, let me know and we'll bring in the police. I don't want you taking matters into your own hands."

Right.

He frowned at the inference. "Whatever do you mean?"

"You know exactly what I mean."

He did, and there was no use playing dumb. "You're referring, of course, to the fracas I got involved in last year?"

"Fracas." She chuckled and shook her head. "More like fracases. Face it, Jack, you have a history. That's partly why I thought you were the perfect person for this job in the first place. But we're playing by the rules. Understand?"

He nodded. "I can do that." Then, he grinned.

Maybe.

* * *

Jack had two locations to check out. Leads that could go a long way toward explaining the cause behind the recent shark attacks.

Could one man actually be responsible for all that had happened?

And if so, why?

At this point he could only wonder, but it was certainly possible. And the Keehi Small Boat Harbor at #4 Sand Island Access Road, where *Sea Odyssey*—a 1986, twenty-eight-foot Carver—was supposed to be moored, seemed like the logical place for him to start. Get a look at the cabin cruiser in question and then talk to Devlin Maxwell, the boat's owner.

He found it difficult to believe the man had somehow instigated the shark attacks currently plaguing Oahu. But the same boat being present at the location of two separate incidents seemed way too coincidental.

He didn't believe in coincidence, and he intended to get to the bottom of it all.

No matter what.

Though he had never moored a boat at the marina, he was familiar with the area. Located between Honolulu Airport and Honolulu Harbor, Keehi Harbor included the La Mariana Marina, and the La Mariana Sailing Club which had been used for filming episodes of *Hawaii Five-O* and *Magnum P.I.*

Make believe.

He needed no reminder that this wasn't a scene in a TV drama.

It was on Sand Island—known as Quarantine Island during the nineteenth century, when it served to quarantine ships believed to carry contagious passengers—that the drug dealer Yang Li met his demise, thanks to Cherise…and in no small part, *him*.

He'd been lucky that day.

And others.

He hoped his luck held.

The afternoon had heated up into the eighties, and with the approaching storm, the humidity was on the rise as well. He left his Jeep in the parking lot and walked to the edge of the marina. Ignoring the oppressive heat, he spent a minute scanning the nearly four hundred yachts berthed there.

The sea of boats bobbed and creaked in the tide.

It was impossible to pick out *Sea Odyssey* in the forest of masts. Not that he expected to on first glance.

If she's there, I'll ferret her out.

He located the slip number he had been given and sighed. His fear that he would find the berth empty was replaced by relief when he saw *Sea Odyssey* gently tugging at her mooring lines. The cruiser had been tied bow first. From where he stood, he couldn't see the name painted on the transom but the vessel was a white, twenty-eight-foot Carver as listed on the registry. He walked onto the finger of pier extending starboard of the boat and confirmed the name.

Large, blue, easy-to-read printing.

No mistake.

The hull, he noticed, showed some wear from age, but the vessel appeared to have been well cared for. The curtains on the cabin were pulled, preventing him from seeing inside; a mild disappointment. For a fleeting second, he considered climbing aboard and forcing the lock on the door. Certainly not what his boss would want him to do, and not a wise move if people were watching.

There were always prying eyes, it seemed.

And it wasn't a necessary risk.

Not yet.

He noticed a hand-sized dark smear on the gunwale. The boat nudged an aft rubber bumper against his side of the pier, allowing him a closer look. He grasped the top edge of the hull and leaned in to satisfy his suspicion. He had seen enough dried blood to know what it looked like, and he had no doubt that's exactly what it was.

But the presence of blood on the stern of a boat was not necessarily cause for concern. It could have easily come from a fish being hauled over the side. Any fish. And that brought to mind the recent rash of dead sharks that had been found washed ashore. *Speared.* His hunch was further confirmed by a seven-foot-long harpoon cleated to the port gunwale.

Not a crime in itself.

But when people die…

Devlin Maxwell definitely had some explaining to do.

CHAPTER 18

Jack parked in front of the address he had been given for Maxwell's residence on Booth Street in the lower Pacific Heights area of the island. A WWII-era house similar to others in the area with a newer model, red, 4-door Nissan sitting in the drive. A good sign someone was home.

He checked his dive watch. Not quite three.

On the drive over, he concluded there was no need for stealth. He wasn't there to bust in and arrest the guy. He only intended to talk to the man. Anything more than that would fall in the hands of the police.

He had promised Meg; he planned to keep that promise.

Unless…

He hit the electric door lock on his key fob and followed the concrete walkway leading to the front door. Several mature mango trees laden with immature fruit the size of marbles, banana trees, and plantings of heliconia, hibiscuses, and birds-of-paradise as tall as the windows on the house, gave the place a secluded feel. At the base of the steps leading up to the porch, he paused and peered over his shoulder. Waikiki and Diamond Head loomed in the distance. The Pacific Ocean beyond.

A million-dollar view.

Not to mention, a waste, he couldn't help thinking, if it turned out Maxwell *was* behind the shark attacks.

He thought about the strangeness of the situation.

The question that continued to nag him was not so much who was involved; it appeared Maxwell was their man. But what motivated him to do what he had done? And how had he engineered it?

This was no act of Mother Nature. Sharks don't hunt people.

Until now.

He started up the steps and was greeted with a meow from a large, silver tabby that loped out onto the edge of the porch to meet him. He reached down and gave the cat a scratch and a stroke the length of its back that got him another meow and a loud purr.

The animal rubbed both cheeks on his hand, clearly wanting more attention.

"You've got quite a swagger there, big boy. Swagger, that's a good name for you. So, what's the matter, your master not home?"

He gave the cat another couple of strokes and stepped past the animal. There had been no sounds from inside and he feared Maxwell wasn't home. But that didn't explain the car in the driveway. He knocked on the front door and waited.

The cat's meows intensified.

So did Jack's rising doubts. It began to look as though he had guessed wrong about the car.

He knocked again.

The cat continued its cries for attention.

Still nothing from inside.

He tried the knob.

Locked.

Suspicion ran through him. He stepped to the window at the far end of the porch and strained to see inside through a separation in the curtains where the two panels hadn't been pulled together. He could make out a few pieces of furniture in a living room. A darkened hallway beyond.

No movement. Nothing appeared out of place.

Yet, the ominous feeling that came with the eerie silence, remained.

He hurried to the window at the other end of the porch, slid a wicker chair out of the way and peeked in through a two-inch gap in the curtains. The cat at his feet continued to voice its complaints. The feline, too, sensed something was wrong.

What?

Then he caught a faint odor.

A foul stench.

One he had smelled before and would never forget.

Death.

Fearing the worst, he pressed his nose to the glass and shaded his eyes with the palms of his hands to better see inside. He scanned the interior, his efforts more frantic now. Still, nothing looked out of place. No TV noise or music came from an unseen stereo receiver or MP3 player.

Only quiet.

Then he spied the bare feet protruding from the rear of the couch, a black rubber sandal askew on the right foot. A second sandal lay upside-down on the floor and…something else.

He squinted, harder.

Flies.

And the odor of decay hastened by the heat and humidity.

Nothing more of the person was visible from where Jack stood. Even so, he saw enough to know the subject was male.

His chest tightened.

He glanced at the door and considered kicking it in, but he didn't need to see the body up close to know the man inside was dead.

As was his hope of getting information from him.

It's a matter for the police to handle.

He pulled his phone from his pocket and placed a call to 911.

CHAPTER 19

Jack took a seat in the wicker chair to wait in the relative coolness of the shaded porch. He heard sirens in the distance getting closer as officers raced to the scene. An unnecessary risk for the patrolmen to take under the circumstances.

Maxwell wasn't going anywhere except the morgue.

If that's who lay dead on the floor inside the house.

At this point though, anything was possible, and he would not speculate. Although that is what he had done by giving the victim's name to the emergency operator.

He had made two phone calls: one to 911, and a brief call to Megan O'Connell to alert her of the situation. Definitely not the news he wanted to deliver, nor the update she wanted to receive.

Now a big question remained. One he couldn't answer.

Yet.

Was this the end of Oahu's shark problem?

He wanted to believe the island would now be able to return to normal. That the trouble would end with Maxwell's death.

But would it?

He still had no idea what happened inside the house.

How had the man died? Natural causes? Suicide? Murder?

If it turned out Maxwell *had* been murdered, he had been killed for a reason, and that would mean a wild card remained in play.

But to what end?

He huffed his frustration.

Questions leading to more questions.

Not the first time.

A breeze rustled the leaves of the trees and the plantings around him in a further sign of the approaching storm. He combed his fingers through his hair, smoothing a windblown lock back in place.

Swagger the cat jumped onto his lap and settled in, kneading splayed paws as though making bread.

"Don't get too comfortable," he said.

The sirens that had grown louder, abruptly stopped. He heard the roar of motors speeding toward his location. The police cruisers were close now and would be there any second. He knew the drill. He eased Swagger off his lap and stood in the open with his hands where the officers could see them. A recent upswing of violent assaults on police had law enforcement everywhere on edge.

He would provide no excuse for a nervous trigger finger.

A moment later, a patrol unit rolled to a stop behind his Jeep, lights flashing. A second car followed. The officers exited their vehicles and approached the house, hands poised on their sidearms.

A necessary precaution.

"My name is Jack Ferrell," he said as he raised his hands a little higher. "I'm the person who called."

Swagger took that as his cue to head for the hills.

The officer closest to him tightened his grip on his semi-automatic. "Keep your hands where we can see them and step down from the porch."

Jack did as he was told. "You can relax. I'm not armed."

"We need to check," the officer said. "I'm sure you understand."

"Of course."

The second officer approached from behind and conducted a quick but efficient pat-down search for weapons. Apparently satisfied, the officer stepped back.

Jack motioned his head toward the house. "The body is in the living room. I tried the doorknob and found it locked, so I didn't go in."

"No one else is inside?"

"Not that I know of."

The two officers, appearing not anxious to rush into the situation, stepped back a few feet and conferred with each other. Jack didn't move from his place at the foot of the steps. The officer, who had searched him, spoke into a handheld radio.

A third officer arrived—a sergeant, according to his stripes—and joined his men. They spoke briefly among themselves, and then he looked at Jack. "You're the person who discovered the body?"

Jack nodded an affirmative, and even though he would bet money the sergeant had been briefed by the two patrolmen, he added, "My name is Jack Ferrell. I'm a marine biologist working for NOAA. I called it in."

"I know who you are."

I bet you do.

Jack kept quiet.

"Wait here with Officer Chow," the sergeant added, without bothering to introduce himself.

For whatever reason, he and the commanding officer on scene were off to a bad start. Jack swallowed his irritation, choosing not to argue the point and chance making things worse. He had already decided he wasn't going anywhere anytime soon, even if he was allowed to.

My assignment ends or begins here.

He asked Chow, "Do we have to stand out here in the sun?"

Chow pointed toward a leafed-out plumeria tree with a few early blossoms adding a pleasant fragrance to the air. "Let's wait over there."

From the coolness of the shade, Jack watched the sergeant and the patrol officer climb the steps with their semi-automatics drawn in a two-handed grip, muzzles pointing down, and assume positions at the sides of the front door. The patrolman sidestepped with his back against the wall and peeked through the window that revealed the body. His attention back on the sergeant, he nodded an apparent confirmation. Resuming his position next to the door, he tried the knob and shook his head.

What happened next, happened fast.

Almost like everything came at him at once.

A loud knock on the door, followed by, "Honolulu Police

Department" a fraction of a second before the sergeant kicked the door open, splintering the jamb in the process. In the next instant, they were both inside, service weapons pointed, each of them yelling, "Police!" A bit of an overkill in Jack's mind but necessary for everyone's safety. From where he stood, he saw the officers step past the body, but lost sight of them when they moved deeper into the house.

He craned his neck and heard movement but nothing else.

What were they finding?

He glanced at his watch, anxious for them to return. But not because he would be free to go.

There were questions to be answered first.

CHAPTER 20

Jack stood staring at the open doorway, waiting for the sergeant and patrolman to emerge.

They seemed to be taking their time.

A good sign?

Jack wondered what they were finding.

Had Maxwell been murdered as initially suspected?

Or was the dead body that of someone else?

Eventually, both officers moved back into the living room. The limited view he had of them through the doorway told him nothing. When the officers at last stepped out onto the porch, the sergeant had his phone pressed to his ear. Tight-lipped, he did more listening than talking.

What's that all about?

There was little Jack could do other than wait his turn.

Leaving the patrolman posted at the doorway, the sergeant finally made his way into the shade of the plumeria tree. The scene inside the house, or the call, had tightened his expression even more than it had been when he first arrived.

"Well?" Jack asked.

"I'm afraid we got off to a bad start," the sergeant said. "And I want to apologize."

What the...?

Jack let the words sink in. He doubted the sergeant apologized often. Something had humbled the man.

He read the name pinned to the uniform. "Thank you, Sergeant Kaouli. No apology necessary. I'm here at the request of my director at NOAA looking into the rash of shark attacks we've had. State and county officials from the top down want the problem resolved immediately, if not sooner. So do I."

Kaouli held up his phone as if to reinforce what he was about to say. "So I've been told. It appears your boss has been on the phone with the mayor making sure you get the cooperation you need. The mayor called the chief, the chief called my captain, and my captain called me. I didn't even have a chance to arrive on scene before I was being told what to do. A few minutes ago, I learned the governor is breathing down our necks as well."

Jack could sympathize with the sergeant's frustration. "I've been there myself and found it quite annoying. Is the guy on the floor Devlin Maxwell?"

"According to his driver's license he is. And if I had to venture a guess based on the injuries, I'd say he was beaten to death. Of course, we won't know that for sure until the M.E. is finished with him."

"Beating someone to death would imply a lot of rage was involved. Any idea what the motive might have been?"

"Not robbery. His money and credit cards were still in his wallet. Of course, it is always possible something else was taken."

"Any chance I can have a look around inside?"

"Sorry. I can't allow you to do that." Kaouli glanced toward the house, in the direction of the officer standing guard by the door. "Detective Tokunaga is on his way here. You can ask him when he arrives."

* * *

Jack hoped his prior association with Detective Brian Tokunaga would help smooth over the awkwardness of the situation. Or at a minimum, get him a positive greeting from the man and a firm handshake.

And with luck, professional courtesy when it came to sharing information.

Even a little would help.

After a brief conversation with Sergeant Kaouli and one of the other officers, Tokunaga walked over to Jack, and said, "So our paths cross once again."

Jack couldn't help but smile. Not because the detective's comment came across as particularly amusing. They shared a history that ended well, and he respected Tokunaga for being a straight-shooter.

He offered his hand. "I wish it were under different circumstances."

Tokunaga gave it a firm shake. "You've got people behind you on this one. I'll give you that much."

"You know the governor and the mayor want results fast."

"My captain made that perfectly clear. But it's still my murder case, so wait outside. I'll let you know when I'm done."

Jack didn't argue.

He needed no explanation from Tokunaga to understand the importance of crime scene preservation. The last thing he wanted to do was screw up evidence that would be vital when it came time to bring Devlin Maxwell's killer to justice.

Only when the evidence techs finished going over the place would he get his chance to see inside. Until that time came, he would have to be content to stand in the shade and watch.

"You're on your own out here," Chow said. "I've been assigned to help canvas the neighborhood."

They hadn't talked much, but the little conversation that took place between the two of them in the relative coolness of the plumeria tree had been pleasant.

Jack nodded, happy to be alone. "Be careful."

"Always," Chow said.

Jack checked his watch and realized he had done a lot of waiting around since arriving at the house.

No surprise there.

He resolved himself to the very obvious fact he would be there a while longer, all night if that's what it took to find out what went on inside that house. Until then, he had plenty of time to think.

And to report in.

The Megan O'Connell he'd come to know over the years came across as patient and understanding. The shark attacks seemed to have changed that part of her; she would be expecting an update.

He found a folding lawn chair tucked in among the mango trees. Dirt and debris from the vegetation coated the webbing. He dusted it off the best he could, carried it back to the plumeria tree he had been standing under, and set himself up to make the call among the fragrant blossoms that kept away the putrid smell of death, strong with the door wide open.

It turned out O'Connell was indeed glad to hear from him. Though disappointed he didn't have more to tell her, she thanked him for the update, and requested he keep her posted on any new developments.

She wouldn't expect another call from him anytime soon.

Swagger sauntered over and leaped into his lap. He stared at his new friend and stroked the feline's back amid a contented purr. The cat obviously craved affection. The tabby wasn't alone; the same craving had been on his mind as well.

Thoughts exacerbated by the late-night visit from Kiana.

Some things are right, and some things are just wrong.

He put her out of his mind and focused his thoughts on his much-anticipated sojourn with Cherise that lay only a month away.

Sooner, if she could manage.

Thirty minutes went by and he sat looking at his watch for the umpteenth time. There was no doubt in his mind he would be there for more than just a little while.

Longer than he wanted, but his resolve remained.

A few minutes later, a black Charger with dark-tinted windows stopped out front. The driver got out and walked to the open door of the residence. He wore a necktie, loose at the collar, and had a badge and a holstered semi-automatic clipped on his belt. No suit jacket. Another detective or possibly a supervisor. Detective Tokunaga conferred with the man on the porch a minute before leading him inside.

Jack could hear talking, but from his seat under the tree, the words came across muffled and impossible for him to understand. Detective Necktie walked out a few minutes later, got into his car and drove off.

Jack began to feel like a spectator in the cheap seats at a ball game.

He sat there forty more minutes before he had his fill of sitting idle. He left Swagger in the comfort of the chair and resorted to pacing the yard in order to pass time. The body had been wheeled out ten minutes earlier, but Tokunaga and the crime scene technicians remained inside. He paused on the sidewalk and peered through the doorway, hoping to catch a glimpse of their progress.

A squabble between two myna birds drew his attention away from the house.

He sighed.

How much could there be left to do?

He returned to his seat in the shade. Another full half-hour passed before Tokunaga stepped onto the porch. His chest and armpits ringed with sweat.

Jack gave the detective a moment before walking over and asking, "Any conclusions as to what happened?"

Tokunaga stepped down from the porch and moved to the side, giving the techs leaving the house room to file past with their equipment. He refocused and said, "I understand from Sergeant Kaouli he told you he thought Maxwell had been beaten to death. That was the M.E.'s initial determination as well. But without knowing more about Maxwell, or an itemization of property inside the house, I can't speculate on the motive behind the murder."

"So nothing new?"

"Not yet."

"Meaning?" Jack held on to a glimmer of hope.

Tokunaga gave him a long look. "I'm just getting started."

CHAPTER 21

Jack knew the bulldog resolve driving Tokunaga.

"Mind if I have a look through the house?"

"You think I missed something?"

"I know better than that. But I want to help, and I want *you* to help me."

The detective's gaze went from Jack to the house, then back to Jack. "Hope you don't mind the smell."

Jack didn't waver. "I'll hold my breath."

That got a chuckle from Tokunaga. "We can talk more inside."

They walked next to each other on the sidewalk. Jack saw no need for small talk—evidently, Tokunaga did.

He said, "I heard you've been busy."

Jack couldn't imagine the detective had heard about the mess in Florida a few months earlier. A phone call from the police in Miami, maybe. The detective there checking up on him.

He said, "I bought a boat, if that's what you mean?"

"That's not exactly what I referred to."

Jack never for a second believed it was. "I think you already know."

He took the lead going up the steps. He strode past the posted officer and the splintered doorjamb and stopped in the center of the room. He stared down at where the body had lain, a pool of dried blood still visible on the hardwood floor. Blood spatter stained the back of the sofa.

"How long had he been dead?"

"The M.E. estimated 24 hours."

Jack scanned the floor. "Was there a weapon involved?"

"We think the person who murdered Maxwell hammered his head against the floor until he was dead. A person doesn't do something that brutal without getting a lot of blood on him." Tokunaga swept his hand over the room. "The condition of the furniture suggests Maxwell was killed without much of a struggle on his part."

"So the suspect is a man of considerable size and strength."

"And probably someone he knew."

Jack stepped to a side-table, picked up a framed photograph and studied the image. A woman and a young boy smiled back at him. A happier time.

"He lived here alone?"

"From what we've been able to determine. A couple of years ago his son was killed by a shark while surfing. His wife committed suicide about a year later."

Jack nodded. It all fit. But it didn't explain murder.

He motioned his chin toward the hallway. "How about the bedrooms?"

"There's one room you'll want to see. Maxwell worked at Kahana Electronics on the corner of Auahi and Cooke Street downtown. Looks like he was in the habit of bringing his work home with him, or he had one hell-of-a hobby. I'll be heading over there once I'm done here."

"Electronics, huh. I find that interesting."

"How's that?"

Jack recalled articles he had read in scientific journals. Scientists had determined sharks have distinct personalities, and that they can be trained to recognize shapes and colors, remembering how to complete a task months or years later. Even to the point of teaching other sharks how to do things. He could not imagine something like that being in play here, but what about some sort of electrical stimulus?

The thought was far too scary.

He asked, "How much do you know about shark behavior?"

Tokunaga shrugged. "As much as the next person, I guess. I sure don't want to be in the water with one; I can tell you that much. What are you getting at?"

"It's an accepted fact among scientists in the field that sharks don't particularly like the taste of humans. When sharks encounter an unfamiliar creature that might be a potential food source—like a human—they will sometimes want to investigate more closely. When sharks do approach and take a test bite, they use their teeth the way humans use their hands. Unfortunately, even a quick nibble from a large shark can be life-threatening and accounts for most of the deaths on record."

"Yeah, well, I'll just have to take your word for it."

"You find what I'm saying hard to believe?"

"Jack, as far as I'm concerned, sharks are swimming garbage cans that will eat anything and everything."

"True to a degree. Tiger sharks have been found with things like license plates, tin cans, and even live hand grenades in them. But given options—providing they're not too hungry at the time—sharks capable of chowing down on something the size of a human prefer a high-fat meal, like a seal or tuna."

Tokunaga pursed his lips and motioned toward the hallway. "Have a look in that room and then tell me what you think. It's the first one on the right."

Jack stepped in that direction with the detective following behind him. The door stood open. No padlock on a sturdy metal hasp to keep out prying eyes. Maxwell lived alone with a solitary undertaking.

In this case, sharks.

The room was cluttered with electrical components. A long, wooden table sat off to his right. Large and small screwdrivers, needle-nose pliers, and wrenches hung from hooks on a pegboard panel affixed to the wall behind it. A roll of solder and a soldering gun sat at an angle on the worktop below the tools. Books on sharks and electronics sat in a stack off to the side. Clearly Maxwell spent time in this room, but constructing what? There were no schematics. No unfinished projects to offer a clue.

But he could guess.

The presence of the electrical components in the house tended to confirm his initial suspicion…making it no less scary.

And infinitely more frightening.

Electrical shark deterrents had been around for years with limited success. All claim to work by emitting a small electrical current into the water, which interferes with special sensory organs in a shark's snout. Their organs detect small electrical currents given off by their prey, such as from the heartbeat of a fish. When overstimulated, however, the sensory organs spasm, forcing the shark to turn away.

Only in this case, the sharks attack.

He took the leap in his reasoning. "You wanted to know what I think. I think Devlin Maxwell developed an electrical device that attracts sharks, driving them into a frenzy to feed."

"You got all that from looking at a few electronic components. That's quite a reach, isn't it?"

"Not so much. Electrical shark deterrents have been used for years with limited success. There are claims that in some cases they attracted sharks instead of deterring them."

"And you think that's what's going on here?"

He took another leap. "I saw the sharks attack that poor guy at Hanauma Bay. It wasn't normal shark behavior. Something caused them to go after Mr. Edwards in a feeding frenzy. Then there are the other attacks that have happened recently. Maxwell's boat was seen in the area of at least two of those incidents. Maxwell's son was killed by a shark. A year later his wife ends her own life out of grief over the loss. You can imagine how the man must have felt. I'm thinking the death of his family—particularly his teenage son—was the impetus behind it all."

Tokunaga glanced around the room. "But why would he put together a device that makes sharks attack people?"

"I don't think it started out that way. Initially, sharks were being found washed ashore; dead. Speared, to be exact. I saw his boat. There was blood on the stern and a harpoon cleated to the inside of the gunwale. My guess is his revenge against the sharks morphed into some kind of sick grudge against the people of Oahu."

"Say I agree. That doesn't explain the motive behind his murder."

"It does if someone killed him to get their hands on the device."

Tokunaga's gaze fixed on Jack. "Holy crap."

CHAPTER 22

Jack digested the grim inference in a few seconds of silence.

"What can you tell me about Kahana Electronics?"

Detective Tokunaga shook his head. "Unfortunately, I haven't had any dealings with them."

Jack arched a brow. "Or fortunately, as the case may be."

"Good point. I'm headed downtown now if you want to meet me there. The officers can finish up here."

Jack checked his watch. "It's almost five. Perhaps you should give them a call and find out what time they close."

His comment drew a frown from the detective. A scowl that deepened when Tokunaga Googled the company on his cellular. His gaze came up with the phone poised in his hand. "We might be screwed."

Jack left him to make the call and wandered over to the worktable. He had been correct when he told himself the game would end or begin here. Until a few minutes ago, he hadn't realized how right his thinking had been. He couldn't imagine the situation being worse, but he had a feeling things were about to get a whole lot nastier.

People had suffered grievous injury as the result of Maxwell's actions. A boy had died…some would call it murder.

Now one killer had been traded for another.

Could one be worse than the other?

The thought prickled his skin.

He worried that people on the island were about to find out.

Tokunaga tapped off. “You were right. Place closes at five so we never would have made it there in time. The owner volunteered to stick around and talk to us providing we didn’t take too long getting there. Still want to join me?”

Jack didn’t have to think about his answer. “Whenever you’re ready.”

Swagger chose that moment to walk into the room and rub against his leg. It seemed the cat had taken a liking to him; the feeling was mutual. He squatted and gave the feline a pet.

Tokunaga said, “I think you have a friend.”

Jack straightened, concerned for the animal. “What’s going to happen to him now that his owner is dead?”

“Maxwell doesn’t have any living family on the island so we’ll have to turn him over to the humane society. Hopefully, someone will adopt him.”

“Consider him adopted.” Jack scooped up the cat and walked out of the room. On his way through the house, he detoured into the kitchen, located a bag of dry cat food and two bowls that read “Kitty” on the sides. One for water; one for food. He grabbed the kibbles and dishes, and carried them and his new friend to his Jeep.

Tokunaga caught him at the driver’s door. Chow and another officer stood a few feet away. “Give me a couple of minutes to talk with my officers.”

“Have they turned up any leads?”

He shook his head. “Not so far.”

When Tokunaga stepped away to confer with the two patrolmen, Jack set Swagger on the passenger seat, and the food and “Kitty” dishes on the floorboard. Then he climbed behind the wheel with his phone in his hand so he could call his boss. At least this time he had need-to-know information to pass on to her before she left for the day. While he listened to her phone ring, Swagger curled into a ball on the seat and closed its eyes. No more than a second later, the cat began to snore.

Some mouse hunter you are.

“Perfect timing,” O’Connell said. “I was getting ready to head out the door."

"You spoke with the mayor?"

"I got off the phone with her a few minutes ago."

He could guess the mayor's response. "I gather she's opening the beaches?"

"With Maxwell dead, she didn't see any reason not to."

Figures.

He fought a wave of frustration. "With all due respect, the mayor should have at least waited until she had all the information before she acted."

The comment brought a sigh from O'Connell. "Talk to me, Jack."

She has a reason to be concerned.

He spent the next couple of minutes briefing her on his conversation with the detective and what they observed inside the house. She listened without interruption, leaving him to wonder if she was formulating the same conclusion he had come to.

When he finished talking, she said, "So you think the decision to allow people back into the water is premature?"

Mayor Kobayashi, he feared, had indeed acted rashly. A gamble that island life could return to normal. It might not be today, and it might not be tomorrow, but there would be another shark attack. He remained convinced of that.

"This isn't over, Meg. Someone murdered Maxwell for a reason. My belief is they killed him to get their hands on his device. That scares me."

Director O'Connell fell silent.

After a couple of beats, she said, "Let's pray you're wrong."

CHAPTER 23

Matt Corvin walked into the bar at the Outrigger Hotel and took a seat where he had a view of the beach and the ocean beyond. Sunlight dappled the surface of the water with a glare that made him glad he'd remembered to wear his sunglasses. He ordered a pale ale on draft and watched a lifeguard pull a "No Swimming" sign from the sand. The bright red shark graphic stenciled above the writing accentuated the warning that was apparently no longer necessary.

About fucking time.

He wanted to yell the words loud enough for everyone around him to hear, but kept the thought to himself.

The shark issue hadn't been the source of his current financial problems. In time, sure, if tourism dropped off dramatically. According to the local news, resorts and vacation rentals on the island had taken a hit—a temporary slump in bookings. All that would change now that people were allowed back in the water.

He felt confident he would recover from his latest setback, and that put a smile on his face.

Thanks, Devlin.

He felt a thumping in his chest.

Excitement over his decision.

He had missed lunch, but not out of dread for what happened to Devlin Maxwell; it'd been a mercy killing, after all. Eliminating his coworker and stealing the man's invention had only been a first step. Things were moving fast now.

Coming up with a balloon payment of a million and a half dollars due and payable had seemed unattainable, until he'd heard about an outfit that specialized in situations like his. A dilemma he would never have faced had the short-term rental permits come through on the two houses he had purchased to be vacation rentals.

Guaranteed big money.

Hawaii's gold rush.

Both homes were prime locations situated two blocks from Waikiki beach. An easy five thousand a week, twenty thousand a month. Each. A total of nearly a half-million a year.

Every year.

More than enough to qualify for a refinance loan on the balance due.

The company who helped put the deal together for him, promised the permits would come through in a couple of months. All he needed to do was hold on for another eight weeks and he would be good to go.

But the bank refused to work with him.

Fuckers.

Everything he owned had been leveraged to the hilt, and he had been thrown to the wolves by the asshole money lenders. Pay the balance due or face default on the mortgage and repossession of both properties, along with the house he and his family lived in, which would have left them with nothing. He couldn't let that happen.

So he turned to Li Fang.

The respectable Mr. Fang—tall, good looking, graying at the temples—conducted business dealings from a twenty-seventh-floor office suite in the Ahi Tower at Bishop Square.

"You're in trouble," Fang said when they talked.

"Deep shit," Matt had agreed. "But I'm almost home free. All I need is one-point-five million to get the banks off my ass for the next eight weeks."

When Fang didn't answer him, he figured that was the end of any deal between them.

But it wasn't.

"And the banks have said no to an extension on your loan…. But you're nearly out of the woods." Fang let a few seconds pass. Long enough for the words to sink in. "Okay, a million and a half payable in eight weeks."

The offer Fang presented seemed doable.

But he knew it would cost him.

"My rates are the best you will get," Fang had claimed. "One-point-five million for eight weeks at, let's say, seven-and-a-half percent interest."

Matt recalled how good that sounded until he did the math.

A fucking rip-off.

"That's almost fifty percent a year," he'd said.

His complaint only made Fang smile.

Matt remembered that grin being more of a smirk.

"Ninety thousand dollars," Fang had said. "If you choose to do business that is my price. Trust me, you won't do better anyplace else."

"And the property?"

Again, that self-satisfied smile. "Security for the loan."

One balloon payment for another.

The thought left him feeling punched in the gut. But at least Fang had agreed to lend the money.

Plus seven-and-a-half percent interest for eight weeks.

He had run out of options, and so he agreed.

"Sure. Let's do it. One-point-five million for eight weeks."

Fang nodded. "I know there won't be a problem with you paying the money back."

Matt stared at his hands. Recalling his thought at the time, the comment sounded as though Fang knew something *he* didn't.

Now he knew what that something was.

CHAPTER 24

There was still plenty of heat and humidity in the day when Jack parked in the shadow of a palm next to Detective Tokunaga's cruiser in downtown Honolulu. Other than a Mercedes SUV, they were the only cars in the paved lot next to Kahana Electronics.

He dumped bottled water into one of the dishes, and a handful of dry food in the other. The temperature in the shade was cool enough for Swagger to be fine in the Jeep. He lowered the windows on the doors a couple of inches and joined the detective at the rear of the officer's car. "You're sure the owner told you he'd be here?"

"He assured me he'd stick around." Tokunaga pointed at the Mercedes. "That's probably his SUV."

Jack scanned the building. Not much larger than the corner liquor store. "For some reason I pictured the business being larger than this."

Tokunaga cocked an eyebrow. "How big does the place have to be?"

A passing car honked as if driving home the point.

Jack motioned Tokunaga forward. "After you."

They found the front entrance unlocked, walked inside and stood at a scarred Formica countertop, not unlike what a person would find in a neighborhood auto parts store. Beyond that was a wall with a door, and a space large enough to accommodate a scarred wooden desk with a phone and a computer. Two-way radios, fish finders, handheld GPS units, and a few electronic devices Jack didn't recognize sat on shelves at opposite ends of the room. A few tagged devices sat on a shelf next to the desk.

The door behind the counter opened and an athletic looking, dark-skinned man—maybe fifty—stepped through. His collar-length dark hair hung over his ears in a gentle curl, and he wore a pleasant smile.

"I'm Gordon Kahana," he said.

Tokunaga took the lead and extended his hand. They shook. "Thank you for waiting for us. I'm Detective Tokunaga. This is Jack Ferrell, a marine biologist with NOAA. He's assisting me on my investigation. Is there somewhere we can sit and talk?"

Kahana motioned toward the door behind him. "I have an office in back. Give me a moment to lock up out here, and we can talk in there."

They waited while the owner used a key to set the deadbolt. No more than a minute.

Kahana said, "I hope this won't take long. I need to get home for dinner."

Tokunaga's stoic expression didn't crack. "We'll try to be brief."

On his way through the building to the back room, Jack got a glimpse at the innerworkings of the business. There were a half-dozen individual workstations similar to what Maxwell had set up in his home. All of them were unoccupied at the moment. Judging from the quantity of devices sitting on shelves and in pieces on the workbenches, there was no shortage of projects to keep the employees busy.

Jack and Tokunaga took seats in padded, straight-backed chairs while Kahana settled into a swivel chair behind his desk. When they were all seated, Kahana asked, "On the phone, you mentioned you needed to talk to me about Devlin Maxwell. I hope this doesn't mean he's in some kind of trouble."

Tokunaga said, "I'm sorry to have to tell you this, but Devlin Maxwell is dead. Someone murdered him."

Kahana's eyes flared. "When? Where?"

When Tokunaga let the question hang a beat, Jack could tell the detective did not take pleasure in being the bearer of bad news.

The obvious downside of his job.

"At his house," Tokunaga said. "He was found dead in his living room earlier today. The preliminary report indicates he was killed sometime yesterday afternoon."

Kahana slumped in his chair, clearly shocked. After a moment, "My God. This is terrible. Why would someone want to kill Devlin?"

Jack kept quiet, letting the detective do his job. He had faced the officer's probing stare and knew what it felt like.

Tokunaga fixed it on Kahana. "We're hoping you could tell us."

A pause; then, "Honestly, I don't know much about the man's private life other than what happened to his family. That ripped the poor guy apart. We all felt it."

"How long had he been employed here?"

"Ten years. Longer than anyone else. And as far as I know, he always got along with his coworkers."

"Any close friends that you're aware of?"

"Here at work?"

"That's what I'm asking."

He shrugged. "Like I told you, he got along with all of his coworkers, but I wouldn't say he was friendlier with one more than another."

Jack hated to interrupt, but felt he had to ask: "What exactly is it you do here?"

Kahana swept his hand toward the stacked storage shelves visible through the window that offered a view from his office. "We repair just about anything electronic. Marine two-way radios, fish finders, GPS units—all types of navigation equipment—those are the most common items."

Tokunaga let the owner talk without interruption. Jack had seen the detective work. Patient. Until it came time not to be.

This wasn't one of those times.

Kahana silent once again, Tokunaga asked, "Have you ever seen Devlin Maxwell work on a project of his own?"

The business owner's brow furrowed. "You mean something we weren't repairing for a customer?"

"Exactly."

Kahana gave him a long look as though giving his answer

careful consideration. "The loss of his son messed Devlin up bad. And then his wife—her death put him over the edge. His work productivity suffered, and he moped around the place depressed. But I kept him on, thinking he would eventually get over his grief. After some time, he did come around."

"You're saying Devlin found a way to cope?"

"But not the way you might think. He replaced the pain that was eating away at him with something far stronger: hate. Like I said, he'd been moping around the place. Then one day he started working on an electronic shark deterrent. His own design, he claimed."

Jack said, "Electronic shark repellents have been around for a long time."

Kahana nodded. "We've even repaired a few. Devlin thought he could build a device that was one-hundred-percent effective. Then one day, a couple of months ago, I noticed he stopped working on it."

"And?"

"I asked him how it was going with his project. He got this kind of strange smile on his face and said better than he expected. I left it at that."

"And you weren't concerned about his hatred of sharks?"

"Why would I be?"

The puzzle pieces fit. Jack let the man's answer lie. "Did any of his coworkers show a special interest in his invention?"

"Matt Corvin, maybe. You might try him."

"Tell me about Corvin." Tokunaga fixed his stare on Kahana. "What kind of guy is he?"

"Nice as anyone, I guess. A little rough around the edges at times, but he's good with electronics. He's worked here nearly as long as Devlin."

That last detail caught Jack's attention.

The news must have gotten Tokunaga thinking as well because he said, "People who work together that long know things about each other."

Kahana shrugged. "I guess so. You'll have to ask him."

CHAPTER 25

Matt Corvin downed the remainder of the IPA he'd been nursing for the past half-hour and checked the time on his phone. With every working stiff headed home for the day, six-thirty in the evening seemed like an odd time to meet. But not when it came to conducting the kind of business he had in mind.

It was his turn to make an offer to Li Fang.

While there was still time.

He stared into the foam in the bottom of his glass, picturing the device he had left hidden in the hidey-hole under the rear seat of his pickup: a black box slightly smaller than a cell phone, watertight, a stubby antenna, a simple on/off switch, no markings of any kind to offer a clue to the apparatus's purpose, how to operate it or its affective range. A complication further exacerbated by Devlin's adamant refusal to divulge the information.

His coworker disappointed him.

A fool to the end.

He would not repeat Devlin's mistake.

He made the drive across town to Bishop Square in heavier than normal traffic. Or perhaps the traffic was no different than any other day at this time and it was just his impatience that made it feel that way. He didn't care which, but he did notice his mood had soured by the time he stepped onto the elevator. Not good when he was about to enter into a negotiation with a man like Li Fang.

He straightened his back and forced aside all thoughts about the traffic he had fought to get there.

Calm in the eye of the storm.

The doors opened on the twenty-seventh floor of the Ahi Tower. He took a deep breath, squared his shoulders in resolve, and strode inside the air-conditioned reception area of Fang's corner office suite with its million-dollar panoramic view of Honolulu Harbor, Sand Island, and Mamala Bay.

It surprised him to see a man—Asian, like Fang; clean-shaven, a scar from a cleft lip—sitting at the desk, his feet propped on the corner of the polished Koa wood, and not the accommodating, pretty, young Asian woman he had met two months earlier. He had hoped this would be a private meeting.

Apparently, Fang had other ideas.

"Mr. Fang is busy at the moment," the man at the desk said without introduction. "You'll have to wait." His right hand came up and he pointed at a straight-backed chair on the far side of the room.

Nothing more…

A stall tactic, Matt figured, to make him sweat.

He didn't have to know what was going on in Fang's office to imagine it wasn't good.

* * *

The middle-aged man stood in silence with his shoulders slumped, his back bowed, and his eyes downcast in an obvious effort to not look directly at Li Fang who sat staring at him from across the top of an intricately carved desk. A squat brass Buddha statue the size of a pineapple smiled up from its place next to a desk phone. The heavy blinds covering the office windows were pulled tight against the probing sun, shading the room in gloom. Two bright spotlights from track lighting above the desk were angled so that they shone directly on the man's face.

Simon Goddard made no effort to flee, or even move.

Fang had nothing to fear. He had complete confidence his bodyguard Chen Woo, who towered over Goddard, would make sure the man didn't cause trouble.

Fang nodded to Chen. "I want him to look at me."

Chen placed a beefy hand on Goddard's bony shoulder to hold him firm, grabbed a fistful of curly dark hair with the other, and jerked the man's head back.

The desired effect was immediate.

Fang stood, taking pleasure in seeing the fear in the wide-eyed expression staring back at him. He had found this technique to be particularly useful when asking questions he wanted straight answers to. He rarely had to ask twice.

"I see I have your attention," Fang said. "I want to know what makes you think you can steal from me and get away with it?"

Goddard struggled to shake his head back and forth—perhaps a show of denial, or maybe a silent plea for his life. The grip on his scalp prevented movement little beyond that of a panic-stricken shudder.

Fang's anger spiked, but his stoic expression did not change. "I asked you a question, Mr. Goddard. I will not ask it again."

Chen eased off on the backward pressure he exerted on Goddard's neck but not the grip on the guy's hair. The frightened man blinked several times, regaining some composure. He squinted into the glare of the spotlights, and said, "I assure you, Mr. Fang, I never stole from you. You'll get the money you loaned me, plus the interest. My freight company is starting to turn around. I'm making money again…and there will be a lot more with the new contract I secured last week. I only need a few additional days."

Fang nodded, and Chen's grip tightened.

Goddard's head snapped back.

"The meaningless words of a desperate man," said Fang, enjoying the man's pain. "Your time was up two days ago. Goddard Freight no longer belongs to you."

"You can't take my company. You wouldn't…"

"I can and will. We had an agreement, Mr. Goddard, and you tried to take advantage of me by not paying back the money you owe. To me, that is the same as stealing. Do you know that in some Middle East countries, if you're caught taking something that does not belong to you, they cut off your hand?"

Goddard's eyes widened.

In an even tone, Fang continued, "Ninety percent of the population performs tasks with their right. Tell me, Mr. Goddard. Which is your dominant side, right or left?"

"I'll pay back the loan, I swear."

Fang directed another nod at Chen. It was all that needed to be said between them. In an instant, the big man's left hand clamped over Goddard's mouth while his right flattened the fingers of the guy's right hand on the desktop. The brass Buddha was already in motion. Fang hammered the statue down hard on Goddard's exposed fingers.

The solid thud shook the desk and shattered bone and cartilage.

Goddard bucked and jerked violently to no avail; his screams muffled by the vise-grip hand clamped over his mouth. After nearly a minute, the screams settled into a series of deep-throated moans.

Fang watched no display of emotion other than a satisfied nod.

"Use the freight elevator," he said. "Take him to the boat and make sure he stays below deck until I decide what to do with him."

Chen merely smiled.

* * *

Fifteen minutes later, the receptionist's phone buzzed. The Asian man seated behind the desk lowered his feet to the carpet, picked up the receiver, listened a moment, and returned the receiver to its cradle. "Mr. Fang will see you now."

Matt swallowed hard and followed the man inside. The inner office looked exactly how he remembered it: opulent paneling, lush carpet, two sofas and a chair, end tables with lamps, and a large coffee table in the middle. The vertical blinds covering the wall of windows on the far side of the room were open enough to let the setting sun on the other side of the glass cast a golden hue on the room. The setup looked as though it could have once been a display in a furniture store.

Fang sat behind his desk, a long walk from the door. The man leveled his gaze but made no attempt to stand.

"Please sit, Mr. Corvin. I trust you've come to pay me my money?"

"Better than that." Matt steeled himself the best he could and took a seat in the chair facing Fang. The man from the reception desk sat on the sofa to the left. "I'm here to make an offer you won't want to turn down."

"That remains to be seen," Fang said. "Am I expected to accept this proposal of yours in lieu of the money you owe me?"

Matt leaned forward and set the cellphone-sized black box on the coffee table in front of him. He struggled to maintain eye contact with the man, having lost confidence in the awkwardness of the moment. Something he had not anticipated.

"Please," he said, regaining some of his poise. "Hear me out."

Fang sat with his elbows on his desk and his fingers tented in front of him. "I'm in no mood to tolerate disappointment. You have two minutes to convince me what you have to say is worth my time."

Matt's stomach lurched.

He swallowed the sour burn rising in his throat. "You know about the recent shark attacks. The device on the table in front of me is what caused those sharks to behave the way they did. On command, if you will."

A second or two of silence descended on the room.

"Very well," Fang said. "Keep talking."

Matt's confidence returned. "The man who developed the device was a coworker of mine. That's how I became aware of its full potential. His son had been killed by a shark, and he never got over the loss. Instead, he went to work designing the perfect electronic shark repellant. When he discovered the apparatus attracted sharks instead of repelling them, he used it to carry out a personal vendetta against the man-eaters."

"Get to the point," Fang interrupted.

"Think about it. I'm sure a businessman such as yourself can see there is a lot of money to be made on the world market with such a device."

"From extremists?"

Matt shrugged. "Who cares as long as they pay?"

Fang nodded almost imperceptibly. "And you will turn it over to me in exchange for the one-point-five million you owe me?"

"Plus the interest," Matt said. "But that's not all. I want to be your partner in this deal."

Once again, Fang tented his fingers and peered across them. Hard and silent, his stare was intense, even from eight feet away.

More silence.

Finally: "If there is so much money to be made, why offer the device to me when you could sell it and keep all the money for yourself?"

"Indeed I could. But with your connections and expertise in this area, you can make the deals happen better than I can."

Matt noticed Fang glance toward the man on the sofa. The communication they had with each other passed silently between them.

Fang's eyes shifted back. "Any further discussion will wait until you prove to me the device does what you claim."

"You've seen the news. What better proof do you need?"

Fang said nothing.

Matt sunk into his chair. "When would you like this demonstration?"

Fang lowered his hands to his desktop. "The money you owe me is due by the end of the business day, tomorrow. You have until then."

"And the plan?"

"I have a yacht, *China Doll*, moored at the La Mariana Sailing Club. Do you know where that is?"

"Sand Island. What time?"

"Ten o'clock in the morning; outside the entrance to the tiki bar. Don't be late."

CHAPTER 26

Jack checked his watch and frowned. Traffic noise from the H1 filled the evening air. The sun had set below a layer of dark clouds, and he and Tokunaga were on the verge of losing what rapidly fading daylight remained. The problem as he saw it was they had a person of interest but no solid suspect, so they had to suspect everyone.

A gigantic haystack with only one needle.

"It's almost seven, Detective. What's your plan?"

"If Matt Corvin is home, I'll talk to him. What I do after that depends on what he has to say."

"I'd like to go with you, if it's okay."

"You're not a cop, Jack. It's been a long day for you. Go home and get some rest."

Jack wondered when the boom would be lowered. Now that it had, he was surprised the issue hadn't come up earlier.

He said, "You let me join you here."

The comment brought a rueful nod from the detective. "And I probably shouldn't have."

Jack couldn't resist a smirk. "But you did."

Tokunaga sighed. "Only because I know you. You would have come here anyway. If not tonight with me, then tomorrow. So let's not get into an argument over this. What I will do is make you a promise. If Corvin gives me information about the shark attacks that I think you should have, I'll call."

The detective's comment made Jack realize where he fit in the scheme of it all. Megan O'Connell had pulled him away from his research in the Philippine Sea to find out what caused the sudden rash of shark attacks off Oahu's beaches. His extreme dislike for killers had fueled his desire to see the man who murdered Devlin Maxwell locked behind bars, but there was no reason for him to be involved in the officer's investigation.

I'm not a cop.

Solving Maxwell's murder is Tokunaga's responsibility, Jack thought. *The shark problem is mine.*

He wouldn't allow himself to forget that.

My job is far from finished.

The motive behind Maxwell's murder remained unclear. A Pandora's Box, of sorts. That when the lid was fully opened, would provide the answer to where he was headed next…hopefully soon.

He said, "Good hunting, detective. I'll hold you to that promise."

Tokunaga nodded. "Get some rest, Jack. You look like hell."

The detective drove off and Jack joined Swagger in the Jeep. The cat greeted him with a yawn and a meow. Most of the food in the bowl had been eaten, and it looked as though some of the water had been lapped up.

"Let's go home," he said.

The first drops of rain hit his windshield before he made it out of the parking lot. By the time he entered the Pali, most of the rain was behind him. It seemed he had been racing the storm on his drive back to Robert and Kazuko's place.

As he pulled up to the house preparing to park, his headlights lit up Kiana Parker and a young man close to her age that he didn't recognize. Accusatory fingers pointed and hands moved in exaggerated gestures amid intense expressions. Obviously caught off-guard, the two peered into the headlights like deer on a country road. He had no idea what had them worked up, but their tempers appeared to cool with his arrival.

Doing his best to ignore them, he exited the Jeep, collected Swagger and the cat's food and dishes from the passenger side, and carried them toward the lanai at the back of the house. Why Kiana was there or what had transpired between her and the young man was none of his business. He had plenty on his mind without involving himself in their problems.

Easier said than done.

He stepped around the rear corner of the house and found Kazuko standing with her back to him. When she turned at his approach, her eyes widened in a stunned expression. He figured it was the cat and not him that surprised her.

"Meet our new friend," he said. "His name is Swagger. I kind of adopted him."

"Kind of?" she said.

Robert, who unseated himself from a deck chair, joined them and relieved Jack of the food and kitty dishes. "Seems you have a knack for collecting strays."

Free of his load, Jack stroked the cat. "I'm surprised you would say something like that. Rebel turned out to be a great addition to the family."

"Right," Robert said, "but how will she take to having a cat around?"

Jack chuckled. "Shouldn't bother her. She just naps in the shade all day, anyway."

Robert faced the lanai and nodded toward the basset hound lying on her belly—ears and legs splayed. "I'll take this stuff inside, but you're going to have to be the one to break the news to Rebel."

"Give the cat to me," Kazuko said. "I'll be the judge of that."

Jack handed Swagger off to her waiting hands and nodded toward the front of the house. "What's the deal with Kiana and that guy she's with? When I pulled up out front, it looked like they were about to go to blows."

She stroked the top of the feline's head, which earned her a contented purr. "We invited Kiana over for dinner and he just showed up here."

Jack didn't think for a second the problem out front had anything to do with him. There was no him and her, hadn't been and wouldn't be. Ever. Besides, he hadn't told Kazuko about Kiana's midnight visit. He also doubted Kiana had; or, that she had told anyone else.

He said, "The guy wasn't invited?"

She answered with a sad shake of her head. "Jeremy works at

the aquarium. Has since before Kiana came on board. He's sort of her boyfriend."

"Sort of?"

"They've dated a few times. According to what Kiana told me, he won't leave her alone. Drives her crazy."

"Possessive." Jack knew the type.

"He always watches what she does at work. More than once, I've caught them in a heated discussion."

"You talked to her about the arguments, I'm sure?"

"She always shrugged them off, claiming it was no big deal."

"Interesting," he said.

"You might call it that. I say it's a pain in the ass. When it starts affecting their work, I'll say something to the director. Otherwise, I'm trying to stay out of their business."

"Is he violent?"

"Never known him to be. In fact, I've always gotten along very well with the guy. Be a shame if he lost his job because of inappropriate behavior."

His or hers?

More likely on both their parts, he thought.

He said, "Sounds like it's Kiana who brings out the worst in him."

"Seems so."

Robert walked up carrying a beer that looked to have about an inch of foam in the bottom. "You're talking about Jeremy?"

Jack glanced in the direction of the front of the house. "I'm surprised you didn't ask him to leave."

"I did. Why do you think the two of them were out front arguing?"

"Sorry," he said. "I must be tired. I've never known you to put up with that kind of shit, so it figures you gave him the boot."

"No worries. I just saw him drive off."

"Be interesting to hear what Kiana has to say."

"I'm afraid that will have to wait. She left right behind him."

"So much for a quiet evening," Kazuko said. "I can't believe she would leave like that without at least saying thanks for dinner... something."

Robert drained the suds from his bottle and clapped Jack on the back. "You look like you're ready for a beer. Make yourself comfortable while I grab us all one. Then you can fill us in on how your day went."

"I think I'll need a couple of those," Jack said.

Robert laughed. "One brew at a time."

As he stepped from the house, beers in hand, Kazuko's phone pinged an incoming text.

"Probably Kiana begging your forgiveness," Jack said, unable to resist a grin.

Kazuko tapped the screen. "Closer than you think. She said she's sorry for running out on us, but will make it up to Robert and me."

Jack decided it was best for him to stay out of it.

Robert passed out the beers, and the three of them sat in the glow of the colored accent lighting situated among the plantings around the lanai. Swagger nuzzled Rebel who summoned enough energy to lift her head an inch. While the two animals got acquainted at Jack's feet, he sipped his Lager and gave his friends the condensed version of his day."

"So that's it," Robert said. "Done before we really got started."

"Before *you* got started," Jack said. "It was a full day for me. And I'm afraid it's about to get a whole lot more complicated."

Kazuko sighed. "At least the island can return to normal now."

Jack stared at the label on his bottle, unable to concede the point. Had a device, maybe more than one, been stolen from Maxwell's house? If so, what did the killer intend to do with it?

Two questions that worried him.

He said, "You really believe that?"

"Maxwell is dead," she came right back. "The crisis is over."

Jack brought his gaze up and peered into her eyes. "Be nice if it is. But it isn't. Not until we know for sure the device Maxwell built isn't still out there."

CHAPTER 27

Jack woke up with a tight head and slowly slid his legs off the side of the bed. Burying his face in his hands, he chalked his misery up to one too many beers and a dream bordering on a nightmare about the recent shark attacks that left him with way too much to think about.

Worse, he didn't know what he could do—beyond what was already being done—to keep even one more person from being killed or bitten.

He stepped into the pre-dawn light, happy to see the storm that sprinkled the island with a light rain during the night had moved on. Lights were on in his friend's house so he wandered that direction in search of a cup of coffee.

"Thought I'd find you out here," he said when he observed Robert sitting in the gloom of the lanai. Kazuko stepped from the house a moment later carrying a plastic carafe.

"You're up," she said, as though surprised. "You can join us."

He grinned. "Thought you'd never ask."

He took a seat at the table and watched her pour him a cup of rich-smelling Kona brew. As though to further improve his morning, the sun peeked bright above the horizon in a sky scrubbed clean by the rain.

He felt better already.

"Thank you," he said to Kazuko.

She smiled. "After last night, we didn't expect to see you up this early."

"Me, either." He sipped his coffee and returned his cup to the table. Swagger the cat rubbed its cheek and whiskers against his leg and leaped into his lap.

Robert asked, "So what's your plan for today?"

Jack ran his hand the length of the feline's back and got a contented purr in return. "Good question."

"You can always swing by the aquarium," Kazuko said.

"I just might." He gave Swagger another pet and watched him splay his paws and jump down.

She stooped and ran her index finger between the cat's ears before he trotted off to join Rebel. Her smile returned as she rose to her feet. "Be nice if you did. It's been a while, and everyone there would love to see you. I'll even let you buy me lunch."

"Tempting," he said. "But before I promise, I need to check in with my director and see if she has anything for me to do. Then I'm going to touch base with Detective Tokunaga and find out how his investigation is going."

"Out of curiosity?" Robert asked. "Or are you sticking your nose in where it doesn't belong?"

"What you're saying is, I'm not a cop."

"That, too. But also because the murder investigation doesn't directly involve you."

"We had this discussion last night, didn't we?"

"We did. And I told you the same thing."

"Then there's no reason for us to discuss the matter further."

"What about your research in the Philippine Sea? Don't you have that to get back to?"

"It'll wait another day or two; I'll know pretty dammed quick if some whack job did my work for me."

"Meaning no more shark trouble?"

"That's exactly what I mean."

* * *

At 9:30, with the heat and humidity on the rise, Jack met Tokunaga at a Mom-and-Pop coffee shop two blocks down and a block over from Kahana Electronics. The detective's shirt hung limp and wrinkled on his body as though he'd already been in it a while. They sat in the shade of a colorful umbrella at an outside table with a partial view of the commercial boatyard and sipped a strong mountain roast blend from cardboard cups.

"I'm glad you called," Jack said. "Kinda hoped to hear from you last night."

"You would have if I'd had information to pass on to you." Tokunaga let his answer drop at that and stared at his cup while he gave it a slow turn with his fingers.

Jack let Tokunaga have a few seconds to finish his thought. When he didn't offer more, Jack ventured a guess. "Something's troubling you, Detective. I'm guessing it's Matt Corvin?"

"He wasn't home last night when I stopped by his house. I figured I would talk to him at work this morning but he called in sick today."

"So he's home."

Tokunaga's gaze came up from his cup. "I checked. His wife claimed he left for work at his usual time."

"You think he knows he's a person of interest in Maxwell's murder?"

"Why else would he be avoiding me?"

"Maybe he doesn't like cops."

"I ran a check on him. Other than a couple of parking tickets, nothing. Makes me think something else is going on; that's what bothers me."

"Do you have any evidence to tie him to the murder?"

"Nothing so far. Fingerprints and trace from the scene are being processed now. The problem is, he's not in the system."

"Meaning you don't have control samples to match prints and DNA to."

"That's about the size of it."

Jack bounced the problem around in his mind. "You can always lift comparison prints from his workstation. Maybe even his DNA."

"If it comes down to that. Corvin could save the department a lot of work if he would just talk to me."

"It doesn't appear that's going to happen."

Tokunaga nodded. "And if nothing breaks, I'm out of leads until he does."

"Or until you find him."

Tokunaga raised his cup in a toasting gesture. "Which I'll do."

Jack lifted his and peered over the cardboard brim. "Would you like some help?"

"Sure, if you know where Corvin is hiding."

"Wish I did."

"I appreciate the offer but there's no need for you to get involved. An officer is watching his house and Kahana will call me if he sees or hears from him. I suspect he'll show up at one of those two places."

CHAPTER 28

Matt Corvin stopped at the bottom of the planked steps leading to the tiki bar. Three up, then three strides to the entrance. He checked his watch—fifteen minutes early as opposed to being one minute late. And, if Li Fang or one of his leg-breakers watched him from a distance, not too early to appear over-anxious.

Perhaps the least of his worries.

Which were piling up.

He switched the small duffle from his right hand to his left and dried a sweaty palm on his thigh. Having been told by his wife that a detective showed up at their house wanting to talk to him about Devlin Maxwell, he was even more eager to complete the deal with Fang and return to a semblance of normal family life.

If that was even possible now.

At least the cop hadn't come to the house armed with an arrest warrant.

He envisioned the story he would tell the detective and felt confident he could convince the officer he had nothing to do with Maxwell's death. They were coworkers, after all. He would claim they were good friends on and off the job and that he visited the man at his house on numerous occasions. A lie, but the cop wouldn't know that. And having admitted to being at the residence would explain any fingerprints of his found inside the place.

No one could prove otherwise.

First he had to contend with Fang and persuade him it was in his best interest to agree to the terms of the proposal. The man would get richer. And—Matt took a deep breath—so would *he.*

He scanned the lot and checked his watch a second time.

Getting into the man's office to present the offer had been the easy part. So had explaining the device's potential and how much money could be made from it on the open market—the bottom line for Fang.

And not just for him, Matt thought.

He understood that going in, but now he had to deliver.

That might be a problem.

The device attracted sharks and incited them to attack—indiscriminately and without warning—anybody in the area. The news reports proved that much. And thanks to the switch on the side of the case, he knew how to activate it. Beyond that, he knew nothing about the device or its limitations.

Devlin Maxwell was to blame for that.

Devlin…

The thought of him, even now, soured his stomach.

He decided not to risk lying to Fang. A wise decision, he was sure.

Keep things simple.

The device would work. When it did, nothing else would matter.

Then the only piece of evidence that could link him to Devlin's murder would be in Fang's hands and not his own.

He couldn't wait.

Fang, dressed in classic yachting attire complete with a white and black captain's hat, and two similarly dressed men minus the cap, made their appearance about a minute before ten. No urgency in their step. No smiles, either.

Matt recognized one of the men as the person who had been seated at the reception desk the evening before. The other rough-looking character, bigger and without the scar on his lip, he didn't recognize.

Both leg-breakers; no doubt about that.

Especially the big guy.

"Good morning," he said. "The storm's moved on so it should

be a nice day on the water."

Fang pointed at the bag. "You brought everything?"

Matt raised it as he spoke. "Just like you asked."

"The diagram to build more?"

"In the bag with the device."

Fang nodded. "Let's get going."

Matt followed a step behind and to the side of Fang. The leg-breakers followed a few steps to the rear. Apparently, they had a distance to walk to reach the yacht.

They passed several empty slips. Boaters already out for the day, he guessed. But most were occupied by sail and power boats that bobbed and tugged at mooring lines amid a waving forest of masts.

When at last they stepped onto the finger of pier that was home to the *China Doll*, he stood and scanned her sleek lines from bow to stern. He peered up at the flybridge and thought how nice it would feel to be the one sitting at the helm, taking her out for the day's run. More yacht than fishing boat, but Fang's wasn't the only boat he admired. They were surrounded by a couple hundred vessels equally beautiful.

He asked Fang, "How big did you say this thing is?"

"Fifty-feet." Fang stepped aboard and head-motioned for him to follow.

Matt stood a moment longer taking in *China Doll*'s magnificence, imagining the cruiser being his own.

Soon…

Fang unlocked the cabin door and Matt followed him into the luxury of the salon. "Wow," was all he could think to say. The cabin was fancier than his living room at home.

"Have a seat and make yourself comfortable." Fang pointed at a U-shaped seating area.

Matt settled onto a soft cushion. He set the gym bag on the table in front of him and spread his arms on the tops of the padded seatbacks. He smiled at Fang, and said, "I could get used to this."

"I'm glad you find my boat to your liking."

Matt immersed himself in the ostentatious surroundings. "I assure you, it's way more than that."

Fang took a seat facing him. "I conduct a lot of my business aboard the *China Doll* on the ocean, far away from prying eyes and ears. Safer that way."

Matt heard a muted rumble and felt a slight vibration through the deck that told him the motors had been started. Through the narrow gaps in the blinds covering the window next to him, he watched receptionist-man casting off the lines. That meant the big guy with no neck manned the controls topside.

Skipper, but not captain.

Only one man gives the orders aboard ship.

It was clear who that man was.

Fang's gaze held steady. "Show me what you brought."

Matt felt the yacht move. There were footfalls on the deck overhead. He asked, "Where are we going?"

"Waikiki. Does that bother you?"

"If it did, I wouldn't be here."

Fang tented his fingers and tapped them against his lips.

Matt read the impatience in the man's eyes. He opened the bag and set the device and the schematic for the apparatus on the table in front of him. He hoped it was enough to hold Fang's attention.

"I only have this one working model," he said. "But there should be no problem building as many as we want."

Fang spread the electrical diagram out before him and scanned it. "You studied this?"

"In detail. The schematic is complete."

Fang slid the paper aside. "I know nothing about electronics. But I have men on my payroll who do."

Matt scooted to the edge of his seat. "Trust me—"

Fang cut him off with a lifting of his hand. "There can be no mistake. The money is not in the device alone, it's in the ability to reproduce the apparatus on a mass scale that will appeal to buyers."

"I realize that."

"I'm glad you agree."

Matt felt suddenly small.

He pointed at the items in front of him. "We're not talking high-tech components here. I assure you, any electrical engineer can easily build a dozen of these with minimal expense."

A sour taste rose and lodged in his throat.

Had he said too much?

For sure his enthusiasm had gotten the better of him.

He needed to be careful.

A long few seconds passed before Fang spoke. "That is one more thing I intend to find out if you're correct about."

Fuck.

Matt swallowed hard, his confidence slipping. Realizing the need for damage control, he searched for the words to reaffirm his vital role in the success of the scheme. "I may have overstated the simplicity of duplicating the device. Don't worry, it's not a deal breaker. I can help in the assembly."

Fang smiled. "Providing the device works the way you *claim* it does."

Matt took a chance, hoping the demonstration went the way he wanted it to. "Believe me, I would not be here if it didn't."

"So you say."

Matt turned at the sound of the salon door opening, and watched the ape-of-a-man with no neck step inside and fix his gaze on him. A nervous chill prickled the hairs on his neck.

Fang looked towards his bodyguard. "Chen, go below and check on Mr. Goddard. Have him slip on a swimsuit and bring him here."

Matt didn't know what to think. "I understood this deal was between you and me. Who is Mr. Goddard and what does he have to do with this?"

"I want proof. You assured me you would deliver. We'll see if you are right."

CHAPTER 29

When Jack stepped into Megan O'Connell's office at eleven-thirty that morning, he found her on the desk phone engaged in what sounded like a serious conversation. She motioned him to the chair next to her desk.

He took a seat in the relative coolness of the air conditioning, feeling like a schoolboy who had been called to the principal's office. Clearly, something had happened...and it wasn't good.

She listened, nodded, and said, "We will, Madam Mayor. Doctor Ferrell is here now."

She returned the receiver to its cradle, and he asked, "Problems?"

"Two more shark attacks." She stared toward the lighted monitor on the wall. The red dots denoting the locations of the prior attacks were still visible. "I thought this crisis had been resolved. Unfortunately, your fears were correct."

"We hoped for the best. That's all we could do under the circumstances." He followed her gaze to the screen. "Where this time?"

"Waikiki, again. A young surfer and a forty-year-old swimmer who ventured beyond the swell were killed less than a half-hour ago. The mayor called me the second she received the news."

"Good news travels fast." He stood and stepped to the monitor. "Bad news travels even faster."

She turned a worried look on him. "What are we going to do?"

His eyes flicked to each of the red dots on the screen—injury and death reduced to points of colored light. He imagined the board full of them.

He clenched his jaw and took a calming breath. Then, "The only choice we have is to find the person who murdered Maxwell to get their hands on his device and stop them before someone else dies."

"I want you involved."

Steel crept into her voice. An undercurrent of resolve he'd heard before.

No less than his own.

He fully intended to play this out.

His jaw set, he turned a hardened gaze on her. "Count on it."

"I knew I could."

"One problem." He hated the thought that came to mind. "Detective Tokunaga has been allowing me to tag along. That could change if the police chief has something to say about it."

"I anticipated that possibility," she said. "The mayor is addressing that issue as we speak. And I haven't forgotten my promise to get you some help. Doctor Susan Price—you might know her—will be flying in from Australia. She plans to be here by Wednesday of next week."

He had hoped the enigma had been an act of nature—an unbalance in the sharks' natural habitat—a problem science could resolve. That was proving to not be the case.

"We've met several times," he said. "Strictly on a professional basis; in case you're wondering. She's a nice lady; quite the expert on sharks. But this isn't about shark behavior any more. It is, and it isn't. Someone is manipulating them. So I suggest you save her the trouble. Her expertise is not going to help in this situation."

She gave him a long look. "Maybe not. But I'm bringing in help just in case you need it."

He walked back to her desk. "A twenty says I'll have this mess resolved before she gets here."

"You know I'm not a betting person."

"There's always a first time for everything." The stern look he got back said stick to business. He agreed. "If we're done here, I have work I need to get back to."

She stood and met his gaze. "Be careful, Jack. It's no secret you have a history of taking chances in situations like this, and I certainly don't want anything to happen to you."

He nodded. "That makes two of us."

On his way out the door, he placed a call to Tokunaga. "You heard?"

The question brought a sigh from the detective. "I'm at the morgue now."

Jack swallowed and asked, "The cause of death has been confirmed?"

"Definitely shark attack. I was here waiting when the bodies were brought in. They weren't pretty."

Jack could imagine. "Any luck running down Matt Corvin?"

"Not yet. You think he's behind this?"

"He's the only lead we have at the moment."

"Where are you?"

"Just leaving my boss' office. I think it's time you and I join forces."

"You're not—"

"Don't say it," Jack cut the detective off before he could get started. "The situation is way out of hand. My director insists I be involved in the investigation. She's tight with the mayor on this issue, and I'm in full agreement. They made a bad call yesterday and they need this problem wrapped up fast to save face. You can check with Mayor Kobayashi if you want."

After a couple beats of silence: "What do you have in mind?"

"You need to make another run at Corvin's wife. And this time, I want to be there when you do."

"You have a pen and paper?"

"In my hand," he lied.

Tokunaga gave him the address and he committed it to memory. "Got it."

"Meet you there in an hour."

Jack tapped off and felt a familiar prickle of the skin.

It felt good to be back in the game.

He sat in his Jeep a moment and jotted down Corvin's address on Waikai Street in the Kalihi Valley. He had an hour to get there.

That left him fifteen or twenty minutes to kill. Not nearly enough time to drop by the aquarium for a visit, and definitely not enough to take Kazuko to lunch.

She'll understand.

Not that she has a choice.

He tapped out an apology text and pressed send. Then he placed a call to Robert to keep him in the loop on the off chance he would need his help, as he had so many times in the past.

"Have a minute?" he asked when Robert answered.

"Let me guess. You're calling about the shark attacks this morning?"

"You know about them?"

"Got the news alert on my phone."

"Then you know I won't be having lunch with Kazuko. The mayor is in a tizzy and Meg wants me to be part of the investigation."

"You would have involved yourself in it, anyway."

"It's better this way," Jack said. "You remember the name Matt Corvin?"

"You mentioned him last night."

"After I left Tokunaga, he tried to talk to him at his house. He wasn't home then, or this morning when Tokunaga dropped by. He also wasn't at work—called in sick, according to his boss."

"He's avoiding the detective?"

"We think so. His wife said he left for work at his usual time this morning. Claims she doesn't know where he is. Tokunaga is going to make another run at her, and he's agreed to let me tag along."

"I suppose you'll use your charm to convince her to give him up?"

Jack smiled into his phone. "If that's what it comes to. But I doubt it will. I'm thinking Tokunaga will threaten to arrest her if she doesn't."

"He can prove she's covering for her husband?"

"No, but it might scare her enough to get her to tell us where he is."

"How convincing can he be?"

"Very. From experience, I know he's a tough SOB when the situation calls for it. I think this qualifies."

"I'll have a beer waiting for you when you get back here."
"I'll hold you to it." Jack clicked off.
When I get there.
He had no idea when that would be.

CHAPTER 30

Jack drove onto Waikai Street five minutes early and saw a patrol car parked at the end of the block. Not the covert surveillance he expected to find.

He pulled to the side of the road opposite the marked unit and parked, drawing the cop's attention. He got out, careful not to make any sudden movements, and crossed the street to check in with the officer.

The stocky, young patrolman exited his vehicle, hand on his gun, and met him with wary eyes. "Can I help you?"

"My name is Jack Ferrell. I'm meeting Detective Tokunaga here. In fact, he should be arriving any minute."

The officer removed his hand from the grips of his semi-automatic. "He radioed a few minutes ago and told me to expect you. Said he might be a little late and gave me strict orders to make sure you stay put until he gets here."

"Sounds like the detective," Jack said. "I'll wait in my Jeep."

When he saw Tokunaga drive up and park at the curb in front of the house next door to the Corvin residence, he glanced at his watch, anxious to get started. He got out and followed the uniformed officer over to the detective.

"No sign of him?" Tokunaga asked, speaking to the patrolman.

"None, sir," the officer said.

"His wife's inside?"

"She walked next door for a minute, but she's back home now."

Tokunaga turned to Jack. "Let's find out what she knows."

Jack picked up on the no-nonsense tone in the detective's voice. Game time over. He was glad he wouldn't be on the receiving end of the cop's questions.

He asked, "Is there any information I need to know about before we do this?"

The question stopped Tokunaga. "What I can tell you is the details on today's attacks are sketchy at best. Plenty of people heard the boy scream and saw him go under, but not a single person who witnessed the attack on the swimmer has come forward to make a statement. In fact, no one knew the guy had been killed until a Coast Guard chopper did a flyover and saw his body."

"Identification?"

"The boy's name is Derrick Kenoi. The swimmer has been tentatively identified as Simon Goddard. He owns a company on the island: Goddard Freight.

"Tentatively?"

"Pending the coroner's confirmation. There wasn't a lot left of him that could be easily identified. While I was there, a woman who presented herself as his ex-wife showed up quite hysterical because this morning their daughter called her saying he failed to come home from work last night. According to the ex, she learned of the attacks when she called the department to report him missing."

Jack didn't envy the detective's job.

He looked at the house. "Let's find this fucker."

They followed the walkway to the front door. Tokunaga did the knocking—loud and unmistakable.

Ms. Corvin cracked the door, then opened it wide. "What do you want, Detective?"

"We need to talk."

"Matt's not here." She held onto the door and pulled it close to her side.

"Have you heard from your husband, Mrs. Corvin?" Tokunaga's tone was a couple of shades less than cordial. "It's very important we talk to him."

"About what?"

"Devlin Maxwell, for starters."

"I've already told Matt you want to talk to him. That's all I can do."

"I think it would be best if we talk inside. Now, if you don't mind."

"Out here's fine." She gripped the door.

The detective inched closer; Jack feared the officer would bull his way past her and kick the door in if she resisted.

Tokunaga held his ground.

Jack relaxed.

"If you insist." Tokunaga gave it a beat. "Tell me, Mrs. Corvin, do you and your husband discuss things?"

She leveled a glare on the detective. "What are you getting at?"

His gaze held steady. "When you told him I wanted to talk to him about Devlin Maxwell, what did he say?"

She fell silent a second. Then, "He said it was about a guy from work and not to worry about it."

"But you *are* worried, and rightfully so."

Jack noticed her sag a bit, some of the wind gone out of her sails.

He spoke up, "There's been a murder, Mrs. Corvin, and your husband seems to be dodging us. All we want is to ask him some questions about his coworker."

"Are you this man's partner?" She flashed a frown from him to Tokunaga, and back.

"I'm not a cop. I work for the National Oceanic and Atmospheric Administration. I'm a marine biologist."

"You work for NOAA?"

"That's correct, as a contract employee."

"So why are *you* here?"

"Have you seen the news?"

"So what if I have?"

"I'm guessing you have children?"

"Three. Our oldest is eighteen. They're off-island for spring break."

"They like to surf, I'm sure?"

"Most kids their age on the island do."

"My specialty is apex predators, Mrs. Corvin. Sharks. You know about the recent attacks. Are you aware that this morning two more people were killed in Waikiki? A kid your sons' ages are dead. And an older man."

Her brow furrowed. "On the television last night, the news, they said it was safe for people to go into the water."

She doesn't know.

"Not any longer," he said. "NOAA asked me to find the cause behind these attacks and put a stop to them. That's why I'm here."

Her gaze dropped, and came back up. Her eyes flared when they met his. "If you're at my house insisting you need to talk to Matt, then you think he has something to do with these deaths."

"Do you believe in *Ho`oPonoPono*?"

"I'm not sure what it means."

"It's Hawaiian, Mrs. Corvin; it means making things right. That's what we're here to do, and we believe your husband can help us."

She leaned her head to the side and craned her neck, as though trying to see past his shoulder. "That's why you have an officer sitting out there in his patrol car watching the house…because you want Matt's help?"

She likes answering a question with a question.

Frustrating.

He sighed, then said, "Please understand how important this is. People have died. There could be more deaths…more kids your sons' ages. Deaths you could help prevent. If that happens, is it something you can live with?"

As a mother she had to care.

It's what mothers do.

His comment failed to precipitate a response, and that concerned him. It had to be something else that prevented her from answering. Perhaps the reality of his inference was too real for her to accept.

He gave her a moment more. When she remained silent, he asked, "How well did you know Devlin Maxwell?"

She shrugged.

Tokunaga edged closer, and in an even tone said, "You did know him?"

Her gaze settled on his. "Not well at all. I spoke to the guy briefly at a few of Matt's company's Christmas parties, but that's it."

"I'm guessing you and your husband never visited him at his house, or had him over to your place for a barbeque?"

"I can't speak for my husband, but I can assure you I've never been anywhere near his house, and he has never been invited here for a barbeque or for any other reason. Matt and I weren't that friendly with him."

"Did he and your husband have any arguments that you know of?"

"Sorry, Detective, I can't help you. Now if you'll excuse me, I have things to do."

Tokunaga held his ground.

Jack did the same, and noticed her eyes tear as she shut the door in their faces.

Crying complicated things.

He hated seeing a woman cry.

"I don't think she knows anything," he said to Tokunaga.

"Matt does. I'll bet on it." Tokunaga turned and started down the walkway.

Jack followed; his long stride narrowed the gap. From experience, he knew that sometimes it's what people don't tell you that says the most.

"You're thinking the same thing I am," he said to Tokunaga's back.

"What's that?"

Jack wasn't fooled.

He said, "Matt Corvin killed Devlin Maxwell." That leap led to another. "And there's a bigger picture to this enigma we're not seeing. A much bigger one. You need to check into the man's financials."

CHAPTER 31

Jack accompanied Tokunaga to his car. The bulldog determination he had seen in the detective the year before showed in his expression.

A bloodhound on the scent.

Of what, exactly, they still didn't know.

But they could make an educated guess.

The logical next step was for Tokunaga to return to his desk at the police station and run Matt Corvin six ways from hell. Jack started to ask if that was the plan when the detective's phone pinged: a text, not a call.

He waited.

"Results of the evidence are back," Tokunaga said when he'd finished reading.

Jack felt an adrenalin jolt. "Any surprises?"

"I won't know until I get back to my office. Do you have something you can do for an hour or so? It'll give me time to see what CSU has for me, and to run Corvin's financials. We'll meet up when I'm done."

A lot depended on the crime scene unit's findings.

Jack clenched his jaw.

I'll just have to wait.

"Actually," he said, "there is something I can do. Call me when you're ready."

He left the detective standing at the driver's door of his Crown

Vic, one of the few left in the fleet, and walked back to his Jeep. The drive to the aquarium would take a full twenty minutes if he didn't waste time. It bothered him that he had missed his lunch date with Kazuko but he could take the time to drop in and say hi.

She would be happily surprised.

On the way, he placed a call to her. She answered with a tone of irritation that disappeared the moment she heard his voice. According to her, he had made her day. She didn't elaborate on the phone, but she did say that in addition to the shark attacks that morning, she had issues at work to deal with.

He didn't press.

She met him at the entrance and escorted him inside. He always enjoyed his visits to the aquarium but rarely made it over this way. Why, he didn't know, but chalked it up to one of those pleasures a person forgets about until they do it again.

He was glad he decided to come.

"I can't believe those two people were killed this morning," she said. "When you told me about that man's murder, I really believed that was the end of it."

"You're not alone. My boss and Mayor Kobayashi had been quick to buy into that assumption, themselves. Otherwise, that young boy and the older gentleman would never have been allowed out on the water."

"It's just so tragic," she said.

"And avoidable." He left his response at that.

"You still believe someone is behind what's happening?"

"My feelings on that haven't changed. In fact, Detective Tokunaga and I both do. I just hadn't expected it to happen again this soon."

She pushed through the doorway into the gallery where the tanks of various sea creatures were housed, and held the door for him. "None of this makes sense."

"The answer's out there," he said, stepping through. "I'm going to find it."

"Soon, I hope."

An understatement.

He said, "Enough about the shark business. You mentioned having issues you needed to deal with here."

"Really? You're interested?"

"Sure. I'm a good sounding board."

While they walked, she spent a minute raving about recent additions to the moon jelly display. A young couple exited the jellyfish exhibit as he and Kazuko approached the gallery of cylindrical tanks. Around him, several species of jellies drifted up and down in a hypnotic motion within a continuous current of sea water.

"It started in here," she explained, "and escalated outside by the monk seal pool a few minutes before we opened. I always like to do a walk-through before the visitors come in. That's what I was doing when I found Kiana and Jeremy in here…engaged in a heated discussion."

A continuation of last night?

He asked, "Any idea why they were arguing?"

She shook her head. "I don't really know. They walked out of the room when they saw me. I caught up with them at the monk seal pool. They appeared to be trying to keep their voices down, which wasn't working, and there was a lot of finger-pointing back and forth. I had enough of their juvenile bickering. They were both going to get fired if they didn't stop."

"What did they have to say?"

"Kiana's story hadn't changed. She claimed he insists on trying to run her life. Before I could say more, she bolted, saying she wouldn't stand for it."

"And Jeremy?"

"He said he was just trying to keep her from getting into trouble. I left it at that and told him this was their last warning. They needed to cool it or I'd take the problem to the director and ask for their dismissal."

"Do you think that's the end of it?"

"I can hope."

"Where are the two lovebirds now?"

"Kiana is here someplace." She glanced toward the doorway before meeting his gaze. "Jeremy's out in the Zodiac with two other researchers."

Jack felt a tinge of guilt for not being out on the water, himself—

where he would be if he wasn't convinced the answer to Oahu's shark problem was on dry land.

And Matt Corvin was the key.

"Maybe you and Robert need to get away. Let the difficulty between Kiana and Jeremy resolve itself. Go somewhere exotic. Egypt...Japan, even. How long has it been since you visited your relatives?"

"Too long." She gave a sad shake of her head. "But I'm not going anywhere until this shark issue is resolved."

Not surprising.

He scanned the exhibit. They stood in the quiet company of the free-floating jellyfish trolling their tentacles beneath them as they drifted up and down in the current. *The medusa-phase of certain gelatinous members of the subphylum Medusozoa*, he mused. A major part of the phylum Cnidaria.

Predatory drifters.

Fascinating, elegant, and mesmerizing to watch.

The creatures had been around for over five hundred million years; ninety-five percent seawater and five percent living cells. As close as evolution had gotten to creating intelligence without the constraints of tissue. No brain, no blood, no heart. A simplex nervous system that responds to light and smell and other stimuli.

Hunt. Attack. Feed. Reproduce.

Killers without conscience.

No different than the person behind the shark attacks that morning.

That was no accident.

He could understand Maxwell's grief-twisted mind driving him to do what he did—revenge is a powerful motivation. But the motive behind this recent turn of events had him baffled. Maxwell's killer clearly had some other agenda in play.

But, what?

CHAPTER 32

Jack parked in front of Tiny's Café an hour later. The detective's choice. An excellent one in Jack's opinion, since neither of them had eaten lunch and the place was known among locals to have the best burgers in town.

He got out of his Jeep and pressed the door lock. For some reason he hadn't been able to shake the image of a sea jelly dangling it poisonous tentacles. A solitary killer, like the person they were after.

Tokunaga had already seated himself at a back table. He cradled a cup of coffee in his hands as though staring into it for answers. Jack took the empty chair across from him and picked up his menu for no reason other than to have something to peruse, even though he already knew what he would order.

"I'm guessing you found a thing or two interesting in Corvin's financials?" He returned the menu to the table and gave the detective his full attention.

"I'll get to that in a second," Tokunaga said. "You'll be interested to know; CSU lifted a bloody fingerprint from the floor next to Maxwell's head. They didn't have any prints to compare it to until today when they lifted some from Corvin's workstation at Kahana Electronics. Great suggestion, by the way. The bloody print…it's his."

"So, Matt Corvin's our killer."

"Hard to explain away a bloody print."

"How about his financials?"

"In a nutshell, the man's in hock up to his ears. A million and a half dollars' worth."

Jack grinned. "The plot thickens."

Tokunaga took a sip of his coffee and set the cup aside. "That he is mortgaged up the ass doesn't mean much by itself—it's who he's in debt to that's important. Corvin purchased two homes a couple of blocks from Waikiki Beach with plans to turn them into short-term vacation rentals, only the permits never came through. The loan was one of those creative financing deals with a balloon payment."

"Let me guess," Jack said. "A million and a half smackaroos."

"That's right. And get this: the loan became due and payable eight weeks ago. He paid it off, but not with his own money, and not by refinancing the property through a bank. My guess is no legitimate lending institution would touch him."

"A loan shark?"

"Might as well be. He borrowed the money from a man named Li Fang. An eight-week loan due and payable today. Corvin put up his house and the two rental properties as collateral. I'm sure you know what that means."

"He stands to lose everything."

"Makes you wonder how a man with a modest five-figure income planned to pay off a one-point-five-million-dollar loan?"

Jack didn't have to think about it. As though a light had suddenly clicked on, the terrorist theory that had only been a thought, became all too real.

"Corvin must have taken that short-term loan to give himself breathing room while he worked another angle. Otherwise, why risk everything he owns? I think he murdered Maxwell to get his hands on that device and now he's trying to sell it to pay off the money he owes."

"That doesn't explain the shark attacks this morning."

"It does if you think about the timing. Corvin murders Maxwell for the device. A day later he puts on a demonstration for a potential buyer. And we know who that person is."

Tokunaga nodded, slowly at first. "Li Fang."

"I'm sure you've looked into Fang's activities. Is this something he would get involved with?"

"Personally, I can't say. But the department's white-collar guys have investigated several of his shady dealings. So far, nothing has stuck. But from what I've been told, he will do most anything if it nets him a big payday."

"The only way that would happen is if he had a scheme to use the device here on the island. Which, to me, seems a lot like cutting one's nose off to spite their face. Odds are, Fang would sell it on the open market. We both know what that means."

Tokunaga gave a slow shake of his head. "I prefer not to think about it."

Jack knew he had unmasked a horrible truth. The shark terror generated by the movie *Jaws* was only a beginning. If people in the Hawaiian Islands and the many other popular tourist destinations around the world couldn't go into the water for fear of being ripped apart by sharks, the psychological and economic consequences would be crippling before anyone figured out the cause behind the nightmare.

A sobering reality.

"You might not have a choice."

Tokunaga appeared to give some thought to that before saying, "The problem is, we don't know for sure if Fang's involved. And even if our assumption is correct, we don't have a single shred of evidence to tie him to a crime. Until we do, we need to tread lightly."

"Really, Detective? You mean that?"

"If you're with me, we do it by the book."

Jack didn't necessarily agree with having to play by a one-sided set of rules, but what choice did he have. "Whatever you say. But know this: I'll not hesitate a second to do whatever it takes to stop this madness before it goes any further."

"I agree. Only we can't touch the man without probable cause."

Jack weighed the detective's comment.

Only one answer made sense.

"Corvin's the key," he said. "We find him, we get the whole enchilada."

CHAPTER 33

Jack waded into his burger and fries in silence. He'd have thought the conversation with Tokunaga would have killed his appetite. Instead, it provided fuel to keep his mind alert and on track.

"So where do we stand?"

"I have a BOLO out on Corvin and his pickup," Tokunaga said between bites. "Nothing so far, but his bright orange Dodge 4x4 with that custom lift kit and big tires will stick out like a sore thumb. We'll find him."

Jack had no doubt they would.

When?

He dipped a fry into a dab of ketchup and swirled it around. "I wonder how much his wife knows about their financial situation."

Tokunaga set his burger on his plate, picked up his napkin and wiped his fingers. "Janice, in case you're wondering. That's her name."

Jack hadn't thought to ask, which surprised him. Normally that would be one of the first things he would have done. "So, what do you think?"

"She's probably aware they're on the verge of losing everything, but doesn't know her husband murdered Maxwell."

"We ought to ask her. Might change her mind about helping us find him."

"I sure would like to believe that."

"There's only one way to find out."

Tokunaga nodded. "Just as soon as we finish our lunch. But it's stupid for us to be following each other around; we'll leave your Jeep in the lot at the department and you can ride with me."

Jack wasn't sure he wanted to be tethered to the detective. He recalled the last time he sat in the passenger seat of Tokunaga's Crown Vic. Not the best of circumstances. But the car had a good air conditioner, and this time he wasn't a suspect.

"Fine by me," he said.

They finished their meal, dropped his Jeep off, and drove straight to Corvin's house. The patrol officer's car didn't appear to have moved. Tokunaga parked in the same spot he had earlier and they walked up to the front door together.

Jack figured Mrs. Corvin heard them drive up, and would be watching through cracks in the blinds hoping it was her husband.

She was not going to be happy to see them.

Jack didn't care.

No more games.

He stood to the side of the entry while Tokunaga stood opposite him and rang the bell twice.

Two muffled 'ding-dongs' sounded inside the house.

Mrs. Corvin opened the door with the same caution she had earlier. A television blared in the room behind her—a commercial for bathroom tissue from the sound of it. She hadn't bothered to turn the volume down.

"What do you want now?" she asked in an unfriendly tone.

Jack kept quiet, letting Tokunaga take the lead.

The detective moved in front of the doorway as though he expected her to bolt. "We need to talk."

Her eyes flicked back and forth at them before settling on Tokunaga. She sagged enough to signal resignation, but maintained her grip on the door. "I don't know why you insist on harassing me. I've already told you everything I know."

"Have you, Janice?"

Tokunaga's use of her first name gave her pause, as though she wasn't used to hearing it. A couple of seconds hesitation in answering, Jack noticed. Nothing more. But enough for him to tell the detective's tactic had been effective.

And perfectly timed.

She straightened, but only a little. "I most certainly have."

"I'm not so sure," Tokunaga said. "If you don't mind, I honestly feel it would be best if we talk inside. There has been a development."

"Development?" she repeated.

"Let's talk inside."

At first Jack didn't know if she would let them in or not, then she swung back the door and motioned them inside. A modest room met his gaze: pictures on the walls, a couch with a table and lamp at each end, a rectangular sofa table in front, and two chairs—recliners by the look of them—both faced a large-screen TV. The tissue commercial now over, the channel had switched back to a daytime soap.

He pointed at the television. "You mind?"

She picked up a remote and switched it off. Her gaze came back to him, then to Tokunaga. "What development, Detective?"

Jack held off. It was Tokunaga's show.

"You might want to sit down," Tokunaga said.

"I'll stand." She crossed her arms in front of her, the TV remote still in her hand.

"If you insist." His gaze didn't waver. "First of all, we know you and your husband are on the verge of losing your home and a couple of investment properties."

"I don't see what that has to do with anything."

"We believe it has everything to do with what's going on. Is Matt a violent man?"

"What are you getting at?"

He let her question hang a full two seconds while suspicion filled her eyes. "Janice, your husband killed Devlin Maxwell."

She stepped to the couch and sank into a cushion. Her gaze came up. "How can you say that?"

"We have definitive evidence that places him at the murder scene." He let that sink in, then added, "What do you know about a man named Li Fang?"

She furrowed her brow and glanced back and forth at them. "Nothing. I've never met the man."

"But you have heard his name?"

"Not till now. Who is he?"

"A local businessman who specializes in high-risk, short-term loans."

"You're saying Matt is involved with this man?"

"Your husband didn't talk to you about it?"

"Not a word."

"Is that normal?"

"More so, lately. I know he has been concerned about our finances. Maybe he didn't want me to worry any more than I already am."

Tokunaga paused; Jack took that as an opening to jump in. "The recent shark attacks around the island were Devlin Maxwell's dirty work. But not the man and boy killed this morning. Maxwell invented a device that attracts sharks instead of repelling them. My guess is your husband knew about it. We know he took out an eight-week loan with Mr. Fang, and the money is due and payable as of today. It's our belief he's trying to pay it off with the device he stole from Maxwell when he murdered him."

Her eyes widened. "But you don't know that for sure."

"We know enough that all the pieces fit."

"Well, it's not enough for me," she said; some of the surprise gone. "Not until I talk to him."

"You said he left for work and his boss said he called in sick. That was early this morning. He hasn't come home and, if you're telling the truth, he hasn't called to let you know where he is. So, you tell me what's going on."

She looked like the wind had been knocked out of her. "I can't."

Or won't.

An inflection in her voice betrayed a desire to open up to them, but something kept her from it.

Her husband?

He pressed. "We want to help, but we need you to be honest with us. Fang is not a man you want to get mixed up with."

"If what you say is true, we already are."

The exchange with her left Jack feeling strange, as though he and Tokunaga were at the house investigating not one, but two murders.

He said, "Please, Janice. Help us find your husband before it's too late."

"Don't call me by my name." A tear broke and streaked her cheek. "Don't look at me, and *don't* say another word. Just leave."

Tokunaga stiffened, obviously in defiance of her outrage. "Not until you tell us what we want to know."

She fixed her dewy gaze on him. "You want me to rat out my husband. I won't do that. Not now. Not ever. So unless you have a warrant, get out."

CHAPTER 34

A gentle breeze tugged at Jack's hair and shirt as he strode away from the residence. The trade winds he had felt blowing from the northeast had died down some from what they were earlier in the day. He stopped at the passenger door to Tokunaga's car and waited while the detective conferred with the patrolman on stakeout duty. The officer would have heard the BOLO on Matt Corvin and know the stakes had been raised.

He checked his watch and looked up when a gray sedan pulled into a driveway across the street and parked. A nicely dressed woman got out. A pickup, an older model blue Nissan, rolled past and kept going. People getting home from work, but no bright orange Dodge 4x4 with a custom lift kit and big tires.

He checked his watch for the second time. They were losing the day.

About a minute later, he noticed Tokunaga walking back to the car. The man's stride remained long and purposeful.

The bulldog on the hunt.

He said, "Sure didn't expect that parting outburst from Mrs. Corvin."

"Me either. Until then, I thought you had her."

"What now? Do we start running down this Li Fang character?"

"May not have to. We caught a break." Tokunaga opened the driver's door and, speaking across the top of the car, added, "Officers spotted Corvin's truck. It's parked in the lot at the Pacific Marina Inn over by the airport. I told the officer who located it to hang back until we get there."

Jack realized he had no idea what Matt Corvin looked like. He'd noticed a family photo sitting on the table at the far end of the sofa but hadn't been able to get a good look at the man in the picture.

He climbed into the car and buckled himself in. "You have any idea what Corvin looks like?"

"I've got his driver's license photo, that's it." Tokunaga brought the picture up on his phone and showed Jack.

Jack studied the face. The same man shown in the photograph on the table at the end of the sofa at Corvin's house. He was sure of it now. "Why do you suppose he picked that hotel to hide out in?"

"Your guess is as good as mine." Tokunaga steered the Crown Vic away from the curb and onto the road. "What makes a man commit murder? What makes that same man leave his wife behind to suffer the consequences of his actions? There might not be a single rational thought behind any of what this guy is doing."

Jack was struck by a thought. "The hotel is by the airport. Perhaps that's it. He's getting off the island."

"Won't work. Airport security will detain him if he tries to board a flight."

"Not if it's a private airline flying to one of the other islands. There are several he could fly out on."

Tokunaga mashed on the gas pedal. "Let's hope he's sticking around. If Janice leaves the house to join him, we'll have them both."

The Friday night commuter rush made it difficult for them to get across town in a timely fashion. Twice, Tokunaga chirped his siren to get past a line of slow-moving vehicles. And each time, Jack cringed at the prospect of being rammed by oncoming traffic.

He asked, "Do we have anything that resembles a plan?"

Tokunaga kept his eyes facing forward. "I think we should take it slow. We don't know what room he's in or if he's even staying there. If he is, we don't want to spook him."

Jack regretted having left his .45 behind. He had no particular reason to believe there would be trouble, but there were no guarantees. Never are. And two guns are always better than one if the situation went sideways.

He asked, "What about the patrolman who's sitting on the vehicle? Corvin might already be spooked."

"He's holed up tight; if he's not already gone. I'll have the uniform stay put while we check the place out on foot."

Now Jack really felt naked. In the past he'd made do with a Ping putter when he nailed the asshole in Vegas. Presently, he didn't even have that.

They met up with the female patrol officer at her car parked fifty yards away from the Pacific Marina Inn. Gaps in a wall of plants afforded them a partial view of the bright orange Dodge nosed into a marked space in the hotel's side lot, but they couldn't see the license number.

She pointed in that direction. "No one has come or gone from the suspect's vehicle. I'm confident I would have seen them."

Tokunaga moved a broadleaf aside with his hand and made a hole. "You checked the plate?"

"It's Corvin's, sir. No mistake. I did a drive by before parking here."

"Keep watch while Jack and I have a look around."

Jack asked, "We walking in?"

"Driving. Williams will back us up if we need her."

Jack looked her up and down. She was tall and pretty in an official sort of way. She had dark hair pinned back, an athletic build, and a no-nonsense expression. The uniform looked good on her, as did the Glock 17 secured in a holster on her hip. She no doubt knew how to use the semi-automatic if need be.

He turned to Tokunaga. "Ready when you are."

They climbed into the detective's car and Tokunaga drove in slow. He parked next to a white van in the front lot that sat at a ninety-degree angle to the location where Corvin had parked his pickup.

Tokunaga said, "Let's go."

Jack opened his door and climbed out. The roar of a passenger jet gaining altitude drew his gaze skyward. He couldn't help but wonder if the rooms there were soundproof. A break for them if they were. He followed the detective into the lobby.

The place was about what he expected; nothing special but good enough. They were alone except for a single registration clerk—an older woman dressed in a garish aloha shirt and a plastic-flowered lei. A framed poster of three surfers and a sunset on a red background above a caption that read *The Endless Summer* hung on the wall behind the registration counter.

She smiled at their approach. "Can I help you?"

Tokunaga flashed his badge. "We're looking for a guy named Matt Corvin. He would have checked in sometime today."

She consulted her computer. "Sorry, Officer. No one by the name Corvin."

"Perhaps if I show you his picture it'll jog your memory." He accessed his phone and brought up Corvin's driver's license photo.

She shook her head. "I've only had two check-ins today and one yesterday. I'd remember if he was one of them."

"You're sure?"

"I have a good memory, Detective. He's not staying here."

"That's strange," Tokunaga said. "His pickup is parked in your lot."

She gave a sad shake of her head. "I'm afraid it's not all that unusual. People have left cars parked here before. Usually, junkers. Eventually they get towed."

A depressing reality in the islands, Jack thought.

Tokunaga said, "Thanks for your help. I think we'll have a look around."

Jack smiled at the clerk. She didn't look happy.

"What do you think?" he asked Tokunaga when they were out of earshot of the woman.

"Honestly, I don't know what to think. Depends how desperate Corvin is."

They followed a concrete walkway lined with broadleaf plants, ginger, and palms on both sides. Jack could see the fenced-in pool area. Only a handful of guests were using it this late in the day.

He said, "I'm going out on a limb here and guessing Corvin's very desperate."

"He's avoiding us," Tokunaga said. "That's obvious. He probably ditched his truck here, waiting to come back and get it tonight when it's dark. If that's the case, Officer Williams will be here to greet him. If not her, another officer will be."

"It's also possible he's on a plane belonging to one of a dozen private shuttle services a mile down the road."

Tokunaga stopped. His gaze swept the pool. "We had better hope not. If he has made it to one of the other islands, there is no telling how long it will be before he's arrested."

Jack scanned the pool-goers. A man, a woman, three kids; no Matt Corvin.

He asked, "Where does this leave us?"

"We wait."

"What about making a run at Li Fang? See what he knows."

Tokunaga glanced up at a sky splashed with color and looked at his watch. "Not tonight, we won't. It'll be dark soon. I'll keep cars posted on Corvin's house and his pickup. We'll regroup in the morning. But first, I want to have a good look at that truck of his."

CHAPTER 35

Jack parked in front of Robert's house an hour and fifteen minutes later. The stars were out…bright in the moonless sky. He had wanted to continue the investigation on into the night but understood, though disappointed, there was not a whole lot he and Tokunaga could do for the time being.

Unless circumstances changed.

Nothing had popped when they checked Corvin's pickup. From what they could see from the outside, anyway. The doors were locked, and with the windows tinted dark, they were not able to get a good look inside. But they agreed it was a lot of machine to leave abandoned.

So the night had turned into a waiting game.

Spiders poised on the edge of the web.

When he rounded the rear of the house, he saw Robert and Kazuko seated at the table on the lanai. To his surprise, so was Kiana Parker. They had their eyes glued to the screen of a laptop open in front of them.

All three turned at his approach. He nodded at the computer. "You have the late show on that thing?"

"Deep Blue is back," Kazuko said.

Kiana added, "Isn't that wonderful."

Her gaze held his for a provocative moment longer than Kazuko's.

Young lust?

He wasn't playing her game.

Swagger rubbed against his leg and meowed a greeting. From where she lay flat on her belly five feet away, Rebel opened an eye and closed it.

The extent of their interest in what was going on at the table.

He gave both animals a scratch behind the ears and joined his friends at the laptop. "Is that blinking blue dot her?"

"A couple of hours ago, her tag pinged off of the receiver at the aquarium." Kazuko pointed. "As you can see, she's swimming a couple of miles off Waikiki Beach. That's the general location where she was spotted feeding on a humpback carcass last January."

"Interesting. Only the whales and their newborns have moved on by now. Makes you wonder if the shark attacks have attracted her."

Robert got up from his chair. "That's what we've been tossing around. You want a beer? I'm having one."

"Sure. Colder the better."

Kazuko said, "Great Whites are perfect hunting machines. We know that. But they can smell blood, what…maybe up to a quarter mile away? That tells me she's here for some other reason."

Jack stifled a chuckle and shook his head at her. "You're singing to the choir. I wasn't serious when I suggested she might have been attracted by the shark attacks. And you're right, she's not here to have some poor swimmer for a tasty snack. If anything, she just dropped in for a monk seal or two on her way to wherever she's headed. It'll be interesting to see how long she hangs around."

"What are your plans?'

"About what…the shark?"

Kazuko's eyes narrowed. "You know I'm talking about Deep Blue."

Carcharodon carcharias.

His decision had been made. Having the great white show up in the water off Oahu was an opportunity of a lifetime. Even for a marine biologist like himself. He had seen a hundred such sharks, but never a twenty-footer. Deep Blue had been pregnant when first spotted over a year ago. Most likely the twelve-to-eighteen-month gestation period was over. Her litter of two to ten pups, each four to five feet in length at birth, were long gone by now.

"I'm going out and take a look at her, of course."

"And I'm sure you won't mind if Kiana and I join you?"

Robert handed Jack his beer. "Don't forget about me."

"You're all welcome to come along," Jack said, in spite of not being thrilled to have Kiana join them. "Only I'm not exactly sure when that will be. Meg asked me to join HPD's investigation into Devlin Maxwell's murder. There has been a new wrinkle in the investigation that could break any moment."

Robert retook his seat. "Kazuko mentioned you dropped by but didn't have much to say about the case."

Jack glanced at Kiana, the topic of much of his and Kazuko's conversation. "I only had a few minutes to spend there. We talked about other things."

"This wrinkle you mentioned; you said you and Detective Tokunaga planned to talk to Corvin's wife. Does this have something to do with that?"

"She pretty much fizzled on us. This involves her husband. If I don't hear from Tokunaga tonight, I'll check with him first thing tomorrow morning and plan from there."

"Can you talk about it?"

"I don't see why not. Turns out there's a whole lot more to Matt Corvin than we first thought. Evidence from the crime scene suggests he murdered Maxwell. Judging from the man's financials, we believe he killed him to get his hands on the shark attracting device in order to pay off a one-point-five-million-dollar debt owed to a shady character by the name of Li Fang. According to Tokunaga, Fang's not a nice man."

"I've heard the name," Robert said. "And it's always followed by several choice four-letter expletives. He's a person who owners of failing companies go to for a short-term bailout loan when they have absolutely no other recourse. Usually, the business arrangement ends badly for the client."

"Screw Matt Corvin. And screw Li Fang," Jack said. "It's the rest of the world I'm worried about. There is only one way to make that kind of big money off of a device that attracts sharks: Terrorism. I won't let that happen."

Robert nodded. "The best defense is a good offense. Know your opponent's tactics and cut him off at the pass."

"You sound like John Wayne."

"I've been compared to a hell-of-lot worse."

"Maybe a time or two," Jack conceded. "Never by anyone who matters."

"You're a good friend, but I'm afraid you're speaking out of a gross misconception that everybody shares your high opinion of me."

Jack raised his beer. "That will be our little secret."

Robert lifted his.

After a moment, he asked, "Do you think there is any way the shark attacks this morning could be accidental; nothing more than a fluke? That they have nothing to do with Maxwell's device?"

Jack shrugged. "I can't say for sure they're not. But I have to go with probability, and in all probability those sharks didn't attack and kill that man and boy by accident. My money is on Matt Corvin, and if Li Fang gets his hands on that device, there will be a lot more deaths. And not just here."

"I assume there's a warrant out for Corvin's arrest. Where is he now?"

"That's just it. We don't know."

CHAPTER 36

The next morning at eight, Jack sat on the upper deck of *Pono II* with a cup of Kona coffee in his hand and a bright morning sun reflecting off the bay. He had a discouraged Detective Tokunaga on the phone.

He felt just as disappointed by the lack of good news. "So Corvin didn't come back for his truck?"

"Looks like he never planned to."

Frustration showed through in the man's tone, and Jack knew why.

The detective's expertise evolved around assembling facts he could build into a prosecutable case. Without Matt Corvin to incriminate Li Fang, there was nothing he could act on. And he was chomping at the bit to get control of the investigation.

The same as me, Jack couldn't help thinking.

He said, "You still made a good call having an officer stake out the pickup. Where is the truck now?"

"In the impound lot. CSU will be going over it from front to back; if they aren't already."

"And Li Fang?"

"He's still on the list, but I need something more than a wild assumption and a little cop intuition to make a run at him."

Exactly what Jack figured would be the case.

"What you're saying is we need to find Corvin before the

situation really gets out of hand."

"Jack, it's already out of hand. I'm going to canvas the private air shuttles at the airport and see if anyone recognizes his picture. If he got on a plane, we will at least know which island he flew to."

"Providing he stayed put once he got there."

"That should be easy enough to check out, as well. But we're just talking a lot of legwork. If you have other business you need to take care of, do it. I'll call you if I find out anything that provides us a lead to his whereabouts."

Jack couldn't shake the sinking feeling some other game was in play. "I can't believe he didn't come back for that fancy truck of his."

"Don't worry. We'll get him."

The call disconnected and Jack tapped off.

Yeah. But when?

He stared out to sea; Kaneohe Bay glistened. The sun was warm on his face, and for a full sixty seconds, the only sound came from a gentle lapping of water against *Pono II*'s twin hulls.

Peaceful.

Serene.

Tranquility for the soul…had it not been for the killer on the loose. He didn't need any help understanding the enormity of the danger to the Hawaiian Islands and to the world.

Calamity in the form of attacking sharks.

He prayed it didn't come to that, but he couldn't forget it either.

And he couldn't forget about Li Fang.

"Permission to come aboard." Robert's shout from the dock broke through his thoughts.

Jack peered over the railing. "Coffee's in the galley."

A minute later the hatchway up top swung open and Robert stepped onto the deck with a cup in his hand. "We missed you at the house."

"Had a call to make." He paused for several long seconds. "I've been thinking."

"Anything I can do to help?"

"Corvin is in the wind. Tokunaga's doing what he can to find him, but Li Fang is the man to worry about now. If he has the device—and it's likely he does—it's only a matter of time before he has a buyer."

"Let me guess. Without some incriminating evidence against him, the detective's hands are tied."

"He could talk to him. Providing the man is willing. That's about all."

"Knowing you the way I do; I'm guessing you have something more in mind?"

"Can you get me Fang's address? I'd like to see where he lives."

"Sure…maybe," Robert said. "I'll make some calls. Anything else?"

"You can help me cast off the lines when you're done. You and I are heading out to have a look at Deep Blue, if she's still around."

Robert busied himself on his phone while Jack called Kazuko.

"Good morning," she said after the third ring.

He asked, "All quiet there this morning?"

"I've only been here a few minutes. What's up?"

"Do you know if Deep Blue is still in the area?"

"Give me a sec and I'll check." He waited, and saw Robert nod and disconnect his call. Good news, he hoped. Kazuko came back on. "She's still there. GPS tracking shows she pretty much meandered around in that same location all night."

"Must have found a school of tuna to feed on. You still want to have a look at her?"

"You're going out?"

"You don't think I'd pass on an opportunity like this, do you?"

"Not if you could help it. What about Kiana?"

"You can bring her along if you want to. Jeremy, too, unless you think that's a bad idea."

"I'll bring Kiana. She'll no doubt be excited, but Jeremy has work to do. I assume Robert is coming with you."

"He is. We'll call when we're close. You can have someone run you out in a Zodiac."

"We'll be ready."

Jack disconnected the call and looked at Robert. "I saw you smiling, so you must have done some good."

"You're going to like this; Li Fang has a large estate on Kalaniana'ole Highway just south of Kaiona Beach Park."

"Jeez. That's not far from here."

"And right on the beach."

The shreds of a plan formed in Jack's mind, but it required darkness and presented a mountain of problems. "I want to get going if you're ready. We'll pass right by there on the way to pick up Kazuko."

"And Kiana?"

"Her, too. Apparently, Jeremy has work to do."

"Probably for the best. There won't be any problems that way."

Jack said, "Providing she keeps her mind where it needs to be."

"Kazuko will make sure of that."

Jack relaxed knowing she would do her best to keep the young lady focused.

I have my own problem to deal with.

CHAPTER 37

Jack sat at the topside controls. Wearing a faded yellow Jimmy Buffett parrot tank-top and blue and white board shorts, he envisioned himself being an island version of Captain Kirk in his Kirk-chair on the *USS Enterprise* 'going where no man has gone before.' That's how he felt when he thought about what he might be getting himself into.

Li Fang would not be an easy nut to crack.

He rounded Mokapu Point and put *Pono II* on a course southeast toward Rabbit Island, visible in the distance. According to Robert, the back of Fang's estate fronted the beach directly west of there, across the Pukakukui Channel. The property would be easily recognized from the water by the turtle pond and the seawall.

Legend had it that a chief who once ruled that part of the island liked turtle meat so much, he had a pond built in a way that it kept a constant supply of live turtles.

But not any longer.

Now, federally protected, congress had made it illegal for a person to touch or even harass Hawaiian sea turtles in the wild.

A wise move.

He glanced at his Seiko dive watch, all too aware of the time.

And the impending scourge on the island.

"Grab the binoculars from below," he said to Robert who stood next to him, hand gripping the backrest. "There's a couple of pairs in the locker in the salon. I'm sure we'll need them."

Robert bent his knees and straightened them, maintaining his balance as a swell rolled under the boat. "I assume you have a plan?"

"The real plan comes later. Right now, I just want to have a look at the place."

Robert stared out to sea with a pensive expression. Jack knew the look. He had seen it many times over the years and had an idea what was coming.

His mind is always working.

Robert said, "Did you know that according to Hawaiian myth, the *Kanaka Maoli*—native Hawaiians—believe that when you die your corpse is often times transformed into a shark that becomes their family's *aumakua* or shark god that will steer fish into their nets and protect them from danger?"

Jack recognized the story. Robert always had more to say, so he waited for him to finish.

"*Kamohoali'i*, the brother of *Pele*, is the chief of Oahu's shark gods. He's like Odin to the Vikings and Zeus to the Greeks. *Ka-ahupahau*—second only to *Kamohoali'i*—is the queen shark and Oahu's guardian spirit. Together, they keep out man-eating sharks to protect the people of the island."

At one time, maybe, Jack thought. *But not right now.*

He appreciated island legend, and suspected Robert shared this tidbit of folklore for a reason. "I assume you're going somewhere with this?"

Robert turned his gaze from the horizon. "The great shark war. The shark god, *Keali'ikau 'o Ka'u* is credited with being the hero of the shark war. He and his four shark companions traveled the Hawaiian Islands seeking out and killing sharks that attacked people. After an epic battle, they won the fight."

Jack now understood. "You're saying that the bad sharks have once again risen from the depths, and that we are in the middle of another shark battle? Where does that leave us?"

Robert grinned. "Sometimes even good shark gods can use a little help."

Jack eased the throttles forward.

Time to get a move on.

He said, "If you're done imparting your wisdom on me, you can go below and get those binoculars."

Racing ahead at top speed, it only took a few minutes to reach their destination. Jack slowed the boat to a few RPMs above idle in the gentle swell a hundred yards from shore. The turtle pond lay between them and the beach. The perfect landmark. Robert already had his field glasses pressed to his eyes.

He pointed. "There it is."

Jack raised his 12x50 Swarovski binoculars and scanned the seawall separating the vast estate from a narrow stretch of sand and the turtle pond. He spotted a gate and focused in on it; a no less formidable obstacle, as tall and solid looking as the rock wall on each side of it. Chopper blades were visible but not the cockpit and tail boom. Towering palm trees swayed above the second-story rooflines of a large house on the grounds beyond.

"Nice place," he said as he lowered his glasses.

Robert lowered his. "Should be, for the millions it cost him."

Jack stepped to the safety rail, letting the boat drive itself. Tokunaga needed evidence to tie Li Fang to a crime. A breadcrumb that would get him through the man's door.

A tall order.

He wanted to give the detective his probable cause. At the moment, that seemed impossible. The place would be occupied by staff, if no one else, and definitely wired. Getting over the wall would be no problem, but what then? Getting past an array of cameras and alarms, and most likely armed guards, would be near impossible—and a last resort if there was no other way inside.

Thinking aloud, he said, "Security around that place is going to be a bitch to get past."

His comment drew him a look from Robert that suggested he had lost his mind.

He had to wonder.

Robert said, "That's your plan? You're going over that wall?"

Jack didn't have to give the idea another thought. "Take the controls. I'll make it quick."

Robert scoffed. "What about going to see Deep Blue? Maybe she's that good shark we were talking about a few minutes ago."

"This first."

"And if you don't come back, I'll know you bought the farm."

At that, Jack laughed. "You really think I'm going to let that happen?"

"Might not be up to you," Robert said. "You're not exactly a spring chicken anymore."

The banter did not mask the concern Jack had seen in his friend more often than he could recall. Worry that he knew wasn't totally unjustified. The aches and pains were there. He'd not let minor age issues stop him. He wasn't that old.

Not even close.

"I'll be careful," he said.

"Yeah, well…" Robert gave a sad shake of his head. "Just see that you do."

There was no time to debate the issue further.

"As you wish," he said.

He stripped off his shirt and leaped over the railing in a shallow dive that brought him to the surface of the water clear of the sharp coral heads. It only took him a couple of minutes to swim ashore. He emerged from the surf and moved quickly across the twenty feet of sand between him and the compound. The stone felt warm against his bare back as he scanned the narrow beach from one end to the other checking for camera surveillance.

Seeing none, he chinned himself up on the wall and peeked over the top at the helicopter he'd seen from the boat. The Bell 206 Jet Ranger rested idle on an expanse of grass between him and the main house. A guard of Asian ancestry trailing a Doberman straining on a stout leash, strode past the front of the two-story residence and continued toward the helicopter. The sidearm he carried was clearly visible.

Without warning, the Doberman's head came up amid a low, guttural growl loud enough for Jack to hear. He knew the animal had alerted to his presence. Its pointed ears stood erect, and its dark eyes locked on his. In the next instant, the dog bared its teeth and let out a series of vicious barks as it lunged against the restraints of its leash. The gunman held tight and peered toward the wall.

Jack knew he had been seen. He immediately dropped to the

sand and quickly pressed his back to the warm stone. He'd gotten a closer look at all he needed to see for now.

Getting in there would not be easy.

CHAPTER 38

Jack didn't plan on waiting around to see what would happen. With no time to ponder his next move, he followed the narrow stretch of beach toward the opposite end of the estate. Keeping his stride casual—being careful not to glance toward *Pono II*—he wanted to give the appearance of a nosy vacationer who had grown curious about what lay on the other side of the wall. He was sure more than one person had been caught taking a peek inside.

The barking had stopped almost immediately. He gave himself a full minute before turning and looking behind him. The security guard, with the dog on leash next to him, stood outside the gate. Both stared in his direction.

Obviously, the armed sentry had stepped out to assess the threat. Even having been caught checking out the grounds, Jack couldn't imagine his actions being viewed as threatening. He continued to walk with the same easy stride as before, feigning a lack of concern in what was going on behind him. A minute later, when he checked again, the man and his dog were gone.

Jack felt he'd gambled, and succeeded. The intrusion had not been viewed as serious enough to warrant further action. Or so it appeared.

The situation could have easily gone the other way.

Back aboard *Pono II*, he brought her up to fast cruise and kept her there. He'd just added another memory to this side of the island

and had no desire to linger there even a minute longer.

He was quick to notice that this was not the case with the other people on the water around them. Waikiki Beach had once again been closed to swimmers. So had Hanauma Bay, but not the other beaches. Nor did the order include boats.

That meant divers.

Thrill-seekers.

For them, the temptation to swim with a man-eater would be too strong to ignore—an opportunity to encounter a large tiger or hammerhead up close.

There would be fishermen, too.

He thought about a scene from *Jaws*: Men in overloaded boats, chumming the water, all vying for the reward placed on the killer shark. Thankfully, no rewards had been posted here.

But the enticement was here all the same.

Diamond Head loomed a hundred yards starboard of them when Jack checked his phone for bars. He found he had three and made the call to Kazuko. "Is everything still a go for you?"

She answered, out of breath. "By *everything*, are you referring to what's going on with Kiana and Jeremy?"

"From the way you're breathing, the thought had crossed my mind."

"That issue appears to have smoothed over, at least for now. I think they finally understand how serious I am about not tolerating anymore of their nonsense." Her breathing slowed. "When you called, I was in the middle of moving boxes of supplies. That's why I was out of breath."

"Are you ready to have a look at Deep Blue?"

"I've been ready."

He heard the crackle of excitement in her voice. "Robert and I are rounding Diamond Head now. I take it she's still out there?"

"Since we last talked, she made a slight course change that brought her in closer to shore. Right now, she's about a mile west of Waikiki Beach. I'll grab Kiana and have one of the guys run us out in the Zodiac."

"Before you go, are any of the large tiger's we've tagged hanging out in the area with her?"

"None have pinged off of our receiver."

"Bring along a tagging lance and a couple of electronic tags, just in case she's brought along a friend or two we haven't encountered before."

"Good thinking," she said. "We'll be ready."

Jack ended the call and turned to Robert. "All's good on her end. She and Kiana will rendezvous with us as planned."

Robert pursed his lips, and said, "So everything is cool between Kiana and Jeremy?"

Jack wanted to believe it was.

He said, "According to Kazuko, the problem has smoothed over, at least for now."

Robert's gaze returned to the water ahead of them. "Her warning must have done some good."

"She thinks so."

They rounded Diamond Head and Jack put *Pono II* on a course northward; the aquarium was in view a quarter mile ahead. A surge of adrenalin spiked his excitement when he spied the Zodiac bobbing in a gentle swell.

He moved the boat's throttles to idle and let *Pono II* drift in the relatively calm sea. The gray Zodiac, with two women and a young man aboard, was already speeding in his direction.

When the inflatable neared the boat, Kazuko's and Kiana's faces lit up with smiles.

A happy crew, he thought.

He stepped to the safety rail and peered down at Robert who leaned over the lower-deck railing and lifted aboard a canvas bag containing the tagging equipment. The gear safely on deck, Kazuko and Kiana climbed the boarding steps and waved off the driver of the Zodiac.

Before resuming his place at the helm, Jack spent a couple of seconds watching the inflatable cut a frothy trail in the direction of the aquarium. He half-expected Jeremy to play taxi driver.

Perhaps the friction between them hadn't been resolved.

The hatchway next to him swung open, and Kazuko stepped onto the upper deck carrying her laptop. Kiana followed, wearing a smile she directed at him. Robert brought up the rear and closed the hatchway.

"Anytime you're ready," he said.

Jack waited for Kazuko to access her computer. When she looked up from the screen, he asked, "Do you have a fix on Deep Blue?"

She pointed. "She's still about a mile west of here, but steadily moving in this direction."

He eased the throttles forward, bringing *Pono II* up to cruising speed, and put them on an intercept course with the great white. If she had detected a school of tuna or some other food source, he wanted to be there to study her movements.

Predator and prey.

CHAPTER 39

Time was ticking down.

Jack knew they could locate Deep Blue as long as the tracking device emitted a signal, but that didn't mean the fish would show herself. She could just as easily be content to cruise the depths.

A solitary hunter.

That meant he might have to go into the water with her and trust in his belief that sharks don't intentionally hunt humans. A dive that lost some of its appeal given the recent shark attacks in the area.

Great whites occupied the top of the ocean food chain—a fact he couldn't ignore—second only to the Orca—the shark's one feared enemy. Killer whales were known to actually stalk and kill sharks for a meal of their large livers.

Whales that eat *Jaws*.

Who would have guessed that was possible?

He held onto that thought and glanced behind him at Waikiki Beach. Towels and an array of brightly colored umbrellas were crowded with people lounging on the sand. Others strolled the boardwalk between resorts. But no one ventured into the water.

There would be no human lunch today.

Not off Waikiki.

Kazuko angled the computer screen at him. "She's been on the move."

He could see the blip that marked Deep Blue's location only a half-mile from land. The distance between them and the big fish had closed incredibly fast. Deep Blue now moved in a slow circle.

"We're close," he said. "Real close."

"What's she up to?"

He scanned the water. "I wish I knew."

"There." Robert pointed.

Fifty feet off the starboard bow, her massive dorsal fin sliced the surface toward *Pono II*. Two seconds later she swam alongside, not three yards away, her body over a third the length of the fifty-eight-foot hull.

But she remained there no more than a few seconds.

As quickly as Deep Blue appeared, the dorsal fin slipped beneath the sea.

"She's gone under," Jack called out as though none of the others on deck had seen her disappearing act.

"There's why." Kiana's gaze fixed on something off the port side.

Jack saw the Hawaiian monk seal a dozen yards away making a frantic bid for the distant shore. A full-grown adult, in his estimation; eight hundred pounds of fat-rich food. Then he saw a second seal swimming away from the boat. He guessed the animals sensed the threat.

Too late, he feared.

All of a sudden, the ocean exploded in a roil of blood and foam.

Not Deep Blue.

The shark shook its head in violent jerks from side to side, its rows of serrated teeth ripping a chunk of flesh from the belly of the mangled carcass. Jack recognized the dark stripes down the tiger's body—a six-footer, and plenty deadly. He spied a second dorsal fin slice the water as another shark joined in the kill. Another tiger, but much larger. Judging by the distance from the dorsal to the tip of the tail, this one looked to be twelve- to fourteen-feet long.

Its brain registered a single primeval impulse: Attack and feed.

The creature struck the second seal with the same explosive ripping motion, crushing flesh and bones and organs into a massive mouthful that it swallowed in a single spasm.

Neither animal stood a chance.

The frenzy continued for several seconds. Jack scanned the

carnage. The tigers swam back and forth in water now laced with blood and seal remains, their mouths opening and closing on the lingering bits of flesh.

The disappearance of Deep Blue baffled him.

That kind of behavior out of the massive great white wasn't what he expected.

In the next second, the twenty-foot great white struck the six-foot tiger with enough force to carry the much smaller fish fifteen-feet into the air. Over half of Deep Blue's body was exposed before the massive fish splashed back into the water. Jack recalled research videos that revealed a thirty-five mile-per-hour attack that started in the gloom a hundred-and-fifty-feet or more beneath the surface of the ocean.

Everyone onboard gasped and moved to the safety rail, Jack included, but no one said a word.

He stood in awe, his eyes glued on the great white as she dove and swam away with her prey. The attacks had not been easy to watch. But then the savagery of nature often wasn't. And the sharks were only doing what they needed to do naturally to survive.

Or did Deep Blue have another agenda in mind?

Had Robert been right when he suggested bad sharks had once again risen from the depths to do battle with good, and that the island was in the middle of another shark war?

"Shit," he said, as much to himself as the others.

Robert edged closer. "If I hadn't seen it, I wouldn't have believed it."

Jack turned to his friend. "It's entirely possible you were correct about that good-shark-god theory."

Robert nodded, his gaze still on the water. "Seems so."

Jack couldn't help thinking about the poor sailors from the *USS Indianapolis*. Defenseless men adrift amid all of those sharks....

Was the darkness of night a curse for them...or a blessing for those sailors who never saw the deadly attack coming?

He could only wonder.

Where was the good shark, then?

To Kiana, he said, "Rig the harpoon with a transmitter. That tiger hasn't been tagged, and I'd like to keep tabs on that big-boy."

"I know some researchers call the tagging pole that, but can we call it a lance? I really don't like the word harpoon much."

"I have to agree."

"Great." She pressed her index finger to her lips. "About the tagging: Are you going to do the honor, or am I? To be honest, I've only watched a YouTube video showing it being done."

"I'll handle the lance." He turned to Robert. "You drive the boat."

Kiana opened the hatch and headed down the stairs leading into the salon. He remained long enough to give her a few seconds head start. When he figured enough time had passed, he winked at Kazuko, and said, "She looked like she needed something to do."

Kazuko smiled. "Thank you."

He winked. "See that Robert doesn't break anything while I'm gone."

"I'll do my best."

He chuckled, pulled the hatch closed behind him, and descended the four steps into the main salon. Robert was already making a turn, bringing the boat into position. Jack knew they would only get one chance, and even though *Pono II* was not designed to be a tagging vessel, he would give it a shot.

Better to at least try.

When he stepped from the galley, he found Kiana squatting next to the tagging equipment sitting on the rear deck. He closed the hatchway behind him and watched her finish assembling the lance that would deliver the electronic tag. She appeared to know what she was doing. When she handed it to him, he examined the barbed tip and satisfied himself it would detach from the fiberglass pole as designed when jabbed into the base of the dorsal fin.

He activated the device, carried the lance forward, and stood on the end of the starboard hull. The tiger swam thirty yards ahead of him. He could see the tip of the dorsal fin and tail as the shark moved in and out of the bloody slick—its mouth open, searching out the pieces of seal carcass.

This was the part of the process that left him feeling like Captain Ahab poised above his white whale, harpoon raised. He took a tight grip on the shaft and, at just that moment, the shark rolled onto its side, momentarily exposing a set of claspers.

A male.

He'd wondered since full-grown females reaching upwards of sixteen feet were almost always larger than males.

Kiana pressed in close behind him.

He focused on the tiger.

The fish continued to seine the blood slick for the last morsels of flesh, as though impervious to the presence of the boat.

The perfect opportunity.

He felt his pulse quicken.

"Do it," she whispered.

He maintained his concentration, no urging needed. The shark was practically within arm's reach of him now.

Not a moment's hesitation.

He raised the lance and thrust it at the dorsal saddle.

CHAPTER 40

The four-meter-long tiger shark exploded away from the boat with rapid left and right thrusts of its sickle-like tail. Jack watched the big fish's triangular dorsal fin slice the surface of the water, with the tracking device securely in place, before disappearing from view into the depths. He turned and flashed a thumbs-up gesture at the upper cockpit.

"Good job," Kazuko hollered down to him.

He laid the lance on the deck and hurried topside, followed by Kiana. When he got there, Kazuko had her eyes fixed on the laptop screen.

"I've got a good signal," she said. "Number T-18."

He leaned in to better see the blips. "How about Deep Blue?"

"She's swimming back out to sea in the general direction from where she came. The tiger appears to be sticking around."

"Persistent bugger."

"Maybe he's still hungry?" said Kiana.

Jack shot her a look. "*He*...you noticed the claspers?"

"Hard to miss them on a male his size."

"He's a big one, alright. But it's not likely he's searching for another meal so soon. He just ate an eight-hundred-pound seal. Even so, it appears something is keeping him here."

"Waiting for dinner, maybe."

Jack refocused his concentration at the blips on the screen. The tiger moved in a big, slow circle. He expected the shark to leave the area after being tagged. That proved to not be the case. A thought made him cringe; one he wished he could ignore.

But couldn't.

With so many boaters in the area—fishermen and divers—he wished the shark would find someplace else to hunt.

A male voice boomed from the marine radio: "Coast Guard, Coast Guard, this is Jeremy Lund, a researcher with the Waikiki Aquarium. Come in Coast Guard. I need assistance."

After a couple of seconds' delay: "Mr. Lund, this is the Coast Guard. What is your location and the nature of your emergency?"

"I'm in a sixteen-foot Zodiac approximately a quarter mile west of the aquarium. There's a body in the water here…a man. Dead. It looks like he has been attacked by a shark."

"Copy that. Switch to channel seventy-three."

The radio went silent. Jack didn't wait to hear more. He took the helm, shoved the throttle levers forward, and headed back the way they had come. At top speed, *Pono II* could cover the quarter mile in a couple of minutes. The Coast Guard would likely send a boat from their station on Sand Island eight miles away.

Fifteen minutes in a fast boat. Maybe more.

Not that there was reason to rush.

Except they weren't alone on the water. Other boaters would have heard the distress call. Like lookie-loos to a fatal traffic accident, they would speed to Jeremy's location to satisfy a morbid desire to get a close-up look at the gore.

Robert switched the radio to channel seventy-three and turned up the volume.

Jack continued to scan the water.

We're almost there, Jeremy.

Over the radio, a member of the Coast Guard said, "A rescue boat has been dispatched to your location."

The radio chatter continued, a blur in the background as Jack focused his concentration on what lay ahead. The surface of the ocean was nearly flat, with little more than a gentle rolling swell. He could see Jeremy sitting at the controls, the Zodiac making a slow, tight circle on the ocean. He could guess what floated in the middle of its foamy arc.

Smart thinking.

The prop on the outboard would discourage sharks from doing further damage to the body.

He glanced at the laptop screen and then at Kiana. The grad student stood with a grip on the ladder leading up to the electronics array. She had her gaze fixed on the water ahead of the boat. The furrow in her brow betrayed her worry for Jeremy—their differences set aside, at least for the moment.

To Kazuko, he asked, "What's T-18 doing?"

"As of a few seconds ago, he started swimming a slow zigzag pattern in this direction. I think he's taken an interest in the body."

"Or he's following us," Kiana said.

"Doubtful he'd do that." Jack shook his head. "Probably more curious than anything, but we had better keep an eye on him."

Robert said, "There's also a good chance T-18 was responsible for the attack on that poor guy in the first place."

Jack had entertained that same thought and couldn't dismiss that likelihood. Not any more than he could forget about the six-footer, or a number of other sharks inhabiting the reef. Any one of them could have attacked the man. It was also possible a shark wasn't responsible for the damage done to the body. Another question that needed answering was whether or not the guy was alive or dead when the attack occurred? If it was *indeed* a shark attack.

An autopsy would tell him that.

Maybe…

He eased back on the throttles and slowed to a stop a dozen yards away from the circling Zodiac starboard of them. Robert, Kazuko, and Kiana rushed to the railing and peered over the side. He understood their concern for Jeremy…and their curiosity.

He cringed inwardly, imagining the gruesome sight.

What remained of the body…and what parts were missing.

He stayed at the helm and keyed the mic to the marine radio. "Coast Guard, Coast Guard, this is Jack Ferrell aboard the NOAA research vessel, *Pono II*. I'm on-scene with Mr. Lund and standing by, ready to lend assistance if needed."

The male voice came right back, "This is the Coast Guard, *Pono II*. We copy your transmission and will have a rescue boat on scene in ten to fifteen minutes."

"Copy that, Coast Guard. Standing by."

He glanced to the north—the direction the Coast Guard boat would be coming from. A body recovery; not a rescue operation.

He heard the growl of the Zodiac's outboard motor subside, and saw Kiana wave. Jeremy would be looking up from below, possibly waving back, no doubt relieved to see familiar faces staring down at him. Thankful to have someone to share the seriousness of the situation.

Jack returned the mic to its holder and joined his friends whose grim expressions told the story. He edged in next to Kazuko and peered overboard. Jeremy sat hunched in the inflatable, cradling his face in his hands. The badly mangled body bobbed face-up between the Zodiac and *Pono II*.

A man, no mistake.

Or what was left of him.

Jack stared at the ruined remains. A vague familiarity tugged at his memory. The man in the photograph sitting on the sofa table at the guy's home on Waikai Street in the Kalihi Valley, and the man in the driver's license photo Tokunaga had shown him.

Matt Corvin never left the island.

Not on a plane, anyway.

Jack could only wonder how the man ended up in the water a quarter mile from shore.

And the bigger question.

Was he dead when the first shark attacked?

CHAPTER 41

Jack scanned the shoreline.

Probing ribbons of white marked the leading edge of the waves washing high on the warm sandy beach. With the incoming tide, Matt Corvin's body, or what remained of it, would have washed ashore within an hour or two. A gruesome find for a happy couple on vacation.

And another news headline.

The island had enough bad press over what had been happening.

He swung his gaze to the north and spied a pleasure boat approaching on a direct course to their location; beyond that came another.

The lookie-loos he worried about, drawn by the talk on the radio.

Just what I need.

His spirits buoyed at the sight of the Coast Guard vessel no more than a mile away. The onlookers were their responsibility, as was the recovery of the body.

He had a bigger problem to deal with. And if he was right, so did Detective Tokunaga. One that could affect the world.

Li Fang has the device.

He prayed they weren't already too late.

Pulling his phone from his pants pocket, he saw he had bars and placed a call to the detective.

Tokunaga's phone buzzed three times before he answered. "I'm in the middle of something, Jack. Can this wait?"

"It can't," Jack said. "I found Corvin. At least, I believe it's him."

"What? Where?"

"Floating belly-up in the ocean about a quarter mile off the Waikiki Aquarium. He's been bitten in half. The Coast Guard will be bringing the body in. Meet me at their station on Sand Island. I'll call you when we're close."

"Bitten, as by a shark?"

"Or sharks."

"Cruel justice."

"Only, we're not done."

A moment's pause. Then, "A long ways from it."

"I'll see you there, Detective."

Jack disconnected the call and watched the body recovery process. The Coast Guard doing their job. Not the sort of thing he liked to watch.

Even if the body was that of Matt Corvin.

To Kazuko, he asked, "What's the status of T-18?"

"Circling the area."

Not good.

"Do you mind riding back to the aquarium with Jeremy? Kiana, too. There's nothing more for us to do out here. Not today, anyway."

She took a steadying grip on the shiny chrome safety rail and tilted her face to the sky as though to absorb the sun and the salty breeze. "To be honest, I don't feel much like going back to work."

"I'm sure no one does, including me," he said. "But I've got business to attend to."

She met his gaze. "You're following the Coast Guard in?"

"Robert and I will as soon as the body is out of the water and T-18 is no longer a concern. Detective Tokunaga is meeting us there."

"Not exactly what we expected, is it?"

Jack pointed at the body. "Least of all him."

She sighed, but her gaze didn't waver. "I'm guessing he's the man you were looking for?"

"One of them."

"And now you're going after the other?"

"That might depend on Detective Tokunaga."

"I'd prefer you leave Robert out of it."

The ever-protective Kazuko. He wasn't surprised. "That's up to him. As far as I'm concerned, he's only going as far as the Coast Guard station on Sand Island."

"And you?"

Here it comes.

Hoping to avoid the usual debate, he said, "You'd better round up Kiana and get your stuff together. The Coast Guard is about done here. Jeremy will be anxious to get back to the aquarium."

She shook her head at him. "You're exasperating, you know that?"

"So you've told me. A number of times."

"Conspiring?" Robert asked, having joined them.

"I plan to follow the Coast Guard in. With your help, of course, providing you're willing. I suggested to Kazuko that she and Kiana go ashore with Jeremy."

"That's a good idea." To Kazuko, he said, "I'll help Jack handle the boat and see you at the house later."

She held his gaze. "Promise me the two of you won't talk yourselves into getting involved in something dangerous."

"You worry your pretty little self too much." He kissed her forehead. "Go ahead and go with Jeremy. I'll be alright."

Jack watched his friends say their goodbyes; a process he had witnessed a number of times. When Robert and Kazuko turned from each other, he caught a knowing look from her.

One that said, 'I'm trusting you.'

Not the first time.

It left him with the realization that nothing he could say would put her mind at ease. Too much history existed between them. He offered her a smile and watched her and Kiana step aboard the Zodiac.

Robert said, "She's hard to say no to."

Jack slapped him on the shoulder. "I just want this shit over with."

Robert arched a brow. "You believe this is the end of it?"

Jack had to laugh before turning a sober eye on his friend. "We wish."

CHAPTER 42

The afternoon turned hot, with little more than a breath of wind from the late-morning trades that tend to cool the island. Jack swiped sweat from his forehead and used the boat's bow and stern thrusters to ease her up to the dock across from the Coast Guard vessel. The obvious center of attention.

And for good reason.

He and Robert secured *Pono II* fore and aft and joined the people clustered around a stretcher holding the bagged remains of the man pulled from the sea. Doctor Mayuko Tadeshi, Oahu's medical examiner, had the body bag unzipped and the flaps folded back. Her gloved fingers probed the corpse. Tokunaga, who had arrived ahead of them, stood looking on, along with several Coast Guard personnel.

Jack recalled having met Doctor Tadeshi at a party. It'd been a brief introduction, and under far more pleasant circumstances.

He doubted she would remember him.

A lingering glance from her suggested he might be wrong.

Edging in next to the detective, he asked, "Not very pretty, is it?"

Tokunaga sighed. "Unfortunately, cops have to look at the stuff on the other side of the wall that few people see."

"You sound tired."

"I haven't slept a lot the past couple of days. You?"

"That's a laugh. Sleep is a premium lately. What do you think about this?"

Tokunaga nodded at the body bag. "A shark did that to him?"

"That's how it looks to me."

Jack pictured the body being pulled from the water. Every bit of tissue and bone below the waist gone; bitten away by powerful jaws and razor-sharp teeth. And…what remained of the right arm—a sight he wished he could un-see.

"Anything else you want to add?"

"I'm wondering if the man was dead when he went into the water."

Tokunaga nodded as though he wondered the same thing. He added, "That, and who put him there."

Jack gave some thought to both questions and watched the body being wheeled away. The M.E. conferred briefly with the Captain of the Coast Guard vessel before hurrying after the gurney. The remaining sailors dispersed, returning to their duties.

Robert shifted closer. "Looks like we're finished here."

"Appears so." Jack refocused his attention on Tokunaga. "Well, is it Matt Corvin or not?"

"As far as I can tell, it is. Of course, we can't say for sure it's him until we hear back from Doctor Tadeshi."

"Agreed, but we don't have to wait around for that, do we?"

"What are you implying, Jack?"

Jack thought that was obvious, "Now we go after Li Fang?"

"Like I told you," said Tokunaga, "not without probable cause."

Jack didn't need to be reminded. "Suspicion of murder isn't enough?"

Tokunaga narrowed his eyes. "Corvin took out a loan through Fang. That's all we can say for sure."

Jack didn't understand the detective's reluctance to make a run at the guy. There was more to the relationship between Li Fang and Matt Corvin than an outstanding debt. A lot more. Tokunaga had to know that.

He held the detective's gaze. "And Corvin was on the verge of defaulting on that loan, which would have caused him to lose everything. To the right buyers, the device was worth far more than what he owed Fang. Offering the device to him was his only way out of the hole Corvin had dug for himself."

"I'll buy that. But what proof do we have he offered it to Fang; or anyone else, for that matter?"

"A dead man and a young surfer. But then, I guess that's not enough."

"I wish it was."

"Then I suggest we get the evidence we need."

"And I suppose you have an idea how to do that?"

"I can tell you where I would start."

"Within the law?" Tokunaga asked as a reminder. "You're aware I can't be a party to anything illegal."

"You know as well as I do, it's doubtful Corvin fell from a plane. Which means he was more likely tossed overboard from a boat. With the kind of money Fang has, he probably owns a nice big one. We find out where the yacht's moored, flash Corvin's picture around the marina, and hope someone puts the two of them together."

"If someone does, what then?"

"We search his boat."

"Without a search warrant?"

Jack grinned.

Tokunaga's gaze flicked from Jack to Robert, and back. "You know I can't authorize you to do that."

Again, Jack smiled. "I'm not asking for your permission."

"Sounds interesting," Robert interjected. "You can count me in."

Jack continued to hold the detective's gaze. "All we need from you is the name of Fang's boat and where he has it moored. Robert and I will take it from there, and you can go do your thing."

Tokunaga stood silent for a full five-count before his frown slipped, apparently having warmed to the idea. He nodded. "There's nothing stopping me from helping canvas the marina. All I ask is that you understand I can't take part in an unlawful search."

"Trust me." Jack grinned and added, "I would never expect you to be involved in something as underhanded as that."

"Trust you?" Tokunaga scoffed. "You could have said anything but that. I'll call in and get the info on Fang's boat."

Jack relaxed, confident he could have gotten the information from a number of sources and moved forward with his plan without the detective's help. And would have; if it had come to that. But knowing even the best-laid plan can go sideways in a heartbeat, it was better to have Tokunaga on board with their scheme.

"Robert and I will tuck *Pono II* into a slip across the harbor. Give me a call when you get the info and we'll meet up over there."

"With fingers crossed?"

"With a box of rabbit's feet, if that's what it takes."

We're running out of time.

CHAPTER 43

Jack fought a mounting sense of exasperation. He and Detective Tokunaga had been all-in on finding Matt Corvin and putting an end to the shark threat that posed an immediate danger to the island's populace, before the device could be placed on the world market. The man had been found floating in the ocean off Waikiki Beach, dead—half-eaten by sharks. Now they had a new player in the game, and the stakes had been raised.

Only Li Fang played his cards close to the vest.

A hard man to read.

And harder to catch…

Jack felt the press of time working against them, but there was one more order of business he needed to take care of before moving the boat. Megan O'Connell wanted answers she could pass on to the mayor and governor to calm their concern and put the island on a path to normalcy. She wouldn't be happy with the information he had to pass on to her.

He sat at the helm with the twin engines idling and placed the call.

All we need is one more complication.

"There has been a development," he said when she answered.

An audible sigh. "More bad news?"

"Matt Corvin's dead. Coast Guard pulled him from the water a quarter mile off Waikiki Beach. It appears the sharks got to him;

bitten in half. But we'll have to wait for Doctor Tadeshi to finish her autopsy to get the official cause of death."

"Any ideas how he got there?"

"Pushed overboard, I suspect."

"Do you think his death is connected to the deaths of the man and boy killed yesterday?"

"I have my suspicions. Detective Tokunaga and I are following up on them now, or will be shortly."

"You'll keep me updated?"

"You can count on it," he said at the same time he heard his phone beep. *Tokunaga.*

"Jack—"

"Sorry," he said, cutting her off. "I've gotta go, I'll call you back in a few. Detective Tokunaga's calling and I need to take it."

"Do what you have to do, Jack. We'll talk later."

He tapped on the detective's call and put it on speaker so Robert could listen in. He said, "That was fast."

"Didn't have to dig. Our white-collar guys already had the information. He owns a fifty-foot Bertram named *China Doll.* Has it moored at the La Mariana Sailing Club. I'm sure you're familiar with the place."

"Very," Jack looked at Robert and got a smile. "Robert is a charter member. Do we know which slip it's in?"

"Number eighty-six."

"Should be easy enough to find. Give me time to get my boat situated."

"See you there."

Robert had his phone in his hand when Jack disconnected. He knew Robert and how the man's mind worked. "You have a plan, I take it?"

"Members have privileges." Robert raised the phone to his ear.

Jack sat quiet and listened. It took a couple of extension transfers before Robert got the right person and arranged for a vacant slip large enough to accommodate *Pono II*. Apparently being a member does have its advantages.

Robert tapped off. "We're set."

Jack didn't hesitate. "Let's not keep Tokunaga waiting."

"Fine. You can buy me a beer later."

"Gladly."

"You're easy. Maybe I should have held out for two."

"That's me: Mr. Easy. There's beer in the fridge below. Grab us one. And while you're down there, throw together a couple of sandwiches. No telling when we will get another chance to eat."

Normally he enjoyed every minute he spent on the water… time to ponder the past and what the future might bring. Now all he wanted was to get *Pono II* tucked into a berth and go to work finding a witness that could place Corvin on Fang's boat.

Again, he felt the pressure of time bearing down on him.

From day one, they had played catch-up. Getting close, but always two steps behind in their probe into the mounting threat; the full scope of which remained frustratingly uncertain. Now, Corvin's death. Another unsettling setback that added to a nagging feeling he couldn't shake.

We may already be too late.

It took them longer than Jack anticipated to make the move to the La Mariana Sailing Club. On the way his phone pinged with a text.

"The detective?" Robert asked.

Jack tapped on. "Says he'll wait for us in the restaurant."

Twenty minutes later, they tied *Pono II* off in an available slip and gave the mooring lines one last check. He said, "Let's register and find Tokunaga."

Robert scanned the boats. "You didn't say a whole lot on the ride over. I assume you've thought this through."

Jack started walking toward the tiki bar, turned to his friend and said, "What's to think over? *Ho`oPonoPono*, brah."

Robert nodded. "*Ho`oPonoPono.*"

They checked in. Robert showed his ID; Jack laid down a credit card and Robert signed the necessary paperwork.

Five minutes later, they met Tokunaga at a table in the bar. The detective sat with an empty plate and a half-consumed glass of soda sitting in front of him—a Coke or Pepsi by the color of it, and maybe a shot of Jack Daniels.

Jack never considered himself a saint. And wasn't about to start, now. Considering the day they'd had, he didn't blame the detective if he *had* indulged in a drink.

He asked, "You ready to go to work?"

CHAPTER 44

Jack would've liked to join Tokunaga at the table and sip a cold glass of lager while the three of them tossed around what they planned to do next. But he saw no good reason—other than the lure of a frosty beer—to sit and waste time discussing the situation. It would be an easy matter to walk the docks and flash Corvin's picture to anyone willing to look.

He figured Tokunaga and Robert would approve.

To Tokunaga, he asked, "You brought the photos?"

"You could have just as easily used your phone." The detective handed them each a 5x7 enlargement of Matt Corvin's DL photograph.

"This is better," Jack said. "I'll talk to the bartender. You two spread out and find out what the wait staff has to say."

Tokunaga tossed back the remainder of his soda and rose from the table. "You running the investigation now?"

Jack reined in some of his enthusiasm. "Just suggesting."

"That's what I thought." Tokunaga dug a ten and a five out of his wallet and dropped the cash on the table.

Jack watched the process, his impatience wearing on him. "Can we get started now?"

"Slow down." Tokunaga tucked the wallet back into his rear pants pocket. "I'm a step ahead of you. I've already shown his picture to the staff. They know Li Fang. Apparently, he's a good tipper.

But no one remembers seeing him and Corvin together. There are security cameras in the parking lot and several locations around the marina; I've asked to see the footage from yesterday. Should be ready to go by now."

"That's better yet. We'll start there."

Tokunaga smirked. "Figured you would agree."

He led the way to the security office. A man in uniform answered Tokunaga's knock on the door and let them inside a room not much larger than a walk-in closet. A bank of monitors lined the wall in front of a desk to their left. A single monitor sat atop a second desk pushed against the opposite wall.

They exchanged handshakes and polite nods. The security officer—who had introduced himself as Henry—handed over a business card and motioned them to the secondary desk.

Jack scanned the work space. "They don't give you much room, do they?"

Henry pulled the door closed. "Sorry for the cramped quarters. At least I have air conditioning."

"We'll make do," Tokunaga said.

Henry pointed. "That's my desk. You'll sit over here. I assume you have experience with this type of system?"

"Some. Mostly I have a tech handle it."

"It's pretty simple to operate, really," the officer explained. "The video feed from each camera is stored digitally. The marina consists of six docks with roughly twenty slips each; ten to a side."

Tokunaga asked, "How about offshore moorings?"

"None here at the club."

The security officer tapped several keys on the keyboard and a full-screen color image flared into view on the monitor's screen. "There's twenty-four-hour surveillance, with a camera like this one located at the beginning and end of each dock, as well as four in the parking lot."

Jack leaned in and took a closer look at an elevated view of a planked walkway extending from shore to open water at the opposite end. Boats of various size occupied slips along each side. Masts and raised outriggers bobbed and waved in the tide.

Tokunaga asked, "How about the bar and dining room?"

"There's coverage in there, as well. You can view the data from each camera on the monitor: fast forward, reverse, split-screen or full-frame. I'll get you started, then all you need to do is type in the date and time you're interested in and sit back. If you have any questions, I'll be at my desk."

"How about a couple of extra chairs?"

The officer pointed. "By the file cabinet."

"That should do it for now," Tokunaga said. "You can wait outside. We'll take it from here."

The security officer's eagerness visibly slipped. He said in a reluctant tone, "If that's the case, I'll be doing my rounds. You have my number. Call if you need me."

Robert found two folding chairs that looked like they were leftovers from a revival tent. He set them up and motioned at the monitor. "Allow me, Detective."

Tokunaga motioned toward the computer. "Be my guest."

With Jack and Tokunaga looking on, Robert put his fingers to work on the keys. "I'm thinking it would be best to concentrate on the parking lot and begin our search starting yesterday morning at 0600. That should give us plenty of lead time. It's doubtful they would have arrived here before that."

"Sounds right to me," Jack said. "If he drove that jacked-up orange truck here, it will be easy to spot."

CHAPTER 45

Jack watched the images from the four cameras appear in a split-screen format, one view displayed in each corner of the monitor. Three showed only the parking areas where a half-dozen vehicles occupied spaces in a predominantly empty lot. The fourth included a view of the entrance to the tiki bar and restaurant. A digital clock in each frame displayed the date and time.

Tokunaga leaned close. "No orange truck."

Jack settled back and crossed his arms. "Not yet."

Robert tapped a key and the timestamp sped forward. "I'm fast-forwarding the feed or we'll be here all night."

Jack didn't dare take his eyes off the screen. Hours passed in minutes. Cars and people came and went in comedic movements; gray and white with an occasional black one thrown in appeared to be the vehicle colors of the day. Fortunately, Corvin had chosen orange.

Another minute passed.

An hour in real time.

Jack jabbed his index finger at the screen. "Freeze it there."

The timestamp stopped at 0941 hours. A view of the lot from different angles, all four frames showed the orange pickup he had seen pull in and park. The frame in the upper right-hand corner revealed an arm behind the open driver's door.

"That's it," Tokunaga said. "All we need is for Li Fang to show."

Jack said. "Switch back to regular time."

Robert tapped a key and Corvin climbed out of his truck and pushed the door closed. He held a small duffle in his right hand and looked around.

"That's interesting," Tokunaga said. "Wonder what's in the gym bag?"

Jack noticed the way Corvin clutched the satchel close to his body. "Could be anything, but my money says it's the device he took when he killed Maxwell."

Robert exchanged glances with Jack. "Let's see what he does."

Jack redirected his gaze to the monitor. "He'll have to go inside to access the marina."

"Not necessarily." Robert brought up a full-screen view of the lot and the entrance to the tiki bar and restaurant. "You're forgetting about the locked access to the right of the building. This Fang character no doubt has a key."

Corvin began walking. At the steps leading into the bar, he stopped and faced the parking lot. His left wrist came up and he glanced at it. Then he switched the gym bag from his right hand to his left. He continued his vigil on the lot, and checked his watch a second time.

"Does he look nervous to you?" Tokunaga asked no one in particular.

"He certainly doesn't look happy to me," Jack said.

"Nor me," Robert added. "I'd say his meeting with Fang has him feeling more than a little apprehensive."

At 0959 hours, according to the time display, Li Fang and two Asian men approached Corvin. One man looked trim and fit, a whole lot like Fang. The other was broad and thick and several inches taller. The thinner of the two carried a shiny metal briefcase. After a short conversation, the four of them walked in the direction of the gate at the side of the building.

Robert switched camera views, bringing the group up in a split-screen configuration on the monitor. They now had a visual of the activity in the marina. Corvin, Fang and the two unidentified men walked past the first dock and the second. There appeared to be little or no conversation between them.

Jack could imagine the whirlwind of thoughts spinning through Corvin's head.

If the man only knew what lay ahead for him.

A minute later, the group came into view as they stepped onto the third dock, Fang and Corvin in the lead. The two other men that Jack figured were bodyguards remained in the rear.

"Here we go," he said.

Robert tapped a key and brought up a split-screen view of the cameras located at each end of the dock.

Coming and going.

Jack leaned close.

Nearly three-quarters of the way down the walkway, Fang stopped and motioned toward a boat moored stern-first in a slip on the left. The name *China Doll* visible in the camera feed.

Tokunaga pointed at the screen. "That's Fang's yacht. I checked when I arrived."

Jack arched a brow at the detective. "You've already checked out his boat and failed to mention that fact until now?"

Tokunaga shrugged. "I walked past it while waiting for you to get here."

"Did you talk to anyone?"

"One couple. No help."

"I'm sure you've already decided it doesn't matter what they had to say." Jack faced the screen. "We have the surveillance feed. If it shows him getting on the *China Doll* and not getting off when the boat returns, we know how Corvin ended up in the ocean."

"We would still have to prove Fang didn't put him ashore at another location."

Dot the i's and cross the t's.

Jack gave some thought to what it would take. "And to do that, we need a witness. Someone who saw him pushed overboard."

"And with knowledge of who the killer is and the link to Fang."

"Someone on his payroll."

Robert scoffed. "Fat chance of that happening."

"Before we get creative," Jack said, "let's see if Corvin makes the return trip."

CHAPTER 46

Jack stood on the deserted walkway outside the security office. Robert joined him, followed by Tokunaga.

In the distance, a mini regatta of large and small sailboats was under way.

"I didn't see that coming," Tokunaga said.

None of us did.

Jack turned his gaze on the boats, their billowed sails leaning with the wind. The three of them had stared at the video screen, sharing creased foreheads of confusion when they observed Corvin return and drive away in his truck, with the smaller of the two unidentified men riding shotgun. They weren't able to see if he had the gym bag with him or not.

All seemingly innocent.

And without a willing witness to state what transpired aboard *China Doll*, difficult to prove otherwise.

But not impossible.

He said, "Doesn't change the fact Corvin ended up being shark chum."

Robert glanced at his watch. "What next?"

"Jack has a point," Tokunaga said. "We can say Fang and Corvin were together on the water around the time the man and boy were killed. And we can say *China Doll* returned and Corvin drove away with one of Fang's men. But we can't say for sure Corvin had the gym bag with him, so we have to assume Fang has the device. That leaves us not knowing how long it will be before it's placed on the market. Also, Corvin didn't drive away alone, so Fang's man still could have killed him and dumped his body, leaving the truck at the hotel to throw us off."

Jack nodded in full agreement. "I'm betting Fang knew about the surveillance cameras. That's why he couldn't dispose of Corvin until they were back ashore. Hate to think we have to wait till Monday but we need to check with the M.E. and find out if she has a time and cause of death. That will tell us if we have a murder scene we aren't aware of, or if he was killed at sea."

"You're reading my mind." Tokunaga pulled his cell from his pocket.

Jack arched his brow in surprised to see the phone come out. "Dr. Tadeshi's working on a Saturday?'

"Only because I asked her to."

Tokunaga placed the call, and Jack turned to watch the regatta. The detective's voice was a muted mumble in the background. Instead of gaining ground, they had lost even more. Twenty-four hours was a lot of time for a lot of things to take place. Now a new glitch had been added to the mix. It was like playing a board game where the board keeps growing with new obstacles and new players and a new finish line always moving away. Roll the dice and make your move.

A never-ending contest of risk.

"Jack."

Hearing his name brought him back.

"Sorry," he said.

Tokunaga said, "You weren't listening?"

"My mind was someplace else."

"We have an official cause of death; it wasn't by shark bite. Corvin was dead when he hit the water."

"So the sharks were only doing what evolution bred them to do."

"If you say so." Tokunaga gave Robert a quick glance before making eye contact with Jack. "The M.E. said she found massive pulmonary contusions, pneumothorax, punctured lungs, and perforations of the heart by broken ribs. None of which were caused by shark bite."

"Meaning?"

"She believes the injuries are consistent with Corvin having fallen from a height of several hundred feet."

Robert nodded understanding. "So, he fell or was thrown from a small plane or helicopter."

Jack couldn't resist a grin. "And Robert and I saw a chopper sitting on the lawn at Fang's estate south of Kaiona Beach Park."

"When?"

"This morning, on our way to this side of the island."

"You just dropped by and had a look around?"

Jack shrugged. "We didn't exactly drop by, but yeah, I swam ashore and peeked over the wall. The chopper was a Bell 206 Jet Ranger. Looks like our little foray paid off. Is there a problem?"

Tokunaga stroked his chin. "None that I know of."

"Okay then, what are your thoughts?" Jack could hardly contain his eagerness to get moving. "Do you try for a search warrant to get aboard that boat, or do we concentrate on the helicopter?"

Robert fixed his gaze on Tokunaga.

"Christ, you guys." The detective faced the marina, putting his back to them. The sails on the boats were bright in the late-afternoon sun. "Do either of you know what it takes to get a judge to sign a search warrant? Especially on a weekend?"

"Witnesses and hard evidence that links a person or location to a crime," Robert said. "Probable cause."

Tokunaga directed an exasperated look at Robert. "We can't even put the device in Corvin's hands."

"And that's the damn problem," Jack said. "Has been from the start. It's all theory built on speculation."

Tokunaga turned his gaze on Jack. "So you *do* understand."

Jack realized they had fallen into a trap of having relied so heavily on conjecture, minus fact. Cops have rules they play by; criminals don't. The age-old game between good and bad. He didn't know for sure if Corvin had brought the device with him to put on a demonstration for Fang. Or even if the apparatus was still on *China Doll*. But he knew he was going to find out.

That was a fact.

CHAPTER 47

Li Fang stood on the second-floor lanai of his home and stared out to sea, the island of Molokai a dark smudge in the distance. The sun had dropped behind Diamond Head turning the water between the two islands a deep blue green. A breeze cooled the air enough to chase away the heat.

His favorite time of day.

He heard the door open. "Tell me some good news, cousin."

Yong Fang stepped out and stood next to him. "Three groups have expressed interest in the device."

"Any discussion of money?"

Yong scratched the scar on his lip. "The price of one million dollars is firm. They understand that."

Li said nothing.

Yong asked, "What would you like me to do?"

"We wait."

"If that is your decision."

"You don't sound convinced."

"It's not that. There's a possible complication we need to talk about. I heard from our contact in the police department. The Medical Examiner identified the body and a cause of death. Unfortunately, the sharks did not dispose of the corpse the way we believed they would."

"This complicates things for us how?"

"They know Matt Corvin died from a fall into the water."

Li turned his gaze on the Bell 206 Jet Ranger sitting on the grass. A recent acquisition that raised his spirits every time he looked at it. Collateral on an unpaid debt.

He clasped his fingers behind him. "You've had the helicopter cleaned?"

Yong nodded. "Wiped down inside and out."

Li picked up on the apprehension in Yong's voice, but refused to share in his cousin's concern. "Then we have nothing to worry about."

"What about the police?"

"Why should we be concerned? There is nothing to connect me to Matt Corvin's death; or Simon Goddard's, for that matter."

"Simon Goddard's death is not what concerns me."

"But Matt Corvin's does?"

"I do not deny we took precautions to assure there wasn't. Still, there is always a chance the police will show up here demanding to search the helicopter."

"Let them look. They will find nothing."

Yong pressed closer. "We do not know that."

Li pursed his lips, and asked, "Who is handling the investigation?"

"Detective Tokunaga? Fifteen years on the force. I'm told he can't be bought. There is another man helping him; his name is Jack Ferrell."

"Another policeman?"

"All I know is he works for NOAA."

"A meddling scientist who wants to play police officer."

"I have a feeling he is more than that. Perhaps we should lay low for a while."

"There is too much money to be made. We stick to the plan."

"Are you sure that is wise under the circumstances?"

"There is an element of risk. I do not deny that."

"You agree, then?"

"Only that there is minimal risk. As there is in every business decision I make. One cop and a mister-nobody scientist does not concern me enough to pass up an opportunity to at least double my money."

Yong laid his hand on Li's arm. "I'm only suggesting we wait a few weeks. The offers will still be there."

"I won't allow these men to compromise my plans. Furthermore, I want you to move forward with the repossession of all Matt Corvin's property."

"If that is your decision."

"You still believe I am being unwise?"

"I still believe it is too risky."

Li could not deny his respect for his cousin's advice. He'd always had that respect—even as a young boy when Yong's birth deformity drew laughter and mean-spirited comments from the other kids, particularly the older ones.

Especially the girls.

"A new plan," he said. "Contact the groups who have expressed interest in the device and arrange for a demonstration. In the meantime, sell the *China Doll* and the helicopter to eliminate any possible loose ends that could cause trouble for us. We can be operating in the clear in a week. Two, max."

Yong nodded. "We will likely have to take a loss on both."

"A small forfeiture that will mean nothing in the long run."

Again, Yong nodded. "As you wish, cousin. I will make it happen."

Li smiled. "And do not worry about Detective Tokunaga or Jack Ferrell. They will be dealt with if they become troublesome."

CHAPTER 48

Jack stood with his back to the sun. Though low in the sky, there was plenty of heat left in it on this side of the island. A dozen more vehicles filled spaces in the lot. Business in the tiki bar appeared to be picking up.

A Saturday night Happy Hour at the La Mariana Sailing Club.

There were more people milling about in the marina, too. A few walked the docks; some readied boats.

All appeared to be waiting for sunset.

Tokunaga worked the latch on the door to his cruiser and held it open. "I think we're finished for today. What are your plans?"

"Not sure," Jack said. "I owe Robert a beer. Maybe we'll hang out in the bar for a few."

"I'd join you if I could, but I have a dinner date with my wife."

"Have a good time, Detective. I'll give you a call in the morning."

"I'll call you. Unless something pops between now and then, I'll be taking the day off tomorrow to spend time with my wife. It's our anniversary." Tokunaga slid behind the wheel, pulled the door closed, and ran the window down. "You two might consider giving yourselves some downtime. It's good for the soul."

Jack grinned. "We just might do that."

Tokunaga's gaze lingered an extra beat. "Enjoy your beer."

Jack moved back a step to make room. The window went up and Tokunaga drove off.

Robert asked, "Do you think he knows?"

"What we're planning?" Jack had his suspicions. "Sure he does."

Robert checked the time. "It's almost five. Kazuko will be getting off work. Want me to call her and ask her to pick us up here?"

"Good idea. This shouldn't take long."

More people arrived. More activity on the docks.

"Busy place," Robert said.

Jack clapped him on the back. "I figure that will work to our advantage."

"Too much activity for one security guard to keep track of?"

"Especially for one who is about to go off-shift and already knows we're working with Detective Tokunaga. And as far as he knows, still are."

"Just don't break anything."

Jack walked and talked on his cell, wanting to keep his call to the NOAA Director short. "I know you were hoping for good news. Our hunch didn't pan out. We can place Matt Corvin on the *China Doll* with Li Fang, and we know he got off the boat at the yacht club. What we don't know is how he ended up dead in the water."

"But you have your suspicions?"

"Trust me. Li Fang's our guy. I just have to figure out a way to prove it."

"Do you know how Matt Corvin died? Was it another shark attack?"

"The coroner determined he died from a fall. Probably pushed from a small plane or helicopter. A shark or sharks got to him *after* he was dead."

A couple of beats. "Keep me in the loop. I need to stay on top of this."

"Very well."

He disconnected the call and shoved his phone into his pocket.

Robert moved up next to him. "Sounded like that didn't go well."

Jack quickened his pace. "Let's get this done."

Pono II sat in the end slip of dock six. Each dock had a number affixed to a pole; so did each slip. He and Robert went aboard and directly onto the flybridge. The marina still buzzed with early-evening activity. From where Jack stood, he could see *China Doll* berthed between two sloops—lonely and unattended.

Right in the middle of the goings-on.

To Robert, he said, "If you're ready, I'll grab a stout wide-blade screwdriver. That should be all I'll need to force the latch on the door."

Robert gave him a look that conveyed a degree of uneasiness. "We'd better make it quick and easy, or rethink our idea."

Jack saw no reason to rehash the plan. He understood the risk they were taking, but he wanted to keep the investigation moving forward and that's what he intended to do.

For everyone's sake.

He said, "My thinking exactly."

They strolled onto dock three, looking at the boats as they walked. Casual as to not draw attention. The two sloops flanking *China Doll* were buttoned-up tight.

A break.

Jack had no intention of lingering aboard *China Doll* longer than necessary. How long that would be, he couldn't say until they were inside and had a look around.

He hoped only a few minutes.

"Let's do it," he said.

He stepped aboard as though he owned the boat and went to work popping the door latch with no real expectation of finding the device lying out in the open. Still, they had to look. Robert stood blocking him from the view of any onlookers. Ten seconds later they slipped inside.

Quick and easy.

With minimal damage.

A million-dollar yacht with a two-dollar lock.

After taking a moment to let his eyesight adjust to the dim interior, Jack said, "You look up here. I'll check below."

He had seen this type of cabin configuration before. A salon with U-shaped seating around a polished wood table, a compact galley down two steps, a master stateroom forward, and one aft to port, with two heads: a master and a guest.

He opened the blinds on the side windows a crack to let in light and descended the steps. To complete a comprehensive search of a boat of this type and size would take hours; time they didn't have. He gambled that the device, if it was here, had not been secreted behind a false panel; or inside a safe, if one had been installed.

Working fast and quiet, he searched the storage areas in both staterooms and heads. Ten minutes tops. After coming up empty, he joined Robert in the salon.

"Nothing," he said.

"Found this." Robert lifted a gym bag using a single finger slipped through one of the loop handles. "Empty, of course."

"The bag Corvin carried aboard. Take a picture of it with your phone and put it back where you found it."

"Already done."

"Then let's get out of here."

"Where to?"

"The bar for that beer I owe you."

"What do we tell Tokunaga?"

"Text him the photo of the empty bag. He'll know what it means."

CHAPTER 49

At eight o'clock that night, showered and dressed in a fresh set of clothes, Jack and Robert sat on the lanai at Robert's house drinking their second beer of the evening. The lights on Robert's private dock reflected off the water of Kaneohe Bay.

Jack wasn't ready to let go of the day. The threat remained; he took that personal.

"Li Fang's motivation is money," he said. "We have to go with the assumption he's putting the device on the market. Hell, the dammed thing is probably there already. It's not on the boat that we know of, so it's probably at his house."

Robert scoffed. "Or his office downtown…or someplace else."

"He strikes me as a person who would want something *that* potentially valuable close at hand."

"I agree. Someplace secure, but readily accessible."

"Exactly."

Robert sipped his beer.

Jack took a drink of his.

Robert said, "If it is at the house, it'll take more than a screwdriver to get into that fortress undetected."

"You're saying we don't even try?"

"Too risky. At least at this point."

Jack held onto his brew, visualizing the Doberman and roving armed guard he encountered when he chinned himself for a peek over the wall.

Kazuko stepped from the house carrying a pu-pu platter made up with cold balls of vinegar-flavored rice served with shrimp, octopus, and salmon. A separate tray held dishes of soy sauce and wasabi.

His stomach growled in approval.

"You two need to eat something," she said, setting the food on the table.

Jack couldn't resist her specialty.

Everything on the plate looked delicious. He passed on the soy sauce and Japanese horseradish, and selected rice and octopus; he then eagerly slid the entire morsel into his mouth before retaking his seat to wash it down with a swallow of lager.

Kazuko didn't have him fooled.

Not for a second.

She was making a valiant effort to conceal whatever it was that preyed on her mind. The pu-pu platter was a good start after having been unusually quiet all evening, especially on the ride to the house. He had known her more than a decade. They were close—as close as two people can be, short of being married. He knew when something had her worried.

"Want to talk about it?" he asked.

"Talk about what?"

Robert stood and took her hand in his. "Jack's referring to what's troubling you. I've been wondering myself."

Kazuko took a seat. "Finding that body today really shook Jeremy up. He and I were discussing it, when he finally opened up about what's been going on between him and Kiana. In addition to helping me with my dolphin research, she's been taking reef fish from the exhibit tanks and selling them to private aquarium owners in order to supplement her income. He's been pleading with her to stop what she's doing. That's what the arguments have been about."

Jack stayed out of it.

Robert said, "She's resistive."

"Apparently."

"Which means she has to be terminated from the graduate program."

"Essentially, yes. Or worse."

"But that's not something you want to do?"

"Jeremy begged me to give her a break. Quite honestly, I don't know what to do."

"Have you talked to her?"

"Not yet. I plan on doing that tomorrow."

He nodded. "After you sleep on it."

"I want to do what's right."

He smiled. "And you will."

Jack gave them a moment. When she sagged into her chair with a sigh, he got up and took a second piece of sushi; shrimp this time around.

He asked, "Did Jeremy say how she goes about selling the fish? It's not like you can walk downtown and set a bucket of butterflyfish and yellow tangs on the countertop at a pet shop and collect your money."

Her look told him she really didn't want to talk about it.

He dropped the food into his mouth, chewed and waited.

Robert watched.

She said, "Would you get me a beer?"

Jack did. When he handed it to her, she said, "According to Jeremy, Kiana uses the web to conduct business. It's interesting you mentioned the yellow tang; apparently, she gets twenty dollars apiece for them. They're sixty bucks through a dealer, so you understand the attraction to her site. Butterflyfish are right up there. And people will pay as much as a couple hundred for crosshatch triggerfish—five-hundred for a male."

"Decent money, then." He retook his seat.

"Could be, on a large enough scale. In her case we're only talking about a few fish—a couple here and there that she takes from the displays when she has a buyer. Jeremy caught her in the act. That's how he found out what she was up to."

"How long has this been going on?"

"Jeremy didn't say, but I got the feeling it has been a while."

"Makes you wonder if she has done this elsewhere."

"I suppose that's possible."

Kazuko sipped her lager. Jack didn't press and took a gulp of his.

"This Kiana nonsense has me thinking," he said after a moment. "What better place for Fang to advertise the device than on the web."

"The dark web," Robert said. "I don't know why I didn't think of checking that. There is a site for just about anything."

Jack rocked forward in his seat. "Can you access it?"

Robert nodded. "There's one way to find out."

CHAPTER 50

Jack woke with a start.

He swung his feet to the floor and massaged his neck, not happy with himself for falling asleep on the loveseat in Robert's office. He checked his watch: 3:15 AM. Robert was still seated at his PC. The reading lamp on his desk was the only light on in the room. In the gloom, the glow from the screen cast a ghostly pallor on his face.

"Sorry I dozed off," Jack said. "Did you find anything?"

"Plenty."

Jack stepped to the desk and peered over Robert's shoulder; a website was open on the screen.

"What am I looking at?"

"I thought it was a site advertising the device we've been looking for."

Jack fought a yawn. "So you found it?"

"Not yet. But you wouldn't believe what I *have* found. There are sites offering credit card numbers, drugs, guns, counterfeit money, stolen subscription credentials, even hacked Netflix accounts, and software that helps you break into other people's computers. It's a virtual cesspool of criminal activity."

He wondered how people got away with crimes as blatant as the ones Robert described. Why the sites weren't taken down by the Feds.

He asked, "What does a person pay for that kind of stuff?"

"One site I came across advertised three thousand dollars in counterfeit twenties for six hundred dollars. Another offered seven prepaid debit cards, each with a twenty-five-hundred-dollar balance, for five hundred. Of course, there's no guarantee you'll get what you order."

Jack scoffed. "Scammers scamming scammers."

"You're not too far off." Robert leaned back in his chair and laced his fingers behind his head. "A lot of the dark websites are set up by scammers who constantly move them around to avoid pissed off customers—including, law enforcement. Even sites that have been around for a year or more can suddenly disappear if the owners decide to abscond with their customers' money."

That explained a lot.

He said, "As per usual you're an abundance of information. But I'm only interested in the site advertising the device."

Robert rocked forward in his seat and took hold of his mouse. "Which is what I've been focusing on while you were over there sleeping. The problem is my web page requests are routed through a series of proxy servers set up to render the IP address unidentifiable and untraceable. Which makes my searches frustratingly slow; not to mention, unpredictable. That's why it's taking me so long."

"But you're zeroing in on it." Jack retrieved the chair he'd been sitting in earlier and took a seat next to Robert's desk. "Let's keep looking."

Robert queried two more sites without success. He rubbed his eyes. "I'm beginning to think it's not here. At least, I'm not finding it."

Jack had the same feeling, but he wasn't ready to give up. "We have to keep digging."

Robert stifled a yawn. "And we will."

They were both facing the monitor when a scuff in the hallway distracted Jack from what he viewed on the screen. A second later, Kazuko walked in dressed in a robe and slippers. She held two mugs of coffee, one in each hand.

An angel of mercy.

She said, "You boys might need this."

Robert took the cup she held out to him. He smiled. "Thanks, but you should be asleep."

"It's four o'clock. You're the ones who should be asleep."

Jack glanced at his watch: five after. He took his mug from her and set it on the corner of the desk. "Thanks for the coffee. I suppose we'll have to hang it up if we don't find what we're looking for soon."

"I don't think we'll have to," Robert said, his eyes back on the screen. "A site just came up advertising terror through shark attacks. And there's a photograph of a device that *has* to be the one Fang took from Corvin."

Jack read the words on the screen and shivered; a chill brought on by a vision of blood-stained surf, the cries for help, and of all the innocent deaths that would follow. His mind flashed on the men of the *USS Indianapolis*, the water, their screams.

This was not just the scheme of a crooked businessman.

Pure evil was at work here.

He shook off the thought and studied the image in front of him. The apparatus looked a whole lot like he'd expected. "Not very sophisticated. Reminds me of an old transistor radio."

Kazuko peered over Robert's shoulder. "A million-dollar radio. According to what it says, that's the price tag."

"He'll probably get every cent." Robert clicked on a tab and scrolled. "Looks like there are three interested parties."

Jack wanted names. He leaned in, anxious to see the identities of the buyers they would be dealing with. "Do we know who these people are?"

"The names are encrypted, and get this: each interested party has been asked to supply a number to a burner phone, which they've done. My guess is Fang, or one of his men, will call with instructions."

"I suppose there's nothing tying any of this to Li Fang."

"Not even a valid IP address."

Jack set down his coffee cup, slopping a sip onto the desktop. "How about the phone numbers? We should be able to do something with those."

"Dammit." Robert frantically tapped the keys. "No. No. What in the hell—?"

Jack rocked forward. His face inches from the screen.

"Something wrong?"

"The site's gone. I was staring right at it and the damn thing just…disappeared."

"You're kidding." Jack fought an urge to reach for the keyboard. "Were you able to copy any of the information before the page went down?"

His question brought a sigh from Robert. "That's the damn problem. I started to but the site vanished from the screen before I had a chance."

Jack felt like he'd been punched.

Their solid lead.

Gone.

"Fang did it." He sagged back in his seat. "The sonofabitch took the site down."

"And there's no getting the information back."

The reality of the situation sank in, souring Jack's mood.

Terrific.

He picked up his coffee cup; peering over the rim, he met Robert's gaze. "What you're saying is, we're fucked."

"Putting it bluntly, yes." Robert pushed back from his desk; fatigue lines showed on his face. "All we know is the device is out there and we need to stop Li Fang before the deals are consummated."

Jack peered out the window at the wedge of moon low in the eastern sky.

Fucked is putting it lightly.

He said, "Meaning we are back to square one."

"Afraid so. Only the clock has sped forward."

Jack realized that as well. He dug his phone from his pocket. "I need to make some calls."

"At four in the morning?"

"Every second counts."

CHAPTER 51

Jack stared at the name on the screen of his phone and placed the call he dreaded having to make. Detective Tokunaga wasn't going to be happy. Nor his wife, since it was their anniversary.

He listened to the detective's phone go to voicemail.

Dammit.

He left a message saying he had urgent information and to call him back ASAP. There was no reason to explain what the information regarded. Tokunaga would know it pertained to the device.

The clock was ticking.

Jack's next call was to his boss. There could be any number of very good reasons why the detective hadn't answered his phone. Megan O'Connell would. Even if she was in bed, she always answered her cell.

"Jack?" Her voice sleepy, uncertain.

He fought fatigue to sort his thoughts. "Sorry to wake you, but I have vital information you need to be aware of."

Her voice became instantly alert. "At four-thirty in the morning?"

"Sooner, if I had known about it earlier."

"I'm listening."

He told her about the dark web and explained what they had found. The difficult part was admitting the site disappeared before they copied the information. He apologized but made no excuses for the setback.

She said, "It just disappeared?"

"On the screen one moment; gone the next. You know what that means. Time's up. We have to stop playing patty-cake with Li Fang and do something to stop the man from going forward with this sale, and fast."

"I totally agree. But from what you've told me, we still don't have any evidence tying him to the device or the recent deaths. What do you suggest we do?"

He'd anticipated her question. "We have a circumstantial case Detective Tokunaga can present to a judge to get a search warrant for Fang's helicopter. It's a shot in the dark but it could lead to more. Only, without a single piece of solid evidence to back up our suspicions, it's unlikely a judge will sign it. Make your calls. When you speak to the mayor and the governor, call in a favor, whatever you have to do to get them to assert some of their influence to smooth the road for a warrant."

"To pressure a judge?"

"If that's what it takes."

"I can ask. That's all I can do."

"There's something else to consider. The buyers will most likely demand a demonstration."

"And we don't know when or where that will be."

"We lost any chance of finding that out when the website went down. But I know it will mean more blood on our hands."

"Any ideas?"

He had given serious thought to that very question. "It's my opinion Fang won't want to risk leaving Hawaii. And I don't think he'll want to sit on this deal. If my gut is right, whatever is in the works will happen soon; here on Oahu or on one of the nearby islands."

"Sounds reasonable."

He heard his phone beep with an incoming call. Tokunaga's name showed on the screen.

"The detective is returning my call from earlier. Give me a ring after you've talked to the mayor and governor. We need that search warrant."

"Will do."

He clicked over. "I was on the phone with my boss. Thanks for calling me back."

"You said it was important." There was a hint of impatience in the detective's voice. "Or are you just trying to fuck up my day off?"

What choice did he have?

He said, "I'm not trying to fuck up anything you have going. That ticking clock we've been chasing; it sped up."

"What are you saying?"

Again, he explained that with Robert's help they had spent the night searching the dark web, what they found, and that through no fault of theirs the site disappeared before Robert could copy the information.

That last bit of news brought a sigh from Tokunaga. "You passed this on to your boss?"

"And more." He relayed his and Meg's conversation. "I figured getting a warrant to search the helicopter was a stretch, but our best shot. All we need to do is find Matt Corvin's prints in it, and we're off and running."

"That and his blood would be better."

Jack understood the validity of that statement. A fingerprint match, along with traces of blood matching that of the victim, would be instantaneous and give them the probable cause they needed to secure a second warrant allowing them access to the house. DNA evidence extracted from a hair or broken fingernail or even a shred of skin would take time to process—days or even a week before the results came back.

Time they didn't have.

"It's possible there's blood," he said. "Remember, Corvin was alive when he fell into the water, so someone had to have pushed him from the cockpit. I don't think he would have allowed that to happen without putting up a fight."

Silence.

"I hope your director has the pull you're gambling on."

"You know the old cliché: Nothing ventured. Nothing gained."

"I'll write the warrant affidavit and have it ready."

Jack stared though Robert's office window at the darkness over the bay. The first rays of sunlight would dapple the water in an hour and a half. He and Robert had been at it all night, and were facing a very long day.

"Keep your fingers crossed," he said. "We're making this up as we go. And you and I both know we're running short on options."

CHAPTER 52

The call from Megan O'Connell came at two minutes after nine. Jack bolted upright on the couch inside Robert's office and read the time on his phone before tapping on. The sky outside showed bright and cloud free through the window.

Perfect Hawaiian weather.

"It's my turn to ask for the good news."

"You've got your judge," she said. "Honorable Lawrence J. Cooke is home waiting for a call from the detective. Now go get that ruthless S.O.B."

He liked her attitude.

Had from the beginning.

"I'll let Detective Tokunaga know the second I hang up with you."

"A lot is riding on this, Jack. Let's hope it works." She disconnected.

He placed the call to Tokunaga. "You ready to go to work?"

"I've *been* working. So, your boss pulled it off?"

Jack pictured her on the phone to the mayor. "She can be a convincing woman. Do you know a judge by the name of Lawrence Cooke?"

"He's one of the better ones."

"You can move him to the top of the 'good-guy' list. He's at home waiting for your call."

"Before I go, you need to know Robert can't take part in the search. My sergeant insisted. I hate having to leave him watching from the sidelines after he has done so much to help, but I'm sure you understand."

"I was afraid you were going to say that."

His response was met by a pause from Tokunaga. Then, "Just be sure he knows it wasn't my idea."

Jack said, "Just get the warrant."

With that, he disconnected, dreading having to disappoint Robert.

* * *

At ten fifty-nine that morning, Jack parked his Jeep a hundred feet from the entrance located at the front of Li Fang's estate. The gate blocking the gravel driveway appeared to be metal festooned with a bronze and copper dragon, and as formidable looking as the seven foot tall stone wall flanking it. Coconut palms swayed in an onshore breeze. He could see the upper portion of the two-story house but not the helicopter.

Not a good sign.

But the fat lady hasn't sung.

He checked his watch; Tokunaga had said eleven o'clock. He glanced at the rearview mirror and saw a dark grey car coming, followed by a marked patrol unit; a white van brought up the rear. Tokunaga had brought reinforcements and the team of crime-scene techs he had promised.

Good thing.

Fang was beyond careful.

Jack continued to watch Tokunaga in the mirror until the detective's car stopped next to him. He secured his Jeep and climbed in on the passenger side of the officer's gray sedan.

Tokunaga eased the car forward. "Our one advantage is Fang doesn't know we're coming."

They stopped at the gate and Jack pointed at a camera facing them from the top of a pole. "He knows now."

A voice crackled over a speaker set above the keypad mounted to a post on Tokunaga's side of the car. "Can I help you?"

Jack wanted to laugh.

Check your surveillance camera, stupid?

Tokunaga ran his window down and leaned toward the box. "Detective Tokunaga to see Li Fang. Open the gate."

It took a minute before the gate swung open. When it did, an Asian man stood in the center of the driveway—the smaller of Fang's men he'd seen in the camera feed at the yacht club. A golf cart sat on the side of the roadway. Jack knew better than to sit in a car while someone you don't trust walks up on you.

He got out and stood by his open door.

The uniformed officers in the patrol unit did the same.

So did Tokunaga.

Tokunaga's right hand was visible through the door window, poised near his Glock. Everyone ready for a shootout.

Everyone, Jack thought, *except me.*

Where is my gun?

Tokunaga said, "Please move out of the way. I have a search warrant."

The man stepped forward. "I am Li's cousin, Yong Fang. May I see the warrant?"

Tokunaga didn't have a choice.

Yong took a moment to look over the document. "You're here to search my cousin's helicopter. I'm afraid I can't allow you to do that."

Tokunaga stiffened. "You understand that if you interfere with the service of a lawful warrant signed by a judge, you are subject to arrest?"

The threat brought a palms-up gesture of helplessness from Yong. Even his expression softened to the point of showing impotence in the matter.

Clearly not the desired effect the detective hoped for.

"I understand that completely," Yong said. "But I still cannot allow you to conduct your search. My cousin no longer owns the helicopter you seek."

Jack craned his neck. The area of lawn where he had seen the helicopter sitting the day before was a bare expanse of grass. He spoke over the top of the car. "Yong could be telling the truth. The chopper's gone from where I saw it."

Tokunaga's jaw muscles visibly tightened before relaxing enough to talk. "I still need to check. Move aside."

Yong stepped to the edge of the roadway. "By all means, Detective. Do what you must, but I assure you I speak the truth."

Tokunaga turned to the uniformed officer behind him. "Follow me in. Have the van wait here."

Jack got back into the car, fighting his frustration.

Tokunaga climbed in on his side of the cruiser and pounded his palms against the steering wheel. "How in the fuck did this happen? Do you think Fang knew we were coming?"

Of all the questions the detective could have asked, that was the least surprising. "The man is beyond careful. That's what I think."

CHAPTER 53

The wind had been knocked from their sails.

That's how Jack felt.

But it did not keep him from wanting to follow through with the plan he and Tokunaga had started with that morning. The chopper was still out there.

So was the evidence they needed.

He hoped.

Li Fang had stared down at them from the second-floor lanai of his home—a king watching from the ramparts of his castle. His hands clean. But his cousin had been cooperative in providing the name of the person who purchased the helicopter the night before. Freddie Ward had, supposedly, been more than eager to take possession.

The name meant nothing to Jack.

Or to Tokunaga.

Judging from Yong Fang's willingness to share the information, neither he nor his cousin were worried about evidence being found inside the helicopter.

Jack didn't know what to make of that.

He followed Tokunaga to the police department downtown. By the time they arrived, the detective had enough background on the guy to have an idea who he was dealing with. The information had been pulled by two investigators in his unit who had been called in to lend support.

Jack slid a chair in front of Tokunaga's desk and listened while the detective rocked back in his seat and briefed him.

Freddie Ward, it turned out, was a thirty-year-old personal computer gamer turned millionaire in 2017, when he founded a cutting-edge software corporation. Neither of them were familiar with Ward or his company, Innovating Gamer—a graphics card retail business that leases high-end graphics cards to PC gamers, with infinite upgrades, at a low monthly rate.

Apparently, an instant success.

Originally headquartered in Pasadena, the company had relocated to Oahu in 2019. What caught Jack's attention—the detective's as well, judging by the tone of his voice—was the location of the main office. Ward had set up shop on the twenty-seventh floor of the Ahi Tower at Bishop Square.

Hearing that, Jack said, "Ironic, isn't it? The person who bought the helicopter and the person who sold it have offices on the same floor."

Tokunaga rocked forward and planted his forearms on his well-ordered desktop. "Li Fang has been a step ahead of us all along. I don't know why we should be surprised now."

Jack wasn't.

He said, "We still have a chopper to search."

Tokunaga nodded. "There's no time like the present."

"So how do we handle it? Get another warrant?"

"First, we have to confirm Freddie Ward in fact bought the helicopter. Then we have to find out where it's kept."

"I know what I'd do," Jack said. "But then we're playing by the rules here. So how do you propose we do that?"

"Since Ward's not implicated in any of this and shouldn't have anything to hide, best way I know is to knock on his front door and ask permission."

"Just as bold as can be?"

"It's worked for you in the past. Why shouldn't it for me?"

Not always, Jack thought.

And he had his doubts now. But then…Detective Tokunaga had a badge and a gun.

He said, "I'll ride with you."

The house in question was located on Noela Drive—a high-end neighborhood situated on the west slope of Diamond Head. They were both familiar with the area and how much it cost to live there.

"We'll make contact with Ward and see what he has to say. If all goes well and the chopper's there, I'll call in the crime-scene techs."

"And if he objects?'

"I get a warrant and we do it the hard way."

Noela Drive dead-ended at Ward's house—a sprawling estate that sat on an acre or more of land. A gated circular drive led up to the residence. The gate was open to guests at what appeared to be a party.

Tokunaga slowed. "Looks like he has company."

Jack scanned the string of cars sitting outside the entryway leading to the front door. All were high-end models with glossy wax jobs.

"A luau," he said. "And we weren't invited. Go figure."

"Rude, if you ask me." Tokunaga pulled in and parked at the back of the line.

He got out and Jack followed. At the front of the detective's car, they paused. Jack heard the mellow sound of a slack-string guitar mixed with muted chatter followed by a brief outburst of laughter.

He looked at Tokunaga. "You lead."

The detective nodded him forward and they climbed the steps to the polished, intricately carved Koa-wood door.

A tall, thirtyish blonde wearing a flowered turquoise wrap dress answered the bell. She could have been a Tommy Bahama model, and quite possibly was. The wine glass in her hand needed a refill.

She stopped smiling, and asked, "Can I help you?"

A man and woman close to her age and dressed in Hawaiian garb, stood in the room behind her. They continued to chat, seemingly uninterested in what was going on at the door.

Tokunaga flashed his badge and ID. "I'm Detective Tokunaga. This is Jack Ferrell. We'd like to speak to Mr. Ward, please."

She looked Tokunaga up and down and did the same to Jack. Her eyes appeared to linger on him.

He smiled.

She asked, "He's not in trouble, is he?'

Tokunaga said, "I just need to speak to him."

She gave them a final quick once-over. "Wait here."

The latch made a soft click when the door closed.

Jack looked at Tokunaga. "At least she didn't slam it in our faces."

Tokunaga huffed. "I bet she wanted to."

Jack turned and took in the view—several million dollars' worth. After a full two minutes that felt like five, the door reopened. A tall, thin, freckled man dressed in the requisite aloha shirt and flowered board shorts stood in the entranceway.

"You wanted to speak to me?" The man's large Adam's apple bounced when he talked.

Tokunaga flashed his badge and ID. "Sorry to interrupt the party. You're Freddie Ward?"

"Did I do something wrong?"

"We simply need to ask you a few questions."

"Regarding?"

"A helicopter you purchased from Mr. Li Fang. You did in fact buy it?"

"I did. Yesterday afternoon." Ward stepped onto the tiled portico and pulled the door closed behind him. "What's this all about?"

"How well do you know Mr. Fang?"

"I've met him. Our offices are down the hall from each other. Nice man."

"Is that how you learned his helicopter was for sale?"

"I got a call from his cousin." Ward glanced back and forth and narrowed his eyes at Tokunaga. "Why are you so interested in the helicopter?"

"We believe it was used in a murder. When did you get that call from Mr. Fang's cousin?"

"Yesterday afternoon. He offered it to me for a good price."

"An offer you couldn't refuse?"

"That's right."

Jack picked up on the rising friction between the two and decided to step in. "Where's the helicopter now?"

Ward broke his stare from the detective and looked at Jack. "It's in a hangar at the airport. I'm having it detailed and painted."

Jack took a deep breath.

Still a step behind.

"Will you allow us to process it for evidence?"

"Do you have a warrant?" Ward's gaze shifted to Tokunaga.

"I can get one if I have to." The detective reined in his tone. "But we would prefer to have your permission."

The man's gaze flicked back and forth. "Surely you're not trying to implicate me in anything?"

"Not at all," Jack assured him. "In fact, quite the opposite. Your cooperation speaks a lot to your innocence."

"You'll be careful not to damage anything?"

"Promise."

Ward took a moment before nodding. "Is my word good enough or do you have a paper you want me to sign?"

"We'll need a key, too."

"I don't have a key, but I can call the guy who does and instruct him to let you in. If that's all right with you."

"If he can head right over. Time's important."

CHAPTER 54

Jack felt his impatience beginning to get the best of him. It was after two, and they had yet to get a look inside the helicopter.

The Sunday traffic didn't help his mood.

The only saving grace was—thanks to Freddie Ward's cooperation—they hadn't had to waste more time securing a second search warrant.

He asked, "You sure you know where you're going?"

"I have a general idea." Tokunaga kept his eyes on the road. "You're worried?"

"I'm just anxious to nail this fucker."

"Don't feel special. We all are."

Jack kept further comments to himself and settled into the ride.

It turned out the hangar wasn't hard to find. There was no sign of the guy with the key, though. They tried the door, just in case, and found it locked.

Jack scanned the area. "Looks like we got here ahead of him."

Tokunaga checked his watch. "Hope he didn't change his mind."

"Ward promised the guy would drive right over."

"So he said."

Jack noticed Tokunaga pull his phone from his pocket. "What's up?"

"Remember me telling you Simon Goddard owned Goddard Freight here in town? I asked detective's Keala and Donohue to check into his company. Donohue should have gotten back to me by now."

"You think there's a connection?"

Tokunaga scrolled down his phone and tapped the screen. "Just dotting the i's and crossing the t's."

Jack listened to Tokunaga's side of the conversation. From the sound of his voice, the call wasn't going the way he hoped it would.

"What did Donohue have to say?" Jack figured he already had a pretty good idea what the answer would be.

"That was his partner Keala. Donohue wasn't there."

"And the verdict?"

"Keala was a little surprised Donohue hadn't talked to me. Surprised me, too. But then everyone has been busy with cases. Nevertheless, according to Keala, the company's financials tanked during the past year and never got turned around. That, and Goddard's divorce, left him on the verge of going under. He was the perfect mark for a piece of shit like Li Fang but so far they haven't been able to find a connection between the two."

"And with Goddard dead, that's it."

"For the time being, anyway."

Jack checked his watch and looked around. "Where is that guy? He could have walked here by now."

"Relax, Jack. It's only been a few minutes."

They had to wait another ten. When a guy in a white pickup pulled up and stopped, they walked over to meet him.

The driver got out and asked, "Are you the cops?"

Tokunaga took the lead. "You're Ryan?"

"Freddie said you want to have a look inside his helicopter." He dug a set of keys from his pocket and walked toward the door of the hangar. "I assume he told you I'm prepping it for a paint job."

Tokunaga fell in stride. "You work on the weekend?"

Jack joined them, afraid of the answer.

"Sometimes." Ryan grinned. "If the money's right." He opened the door and switched on a bank of overhead lights.

They stepped inside and stopped.

"Shit," Jack muttered when he saw the doors to the helicopter laying on a table and the seats sitting in the middle of the concrete floor.

Tokunaga raked his fingers through his hair. "My sentiments, exactly."

Ryan stood off to the side. "Like I told you, normally I don't work on weekends unless the money is good. Freddie wants the chopper cleaned and ready to go, so he paid extra. Me and my partner pulled the seats and doors and scrubbed them down last night. We'll start sanding and prepping for paint tomorrow."

Jack didn't exactly know what he expected to find at the hangar. He was pretty sure it wasn't this.

Not even close.

His mind reeled with the events of the past few days as he struggled with the shock of seeing their evidence slipping from their grasp. He and Tokunaga knew the players and the part each one had played in the deaths—right down to what Li Fang planned to do next. But they needed proof to support their hypothesis. They *still* needed proof. The sound of a vehicle rolling to a stop outside drew his attention to the open doorway.

Finally.

He held out hope they'd retrieve the evidence they were after, and turned to the detective. "Sounds like your crime-scene techs are here."

"Good," Tokunaga said. "We're going to need them."

Jack heard the exasperation in the detective's voice, and thought it ironic how luck could evaporate right when you need it the most. They were stuck with the cards they had been dealt. Good or bad, to play out their hand remained their only viable choice. Something he was getting used to.

The crime-scene techs filed inside with their equipment. Introductions were made and he stood back to watch them do their thing.

He had an understanding of the process from the detailed explanation Tokunaga gave him on the drive over. The smooth, hard surfaces on the seats, doors, and the entire fuselage would be dusted for prints; luminol sprayed to expose trace amounts of blood; followed by aggressive DNA extraction. Every piece of evidence collected would be meticulously documented and taken to the lab for processing.

He admired the forensic team and trusted their skill, but seeing the helicopter laid out in pieces on the floor and knowing every item had been handled and scrubbed clean by Ryan and his partner, made it hard to believe the slightest trace of Corvin remained for them to find.

It wasn't hard to imagine Li Fang and his cousin laughing as he and Tokunaga drove away from the man's house empty-handed.

The joke's on us.

It had taken the technicians over ninety minutes to make a detailed examination of the helicopter. When he noticed them packing up their equipment, he walked over to where one of them stood talking to Tokunaga.

Akimoto Yoshiko, he recalled.

"Blood?" Tokunaga asked her.

Yoshiko shook her head. "We weren't able to find a single trace on any of the surfaces."

Tokunaga pressed. "How about prints?"

"Plenty. Once we get back to the lab, we can run them and have an answer for you in possibly an hour.

"How about DNA?"

"That takes a while."

"Thank you," Tokunaga said.

Yoshiko nodded and followed her team out of the building.

Jack watched the woman go and set the bezel on his dive watch. So much hinged on the next sixty minutes.

He turned to Tokunaga. "Guess we're done here."

CHAPTER 55

Time became muddled and slow.

Jack recalled Tokunaga driving them away from the hangar and talking about what they would do next. Then, a deafening crash. Glass shattering. His body slamming into Tokunaga's right side. Airbags going off.

He managed to look up and saw what could have been a delivery truck speed away. Duel rear tires; big boxed-in cargo area. No other vehicles were around that he could see. His vision blurred and he attempted to wipe his eyes clear with the back of his hand, but the fog was inside his head.

His arms worked. He tried his legs, and found he could move them with little pain. A drop of warmth on his forehead drew his hand to his scalp. When he looked, he saw blood on his fingertips and realized he had been hurt in some minor way.

But he'd worry about that later.

Sluggish, and not all at once, his senses started to work.

Images began to clear.

He felt as though he wanted to lean his head back and close his eyes but fought the urge. Steam rose from under the hood. The exhaust pipe crackled beneath the floorboards.

He needed to get out.

They needed to get out.

Tokunaga hadn't moved. His body sagged in the restraint of his seatbelt and shoulder harness. Airbags hung like deflated balloons. The car was a ruined mess from the driver's door to the front bumper. When struck, the door and dash and hood had crumpled in a hail of shattered glass and bent metal, canting the steering column several degrees.

Jesus…

"Brian. Are you okay?"

Nothing.

Jack unbuckled and gave the detective's arm a nudge with his hand. "Talk to me, you stubborn bastard. You okay?"

Again, nothing.

He probed the detective's neck for a pulse and heard him moan. The fingers of his right hand curled and formed a loose fist.

Jack debated whether to try and move the officer or wait for paramedics. He looked him over the best he could. There was no way for him to judge the seriousness of the detective's injuries. They had to be bad, but there was no bleeding that he needed to control. He scanned the crumpled fender and hood for signs of fire. Seeing none, he decided it was best to not risk further damage.

Not until he had no other choice.

"Brian, can you hear me? Open your eyes, Brian. I'm calling an ambulance. Did you hear me, Brian? Hang in there."

The man's eyelids fluttered and closed.

Alive.

Jack wrestled his phone from his pants pocket and dialed 911.

* * *

Jack had his door open, his butt resting on the edge of his seat, and his feet on the ground. He raised his head and listened to the sirens. They were like bugles blowing in the distance. The cavalry charging to the rescue.

A marked HPD patrol unit was the first to arrive on scene. He recognized Officer Williams when she exited her patrol car a minute ahead of the arrival of paramedics and fire department. He wasn't sure if she recognized him or not. Her focus was on Tokunaga, where it needed to be.

From the sidelines, he watched the two paramedics—an older man and a younger woman—work through the shattered driver's window to stabilize Tokunaga's neck with a cervical collar and apply gauze to his head. Then the firemen went to work extracting the detective from the wreckage.

Jack cringed at the crunch of metal.

He searched out a large rock to sit on and wait. Not comfortable but he saw no reason to get up. Not even when Officer Williams walked over with her notebook open.

"We met the other night," she said in introduction.

"Officer Williams." He mustered the energy to nod. "You're the officer who found the orange pickup we were looking for."

A hint of a smile formed. "Can you tell me what happened?"

"A truck rammed us from out of nowhere with no indication the driver made any attempt to stop. Tokunaga might have seen the damned thing coming but I didn't. I was lucky to get a look at it as the driver sped away. It had dual tires on back; a boxed-in cargo compartment; shiny metal on the outside. Clean. No writing or logos that I saw."

"Like a delivery truck?'

"That's right. Maybe a five-ton. Seems strange one would be making a delivery out here on a Sunday."

She made a notation. "Anything else you can tell me about it?"

He wished he had seen more. He hadn't, but stated the obvious, "The truck has to have major front-end damage."

She made another notation. "I'll put out a broadcast. Maybe Brian can add to it when he's able."

Jack looked at the detective pinned in the car. "Brian opened his eyes once and made a fist. That's got to be a good sign, right?"

She offered a somewhat sad smile. "Do you have your driver's license with you?"

A formality to complete her report.

He dug it out of his wallet and handed it to her. When she had the information jotted down, she handed it back.

She still had her notepad open. "Phone number?"

He told her, and she wrote that down and closed her book. "Wave me over if you think of something else."

"Count on it."

She left him sitting there and rejoined the activity at the car. He knew the firemen were working to get the door open as quickly as they could. This was not their first rodeo. Nor his. They needed to get the detective out of there.

Fast.

Brian couldn't die.

Not this way.

It dawned on him he had started addressing the detective by his first name. Even in thought. Now he realized how much he considered the man to be a good friend, and how much he wanted him to live.

Life takes cruel turns.

This wasn't going to be one of them.

He sat, trying to come up with an explanation for the accident, and why the driver had fled the scene. His thoughts kept returning to one answer.

Accidents happen.

This is no accident.

Li Fang was hedging his bet. He had taken steps to get rid of the helicopter. Somehow, he found out Tokunaga was at the hangar processing the chopper for evidence. Fang couldn't have known what evidence, if any, had or would be found. Even so, he made no attempt to take out the crime scene investigators or their van.

Any number of scenarios could suggest why. Confidence on Fang's part that all evidence connecting him to Corvin's murder had been erased, surely figured largely into each one. This, in Jack's mind, left the one explanation that made sense.

Tokunaga's cruiser was the intended target.

He narrowed his eyes in a surge of anger as the implication becoming vividly clear.

We were getting too close.

This was personal.

Li Fang wanted them out of the picture, hopefully for good.

The female paramedic walked over to him, and asked, "What's your name?"

He swallowed his rage and told her.

She probed his scalp with gentle fingers and shined a flashlight into his eyes. She took his vitals.

Competent.

He asked, "What's the verdict?"

"You probably have a mild concussion, and you could use a couple of stitches. I think you should come to the hospital."

He didn't argue.

She took hold of his arm and helped him stand. He was more interested in what was being done to help his friend. His own injuries—minor in comparison—were the least of his concern.

The firemen had the crumpled driver's door cut away and were in the process of loading Brian onto a gurney. The detective's left arm was splinted and he didn't appear to have regained consciousness, but the firemen weren't preforming CPR. He took that as a good sign. The male paramedic examined Brian's injuries and checked his vitals while other rescue personnel rolled him toward the ambulance.

Jack stopped and waited out of their way.

Officer Williams had Brian's semi-automatic in her hand.

The detective wouldn't need it where he was going.

Jack had a bad feeling about it.

He had a bad feeling about everything.

This isn't over.

CHAPTER 56

Jack sat in the surgery waiting area at Queen's. The same chair he sat in when Robert had his emergency appendectomy preformed not even a year earlier. As far as he was concerned, he'd already spent way too much time at this hospital.

He would be spending a little more.

There still had been no word on Brian's condition. He watched Officer Williams wander in and out of the room with only a minor acknowledgement of each other's presence. What needed saying, had already been said. Her sergeant showed up as well. Clearly, they were both worried.

One of their own was fighting for his life in the OR.

He pulled out his cell and called Megan. "I assume you haven't heard."

"Heard what?"

"Tokunaga and I were in an accident."

She shot back, "An accident?"

"Not exactly an accident. A delivery truck intentionally broadsided the detective's car with us in it and fled the scene."

"Please tell me you're not hurt?"

His aches and pains were nothing compared to what he wanted to do to Li Fang, but he wouldn't tell her that. "A bump on the head, some bruises, and a few stitches. Tokunaga wasn't as lucky. He's in surgery now."

"I'm so sorry. You're sure you're okay?"

"Brian's the one we need to worry about. I'll give you a call when I get an update on his condition."

"Be sure you do."

"Count on it." He clicked off.

More officers came in. Some were in uniform and some in street clothes. The room went from quiet to noisy with everyone demanding to know what happened, and no one supplying answers.

When a middle-aged Caucasian woman—pretty, in spite of looking like the blood had drained from her face—was escorted in by a uniformed female, the chatter stopped. Heads turned in her direction. All the officers seemed to know her.

He had never met Brian's wife but had imagined her looking much like the woman who had just walked in. Only, from the way Brian spoke of her, beaming and rosy.

She forced a smile and accepted hugs from the men and women huddled around her in a mob of emotional support. It looked like everyone had a turn before she took a seat. The female officer with a genuine look of concern sat beside her.

They didn't talk.

A somber vigilance.

Jack felt odd watching the two women, like he should go to Brian's wife and say something. Apologies. Words of encouragement. Anything to help lift her spirits. But the sad reality was, nothing short of having a doctor tell her that her husband was going to be all right would make her feel better.

Make all of them feel better.

He had the presence of mind to give himself and her the space they needed. He got up from his chair and walked out of the room. A good prognosis and the promise of a full recovery on Tokunaga's part might be enough for them.

Not for him.

This is personal.

On his way to the cafeteria, he ran into an ER nurse he recognized from earlier. She smiled and stopped. "You're still here?"

He reached up and fingered the bandage covering the stitches holding his scalp together. "My friend is still in surgery. Me, and half the police department, are waiting on word from the doctor."

"I'm sure your friend will be all right. But how are you doing? You look like you could use a cup of coffee."

"It so happens I was on my way to the cafeteria."

"I'll save you the walk."

She led him to the breakroom primarily reserved for OR staff. At the door, she paused and said, "I don't think they will mind."

He followed her inside and put a dollar bill in the coffee machine. "Can I get you a cup?"

She gave a slight shake of her head. "I've had my quota for the day."

He collected his coffee and twenty-five-cents change and they stepped back into the hallway. She stood a moment, looking at him as though she wanted to say something.

She had nice eyes.

He sipped his coffee, letting his imagination wander.

Finally, she said, "Take care of yourself."

"I will." He saluted her with a raised cup and watched her walk away. Whatever it was she had wanted to say, she took it with her.

When he got back to the waiting room, he saw several officer's walk out. Williams was on her feet. He approached her and asked, "What happened?"

"A lot." She kept glancing toward the officers who were leaving. "The doctor came out a few minutes ago and informed us that he feels Brian will recover from his injuries okay."

"Okay? How bad was it?"

"His left side is banged up pretty bad, as you can imagine. A broken arm and leg—a bone in his arm had to be pinned. The surgeon's primary concern was internal bleeding. Brian suffered a lacerated spleen that had to be repaired."

Jack's concern buoyed. "Fortunately, the surgeon didn't have to remove it."

"That's what the doctor said."

"When will we be able to see him?"

"Not for several hours. And then, only family."

"You're not sticking around to find out how he's doing?"

"Can't. One of my beat partners found the delivery truck

burning on the side of the road. I'm on my way out there now."

"The one that hit us?"

"We suspect so."

He knew the 'we' she referred to was the HPD, the officers on scene in particular. "Where was it abandoned?"

"Pahounui Drive off the Sand Island access."

"What about the driver?"

She motioned him off. "Sorry, I need to go."

She hurried out, leaving him alone in the middle of the room, and feeling very much like an outsider. In the hallway on the opposite side of the doorway, the hospital buzzed with its usual activity. Visitors paced the hallway. Staff went about their duties. Footfalls scuffed and clacked on the tile floor out of sight from him. He glanced around the waiting area and noticed Brian's wife standing off to the side. Some of her color had returned.

He walked over to her. "My name is Jack Ferrell. I was with your husband when his car was hit by the truck."

She offered her hand. "I'm Joan. He talked about you."

A firm shake. He liked that.

"Guess I screwed up your anniversary."

"That wasn't your fault. I assure you Brian will make it up to me the moment he's able."

He flashed a sympathetic smile. "I'm sure he will."

And I'll make sure he does.

His phone vibrated in his pocket, pulling his attention away from her.

"Excuse me a second," he said, and answered without bothering to glance at the name on the screen. "You're here?"

"We're in the lobby," Robert said. "You ready to go?"

"I'll be right down."

A second after he disconnected, his phone vibrated again. This time he checked the screen for caller ID. He tapped on, and said, "Director, hold on a second."

He covered his phone and refocused on Joan. "I need to take this call. When you see Brian, tell him I was here the entire time and that I'll drop by when I can. He'll understand."

She smiled. "I promise."

He went back to his phone. "I was about to call you."

"Sure you were. Who in the hell did you piss off?"

"Li Fang. But you know that."

"I'm talking about at the police department. The chief called me saying he wants you off the investigation. A new detective will be assigned to it and they don't want you involved."

"And you went along with it?"

"I didn't have a choice."

"I thought you were tight with Mayor Kobayashi."

"Friendship only goes so far, Jack. I made my case to keep you involved, and she felt she had to side with the police chief."

"So, that's it?"

"Officially, yes."

"How about unofficially?"

Silence.

Then, "Just be careful, Jack."

CHAPTER 57

Li Fang took the call, nodded to himself, and disconnected.

His gaze fixed on Yong. "You were saying, cousin?"

"There were complications."

"What do you mean, complications?"

"The calls were made separately to the number of each burner phone. All three buyers demanded the demonstration be done on one of the other islands. They claim the test will provide a more accurate representation of the full potential of the device."

"Not Oahu?" Li smiled. "Afraid of giving me home-court advantage."

"They want an unbiased demonstration."

"So they don't trust me?"

"Not just you. These people don't trust anybody."

"Did they say which island they preferred?"

"I suggested Maui."

"They agreed?"

"It's scheduled for tomorrow at noon. Maui's close, and the beaches will be packed with vacationers."

"Which beach did you have in mind?"

"Kaanapali Beach. Where many of the hotels are located."

He pictured the sand crowded with young vacationers. At that time of day there would be a lot of unsuspecting people in the water. He imagined the chaos: men, women and children, screaming and trampling each other to get to shore. Exactly what he needed for maximum impact.

"Will the devices be ready? We can't afford further complications."

"They are ready now."

"Then we can proceed as planned. Once again, you have made me proud. What is the status of the boat?"

"Freddie Ward was only interested in the helicopter. I planned to list the *China Doll* with a yacht broker tomorrow."

"That will not be necessary. Instruct Chen to bring the devices to the house. We will take two with us on the boat and leave the others here."

"Do you think that is wise considering what happened this morning? What if the police come with another search warrant?"

"Detective Tokunaga and that meddling scientist have been dealt with."

"Yes. But the detective lives, and Jack Ferrell only suffered minor injuries. And—"

Li lifted his hand, stopping him from continuing. He knew what worried his cousin. "You are afraid I may have awakened a sleeping dragon?"

Yong lowered his gaze. "The police will surely suspect you, and want revenge for the attack on their fellow officer. Perhaps it would have been better to let the detective and Jack Ferrell play their games. They were getting nowhere."

"Nowhere? They came here with a search warrant, didn't they?"

Yong's gaze rose to meet his. "And we had taken precautions."

"Just as I did when I ordered the men killed. A decision you feel was unwise?"

"Unfortunately, Huan's failure to carry out your instruction cannot be undone. We can only move forward."

Li did not tolerate insolence from anyone in his organization, not even his invalid father with all his wisdom. But he would make allowances for Yong.

Something he had always done.

"You've dealt with Huan?'

Yong offered a curt bow. "Most severely, I assure you."

Li felt secure Huan was no longer a liability. "I told you

everything would work out. The way it always has, and will continue to. Just as I promised. My actions earlier today may have been hasty, but we no longer have to worry about Detective Tokunaga or Jack Ferrell. They are done. That is what my phone call was about. The detective is in the hospital and Jack Ferrell has been ordered to not interfere."

Yong's gaze intensified. "Does that not mean the police are continuing their investigation of Matt Corvin's death?"

Li stepped to the window and looked to the south, across the channel, past Molokai. In his mind, seeing the island of Maui.

Where the future of the world would soon change.

"Let the police investigate," he said. "They have nowhere to go. Our business dealings with Matt Corvin were perfectly legal. The only link to his death is no longer a threat to us."

"What about the device? They know Matt Corvin was in possession of it. If they haven't already done so, it's reasonable for them to suspect a connection to you."

"Not if our contact continues to do what he is being paid to do. As far as the police know, the device died with Corvin. And after the demonstration has taken place on Maui, two islands south of here, all suspicion will be removed from us. The sale will go through and in two days we will continue to operate the way we always have."

"Two days might not be enough."

"It will. If not, we are still in the clear."

"Your mind has not changed, then. You still want to proceed with the foreclosure on Matt Corvin's property?"

"Take it all."

"His wife and family?"

"They are of no concern to me."

CHAPTER 58

Jack met up with Robert in the lobby. Kazuko was there with the same worried expression he had seen too many times.

He knew there would be a million questions. "We can talk in the car."

Robert hesitated. "What the hell happened?"

Jack put a hand on Robert's back and pointed him toward the exit. "When we're in the car."

Kazuko followed them outside, quiet for now. He was happy to be spared a few minutes of explanation. She had made her feelings clear the day before when she said she did not want Robert involved in anything stupid. It'd been her way of saying she didn't want him taking part in anything that could get him hurt.

Jack squinted into the sunlight.

Maybe she knew something he didn't.

Or envisioned it?

Robert dug his keys from his pocket. "Where are we going?"

"The Sand Island access road."

"The marina?"

"Not that far. You want me to drive?"

"My new Lexus LC? Forget it."

At the door to the car, Kazuko turned and looked at Jack. "I'll ride in back. You ride up front so you two can talk. I'll be able to hear you just fine."

Jack was sure of that.

During the ride he explained in detail everything leading up to the collision with the delivery truck. When he got to that part, he told them what he remembered. Which wasn't much. He even shared his phone conversation with his boss.

From the rear seat, Kazuko said, "I'm glad the police wouldn't allow Robert to tag along with you."

She wasn't done being upset at him.

He turned in his seat. "How were we supposed to know Fang would try something like that?"

She gave him a sober look, but said nothing.

"You couldn't," Robert offered. "You can't even say for sure Li Fang had anything to do with what happened. At least, not yet. But I sure wouldn't put it past him. What are the police doing about it?"

"Besides ordering me off the case?" Jack shifted his body. "I can't say for sure. Providing they identify the diver of that truck; they'll go after him. You can bet on that. They'll also continue to investigate Corvin's death, but that's a dead end unless the lab pulled some evidence placing him in the helicopter."

"Any idea when that will be?"

"Initially it was supposed to be an hour. Which means the detective working the case now probably has the results. The problem is, even that's circumstantial without a witness or a confession. Even if we found blood, which I don't think we did, Fang could claim ignorance. What Tokunaga and I planned to do was use the evidence to pressure him. Make him explain how it got there. That would hopefully get us more names. And if we're lucky, someone who would spill their guts to make a deal."

"So the best chance of stopping Fang before the device is turned loose on the world is to find the driver of the truck that hit you."

"Find him alive, you mean, and make him talk."

"Coerce is the word I'd use."

They found the street. From the police activity, it became immediately obvious where the truck had been dumped. Robert parked a block away and they walked to the scene.

Jack didn't quite know what he expected to see. A suspect in handcuffs would be a good start. He saw Williams filling out a form on a clipboard and walked over to her. "Anything you can tell me?"

She continued to write. "You're not supposed to be here."

"Why do you suppose that is?"

"You'll have to ask Detective Sergeant Edward Liu. I heard the order came from the Detective Commander at his request. Now I think it would be best if you left before I get my ass reamed for talking to you."

He liked this girl. "They can't stop me from looking."

"No, but they can take it out on me."

"Shit detail?"

"Something like that."

Loud talk drew his attention to the damage on the front of the burned-out hulk. An officer stood pointing at the twisted metal. A big, heavy bumper had absorbed most of the impact from the collision with Tokunaga's police cruiser. The truck's grill had taken the rest head on. But, unfortunately, not enough to disable the vehicle.

He asked the question she had left hanging at the hospital, "What about the driver?"

She looked up from her paperwork. "There's no body in the cab, if that's what you're asking."

"I don't suppose there is any word from the lab on the evidence they collected from the chopper?"

"Even if I was inclined to tell you, I can't. In case you haven't noticed, the lab techs have their hands full at the moment. If I were you, I wouldn't expect results to come back anytime soon."

He noticed a lab technician step back from the cab of the truck. Coveralls and gloves smudged with black.

She was right. The lab guys had their hands full.

"Do you know who the truck is registered to?"

"Island Tours. The reason you didn't see a logo is because the truck's new and hasn't been painted yet. They claim it was stolen from the yard sometime this morning."

He thought about that. "You do know Li Fang is behind this?"

She clipped her pen to the report and met his gaze. "I'm sure you're right. Get me the evidence and I'll arrest him."

And I'll help you.

"How do your higher-ups feel about that?"

"Can't say for sure. They're in kind of a holding pattern right now."

He could imagine. "I don't want you walking foot patrol in Chinatown, so I'll leave you to do your work. If something pops, will you give me a call?"

"I can't make you any promises."

He smiled. "But you'll consider it."

CHAPTER 59

On the way to the car, Jack stopped and looked back at the police activity around the scorched truck. The order to have him removed from the case had come from the police chief. He had just been told the order originated with the Detective Commander at the recommendation of Sergeant Liu.

Strange, he thought.

Why now?

He was not so arrogant as to believe the case against Li Fang could not be worked without him, but why would the commander want him removed from the investigation when the only other person totally familiar with the case lay in the hospital?

Robert asked, "Something wrong?"

Jack let it go. "We passed a market on the way here. Let's get a six-pack and take it to the boat."

"There's beer in the galley."

"A couple of bottles. Not near enough for what I have in mind. I'm thinking Foster's Lager."

Kazuko said, "You sound like a man who's had a rough day." She took his arm and guided him toward the car.

He set aside his negative thoughts and played along. "What gives you that idea?"

"That bandage on your head, maybe."

"Good guess."

"Don't worry," she said. "I'm sure a few beers will help."

"What an excellent idea. Why didn't *I* think of that?"

The sun had sunk low, splashing the first rays of yellow and orange across the horizon. Jack carried the beer aboard *Pono II*. He removed three bottles and they took them topside. Robert and Kazuko settled into folding deck chairs and Jack dropped into the seat at the cockpit. He swiveled around so that he faced his friends.

Color from the sky reflected off their faces. In them, he read the warmth of unconditional, lifelong friendship.

He watched a sloop motor out, hoisting canvas as it headed for deeper water on a sunset sail. Other yacht club members moved about on their boats. Hawaiian music sounded in the distance. A warm evening added to the island ambiance.

But it did nothing to soothe his mood.

"Wish I could say I'm surprised by all that's happened."

Robert sipped his lager.

Kazuko asked, "You ready to let the police do their job and come home with us?"

Mother hen, again.

She seemed to be doing her best to steer him away from the case.

He shook his head. "Give up on stopping Fang? Not going to happen. Besides, when someone hurts a friend of yours, you're supposed to do something about it."

"*The Maltese Falcon*," Robert said. "You're quoting Bogart now?"

Jack shrugged. "Not exactly, but it fits."

"What about Homeland Security?" Robert said. "If they haven't already been contacted, you could push your boss to get them involved."

"Wishful thinking. Without evidence of an imminent threat against the country, do you think they're going to want to get involved? And even if they do, they'll spend a week or more getting their ducks in a row. Time we don't have."

"We don't know that, and it beats doing nothing."

Jack stared at the label on the bottle. "You have a point."

"Well?"

Jack checked his watch and pulled his phone from his pocket. He stepped to the safety rail, put his back to the water, and placed the call to his boss's cell. A Hawaiian Airlines 737 on approach to the airport drew his gaze skyward.

Another flock of tourists in search of tropical sun and relaxation in the islands.

Welcome to paradise.

"It's me," he said when she answered. He heard the clank of a dish.

"I'm in the middle of eating dinner, Jack. Is this important?"

"I'll make it fast. Robert and I have been tossing around the possibility of getting Homeland Security involved in this shark business. I'm wondering if that possibility has been looked into?"

"It's been talked about on my end, too. So far the police chief has pushed to keep the investigation local."

"We see what that has gotten us."

A pause. "Are you okay?"

"Just peachy." He fought a wave of frustration. "I think it's time for you to make the call to the Feds."

"You sure you're all right?"

"I'll be even better when this is over with."

"You worry me at times, Jack."

"Trust me. I'm okay."

Another pause. "If you say so. Just make sure you stay that way. I promise I'll run it up the ladder first thing in the morning."

"Thanks. Enjoy your dinner." Jack tapped off and retook his seat.

Robert rocked forward in his chair and planted his elbows on his knees. "What did she say?"

Kazuko looked at him with a similar curious expression.

Jack laid his phone on the ledge in front of the instrument display and retrieved his beer. "She'll make some calls in the morning."

"Some calls?" Robert sat back in his chair.

Jack shared the uncertainty in his friend's expression, but held onto hope.

He said, "Apparently the decision is not hers to make."

"She's trying," Kazuko said. "That's something."

Jack scanned the boats. He had a difficult time taking his eyes off *China Doll*'s sleek lines.

"But will O'Connell's efforts be enough?"

CHAPTER 60

They were halfway through their to-go dinner of ono and chips they had purchased at the restaurant and carried aboard. The sun had dropped lower, adding a deep red to the yellow and orange already coloring the horizon. A pile of pale crimson clouds loomed far to the south.

A quiet time Jack used to contemplate the shark problem.

Kazuko had her own issue to worry about. Robert had to feel caught in the middle.

Maybe the toughest spot to be in.

To Kazuko, he asked, "Have you decided how you're going to handle what's been going on with Kiana?"

She looked up from her food. "I have Jeremy to think about as well."

He had wondered if she would get around to that. "For not going to you with the situation immediately?"

She picked up a fry and looked at it. "I guess I can't blame him for wanting to protect her. I might even have done the same thing if I were in his shoes. Besides, he did finally tell me what has been going on."

"Which brings us back to my first question."

She dropped the fry onto her plate and met his gaze with a sigh. "My first impulse was to report the theft to the police and terminate her."

"Naturally," he said when her response trailed off. "But you're reconsidering?"

She took a moment to answer. "Tomorrow I'll lay out the facts in no uncertain terms. She has to understand her behavior is totally unacceptable and threatens to ruin her future as a marine biologist. Her only choice will be to stop what she's doing and make restitution to the aquarium by putting in extra hours without pay. If that's not acceptable to her, I'll have no choice but to file charges and let her go."

"And Jeremy?"

"I'll have a talk with him. But I think if something like this happens again, there won't be a problem with him doing the right thing."

He looked at Robert. "I assume you and Kazuko have discussed her decision?"

Robert nodded. "At length, and I agreed. It would be unfortunate for a mistake this early in the young woman's career to put a black mark on her future."

Jack had his doubts. "Let's hope for the best."

He let the subject drop and turned his attention on Li Fang's boat. He sipped his Foster's Lager, and watched a familiar thick-chested Asian—in his mind looking a whole lot like Goldfinger's bodyguard Oddjob, minus the hat—step aboard the *China Doll*. In the glow of the sunset, he could see the man carried a metal briefcase in his right hand.

Jack stood from his seat for a better look. "Fang's boat has a visitor."

Robert pushed out of his chair and peered in that direction. "He's one of the guys from the security footage."

"Yeah. Only, in the digital feed we looked at, Li Fang's cousin was the person carrying the case."

"Think he'll notice the pry marks on the lock?"

Jack raised his phone and snapped the man's photo. "Not unless he looks real hard, which he has no reason to do."

"What do you think he's up to?"

"I imagine we'll find out."

The phone trilled in Jack's hand. Unknown caller. He tapped

on and pressed his cell to his ear while keeping an eye on the boat. "This is Jack."

"This is Officer Williams. You have to keep this call to yourself. So far, we have turned up nothing on the driver of the truck. I took a chance and checked with the lab. They struck out on the prints taken from the helicopter. Nothing back on DNA. It will take a while for the results to come through."

"You took a chance and I appreciate the call."

"I don't need to tell you to watch your back."

"You don't. But thanks, anyway."

He waited a couple of seconds to see if she had more to add. Apparently, she didn't, so he disconnected the call.

Robert said, "That didn't sound good."

Kazuko jumped in. "Not to me, either."

Jack wished Tokunaga was there with them to offer his expertise. There were so many unknowns in the case. Facts without proof. What he did know was Li Fang and Matt Corvin had been together on that boat, a swimmer and a young surfer had been killed by sharks, and a few hours later Corvin was dead.

If it walks like a duck and quacks like a duck, it's a duck.

So they say.

It was easy for him to imagine the metal case contained the device. Or even a worse nightmare, multiple devices. The site he and Robert looked at on the dark web showed three buyers on hold. He didn't need it spelled out. The deals were going through. More people would die, and not only in the Hawaiian Islands. No beach in the world would be safe.

Total insanity at work.

And he had no solid evidence to stop any of the carnage from happening.

He bit back his frustration. "The prints the lab pulled from the helicopter this afternoon weren't a match to Corvin's."

Robert pressed. "How about DNA?"

"That takes time. Something we're fresh out of."

"What do you mean?"

Jack pointed. "Look."

CHAPTER 61

Jack saw his theory coming together in the dim light.

Robert stiffened. "That's Li Fang."

"And his cousin."

"You think the deal's going down?"

Jack watched them board *China Doll* and disappear from view inside the salon. A full cast of players. "I doubt they're going fishing."

Kazuko said, "That's the guy you've been after?"

Jack nodded. "He's one smug son-of-a-bitch, too."

Light that hadn't shown a moment before, appeared in the gaps of the salon blinds. Then the sheer curtains covering the portholes in the master stateroom lit up. A minute later, all three men stepped onto the rear deck.

Robert said, "Looks like they're getting ready to head out."

Jack could see that too. The thick-chested man with no neck climbed up top and took a seat at the controls. Running lights blinked on, followed by the faint gurgle of engines. Yong Fang busied himself untying the dock lines. Li looked on; his hands clasped behind him.

Kazuko gripped Jack's arm. "We're not going to let him get away with this?"

He laid his hand on hers. She had been protective of Robert, not wanting him to be involved in something that would get him hurt. Now she begged to not let Fang carry out his deadly scheme, even to the point of putting herself and Robert in harm's way.

"Not if I can help it." He retook his seat at the helm and started the twin diesels, giving them time to warm up. To his friends, he said, "Once they're underway, cast off the lines forward and aft and we'll follow him and see what he's up to."

"You got it." Robert folded his chair and set it aside.

Kazuko asked, "What about calling the police, or even the Coast Guard?"

Jack met her gaze. "And tell them what?"

She glanced in the direction of Li Fang's boat. "I see what you mean."

He winked. "We're not done yet."

The *China Doll* inched forward out of her slip. Yong Fang remained on the finger of pier to starboard, following the boat out. When no more than a few feet of dock remained, he jumped aboard.

Jack fought an urge to speed after them. In his mind, every second counted, but the deal wasn't going down here. They had a fifty-yard head start when he eased *Pono II* away from the dock. He planned to take his time narrowing the gap between him and the yacht. A slow game of catch-up while maintaining a cautious distance behind.

Robert and Kazuko rejoined him at the helm.

Robert said, "Aren't you getting a little close?"

The two boats were within a couple hundred yards of each other now. Jack feathered the throttle levers so that *Pono II*'s speed matched that of the Bertram, and kept it there; not gaining on the yacht or falling back. The only race they were in was a race against the time.

To stop more people from dying.

He said, "We'll be fine until we pass the channel markers."

The *China Doll* picked up speed once she entered open water. He didn't want to crowd the boat, nor did he want to follow directly in her wake. That would be a sure tipoff, and he wasn't ready for that.

Not yet.

Kazuko asked, "Where do you think he's going?"

So far Oddjob had kept *China Doll* on a southerly heading. Jack didn't believe that would change. Li Fang was headed to Molokai,

Lanai or Maui—even the Big Island was a possibility. Some place away from Oahu.

Jack noticed her looking at him. He shrugged. "Wish I could say for sure, but I'll bet money it's one of the other islands."

"Why would he do that?"

"He put the device on the market. By now he's likely to have reproduced several duplicates, which are probably in the briefcase. According to the site on the dark web, he had three interested parties. I'm guessing he's meeting with them."

"But why take the boat?"

He let her question hang as he thought about it.

The sun had slipped below the horizon. The hotels along Waikiki were lit up like a big city skyline. He moved a few degrees to port, resumed the heading they had been on, and switched off his running lights.

This time, Robert answered ahead of Jack, "To put on a demonstration to prove the device works. And that has to be done from the water."

Her eyes widened in the glow of the instrument panel. "To kill more people. Teenagers. Young kids splashing in the surf."

Jack listened to the shock of reality show through the tone of her voice. He and Robert shared that conclusion. It was Kazuko's turn. Over the past days, she had been privy to what Li Fang was up to. But only now did the full ramifications of the man's deadly scheme totally resonate.

And if they were correct, this would only be the beginning.

He said, "I hope we're wrong but that's about the only explanation that makes sense."

Her gaze fixed on him. "So we're not going to let them do it, right?"

"That's the plan."

They cruised another ten minutes. Darkness deepened over the open water, which worked for and against them. Jack knew all too well the danger of cruising blacked out. Fortunately, the Bertram wasn't. Not only were her running lights on, the cabin was lit up as well. That made it difficult for the men aboard *China Doll* to see beyond the light's reach.

Jack was thankful for that.

He checked his watch. "Anybody know what time moonrise is?"

Robert said, "I noticed it come up the other morning when I was digging into the dark web. It was around three-thirty."

Jack thought about how much he loved the romantic moonlit nights he and Cherise had spent together on the water. This was one time he wished there was no moon at all.

He said, "As long as another boat doesn't run into us, we should be good until then. If you two want to go below and sack out for a while, I've got the watch."

Kazuko brushed a strand of hair from her face. "Robert can go below if he wants. I'm staying up here with you."

"So am I," Robert said. "We still don't know what he's up to. Anything can happen and I'll be ready if it does."

CHAPTER 62

Jack set the auto pilot. The two boats perfectly timed and churning along at a constant fifteen knots. The ocean was relatively flat with low rolling swells *Pono II*'s twin hulls sliced through with minimal noise. Her twin diesels were little more than a low drone, undetectable above the rumble of *China Doll*'s own engines.

A stealth boat under the cover of darkness.

But for how long?

Behind them the lights of Honolulu were still visible. He checked his watch, did the calculation of speed and time, and figured they were within five miles of Molokai where only a few lights twinkled in the night.

"Coffee?" Kazuko asked.

"You made a pot?"

"I didn't want to chance turning on a light. This is instant, made with water heated in a pan on the stove."

He took the mug she offered and raised it to his lips. She had a second cup for herself. He noticed she had taken the liberty of helping herself to one of his sweatshirts.

"What's Robert up to?"

"Had his phone's flashlight app on; rummaging around in the dark, when I last saw him."

She turned her face to the breeze. In the feeble glow from the instrument panel, he studied the highlights of her profile. She had answered as though Robert's activity below was one of her husband's humorous and endearing behaviors. Far from the truth. But a response like that would normally have garnered a chuckle or at the very least a smile. That was not the case here. Her expression was fixed with the seriousness of the situation.

A reflection of his own.

"We'll stop them," he said.

She kept her gaze focused forward. "We have to."

An understatement that immersed him in thought.

His attention was drawn to the hatchway next to him. Robert emerged, turning off his phone when he stepped through. "Black as molasses down there."

Jack noticed an object in Robert's hand. Indiscernible in the darkness. "Find what you were looking for?"

Robert held out a holstered semi-automatic. "Thought it would be a good idea to have this handy if things do turn to shit on us."

"My trusty Colt 1911." His gaze went back on the boat ahead of them. "Took you long enough to find it."

"I should have looked in that secret compartment first."

Jack took the .45 from Robert and ejected the magazine into his hand. He could tell by its weight it was fully loaded. He slid it back inside the grip and pulled the slide back a fraction of an inch. Directing the open port at the light from the instruments, he could see the chamber was empty. Safer that way. A round could be jacked-in quick enough if needed.

Robert, who stood watching the process, said, "I wouldn't give you an unloaded gun in a situation like this."

"Of course you wouldn't." Jack held the 1911 up for him to see. "You know what they say about a .45 caliber bullet, don't you?"

"What's that?"

"Big, slow, and deadly." Jack re-holstered the semi-automatic and set it on the ledge in front of the instrument panel. "Let's hope we don't have to use it."

"The way your luck is going, I won't hold my breath."

Jack took the comment as a joke, but knew there was a serious side to what Robert said. "You're saying I'm bad luck?"

"I'm saying you have your moments." Robert peered ahead of

them. "Either way, we'll find out soon enough. At this rate, we'll reach Maui in another two or three hours. If that's where he's headed."

Jack let the subject drop and glanced up at the blanket of stars that had been their companion since nightfall. During the past few minutes, a few million had disappeared from view in the sky ahead. Clouded over, the sea and the sky were dark as any he could recall.

As though announcing the arrival of the impending storm, a gust of south wind scented with the salty aroma of the sea curled back his hair. The hull bucked and rolled under his feet. A sip of coffee sloshed over the rim of his mug and he held onto the rest.

"Waters getting rough," he said.

Robert gripped the upper edge of Jack's seat and kept his balance. "I bet that asshole Fang didn't plan on this."

"Must not have checked his weather app."

"What's our excuse?"

Jack shot his friend a look. "Oops..."

He glanced at Kazuko. She, too, stood holding on to his seatback. Her empty cup dangled from her curled index finger.

She pointed with her free hand. "Is it my imagination or is Fang's boat slowing down?"

Jack squinted at the lights on the boat ahead and throttled back, adding distance between them and the Bertram. "My guess is Oddjob is compensating for the rougher water."

Her gaze met his. "Oddjob?"

"From the Bond movie *Goldfinger*." He pointed into the darkness. "The big no-neck at the helm. That's what I call him."

She nodded. "The name fits."

China Doll's speed dropped to ten knots but the boat's course remained the same. After an hour of rough water, they were able to see the lights of Maui. There was still no indication that was Fang's destination, but it made sense he would want a crowded beach and a surf full of vacationers.

Maximum hysteria.

The night air that had cooled rapidly over open water actually warmed a few degrees under the cloud cover, which also increased the humidity and forewarned of rain that he hoped would come before sunrise. With luck, people would avoid the beaches and stay out of the water completely.

No target. No demonstration.

No one else dead or injured from shark attacks.

That left him with a lot to think about. When Oddjob put *China Doll* on a slight easterly course correction toward the hotel lights in the distance, he knew his theory had been correct. The crowded beaches of West Maui were Fang's intended target.

With *Pono II*'s running lights still off, she was nothing more than a shadow on a darker sea. He maintained his distance and speed and plowed his ghost ship across the murky void. Ahead of him *China Doll*, with Li Fang aboard on a mission of death, did the same.

Jack could only wonder what perverse thoughts warped the man's thinking.

A shiver danced across the skin beneath his shirt.

CHAPTER 63

Jack figured nothing would happen that night, and probably not first thing in the morning. Li Fang would wait for the heat of midday for his show.

When people flocked to the water in droves.

There was only one place to dock on this side of the island. One that Jack was familiar with; the Lahaina small boat harbor with its fleet of sport-fishing boats…and its' long waiting list for vacant slips. The other option would be to anchor offshore and ride out the night buttoned up tight against the storm.

In his mind, the more likely choice.

When at last *China Doll* slowed to a stop it became obvious Li Fang intended to anchor among the flotilla of boats moored offshore from Lahaina Town. Gone were the two- and three-mast whaling ships that crowded these waters a hundred and seventy-five years earlier. The crux of the town's economy for a quarter century.

Now the fleet consisted of a mixture of new and old privately-owned watercraft of various size, type and condition.

Jack drew a certain amount of satisfaction from having anticipated Fang's moves correctly.

I know what you are up to, asshole.

The incoming tide had swung the moored boats' sterns toward land. He pointed the bow toward the outer channel and pulled back on the throttles. *Pono II* slowed and settled to a stop in the swells. Satisfied with their position, he switched off the engines and dropped anchor in an open area of water on the opposite side of a deserted sloop fifty yards away from Li Fang's Bertram. After hours of listening to the drone of the diesel engines, the night fell deathly quiet. In the silence, he studied the other boat. Even with the schooner moored between them, *Pono II*'s flybridge afforded a view of the yacht.

If Li Fang made a move to deploy the device, Jack would know about it.

So far, nothing Li Fang had done since leaving the yacht club came as a surprise. Come daylight that might be a different situation.

One he'd deal with when the time came.

Sitting among the other boats, he saw no reason to maintain his stealth vigil any longer. He went below, switched on a light, and proceeded to start a pot of coffee brewing. It would be a long night.

Robert and Kazuko had come in through the starboard hatchway after having helped set the anchor. On his way through the main salon, he had seen them enter and follow him into the galley. They both looked fatigued from lack of sleep.

He said, "We're all beat. I'm going to stay up for a while longer. At least until Fang turns off the lights in the salon. You two get some sack time and we'll put our heads together at sun-up. I'm sure he'll still be there."

Robert's shoulders sagged. "You *will* get some sleep, right?"

"I won't be much good if I don't. Now, go."

"You're sure?"

Jack looked a Kazuko. She fought a yawn.

He said, "Take Robert below and put him to bed. I'm sure I'll be hitting the sack shortly."

He got no argument from her.

She took Robert by the arm and led him out. Jack watched them all the way though the main salon, until his friends slipped from view down the forward companionway. They would thank him in the morning.

The coffeemaker beeped and he filled his mug from earlier. He dug a lightweight coat out of a storage locker and shrugged the jacket on to ward off the late-night chill. Something he should have done earlier. He carried the steaming cup topside and took a seat at the helm. Fifty yards away, *China Doll*'s lights continued to illuminate the cabin. By all appearances, he would be up longer than he anticipated.

A half-hour into standing his watch, the salon door on *China Doll* opened, spilling light onto the rear deck. He straightened in his seat, instantly alert when Oddjob stepped out and took a quick look around before stepping back inside.

What's that all about?

Just checking things out, Jack thought. He sipped his coffee and pulled his coat tight around him.

He sat like that for another thirty minutes. The light in their cabin a long throw across the water from him still hadn't gone out or dimmed. The auxiliary generator droned on.

Having spent a few minutes aboard the yacht, he knew *China Doll* only had two staterooms. The master forward and guest quarters aft on the port side. Most likely that's where Li and his cousin would sleep. That meant Oddjob had been stuck with the couch in the salon. And, Jack mused, the night watch.

He got himself a refill of Joe, switched off the light, and resumed his vigil topside. The breeze had picked up and so had the swell. The sky remained a mantle of black. Rain, he hoped, would come next.

If we're lucky.

Holding onto the hope for a day of rain, he set his mug on the deck and opened the storage locker built into the bottom of the helm. His holstered 1911 sat near the front edge of the shelf where he had left it; so did his flare gun. He removed the .45, a pair of binoculars, and the waterproof canvas cover for the instrument panel. Once he had the cover snapped in place, he picked up his mug and sat back in his seat. There was nothing more for him to do except sip his coffee and keep watch.

The sailboat next to him creaked and waved its masts. Five minutes later, he had the binoculars held to his eyes. Even in darkness, the lenses captured enough of the town's light to give him a dim view of the Bertram. He still had the field glasses raised when he saw the salon door open and Oddjob step out. Again, light spilled from the cabin to illuminate the aft deck.

Jack fine-tuned the focus. This time, however, the thick-chested man did not look up or scan the boats around him. He lifted a pair of binoculars to his eyes…and aimed them directly at *Pono II*.

The staring contest went on for a full thirty seconds. Jack could envision the guy's lips spreading into a smug grin, and the man thinking, *I see you*.

The fact was, they were looking at each other.

Now Jack smiled.

You can bet I'll be seeing you again.

Soon.

CHAPTER 64

Li Fang found it difficult to sleep. His bouts of insomnia had gotten worse. Especially when he was troubled, like now.

They had come this close to closing the deals.

He knew what needed to be done.

His cousin sat across the table from him; their custom whenever seated together. He watched the younger man struggle to keep his eyes open. Though they were related and more like brothers, being only two years apart, Yong did not suffer from similar bouts of sleeplessness.

Li clenched his jaw. He would like to have gotten the two hours of sleep Yong had—even one of those hours. But the affliction was his to bear alone.

"Is it too early for you to get up, cousin?"

Yong stifled a yawn. "Surely we could have slept another hour. It's still dark outside."

"You know I do not give up easily. There is too much money involved to walk away from this now. The deals are in motion. We can still make this work."

Yong came alert. "What do you suggest?"

The open salon door let in a breath of humid air from the storm brewing outside. The rain-slicked aft deck glistened in the light spilling from the salon. From where he sat, he couldn't see Chen standing his watch, but the bodyguard's unmitigated dedication was never in question.

Li returned his attention to his cousin. "Tomorrow morning we will put an end to Jack Ferrell's troublesome meddling once and for all."

"You have a plan?"

The storm outside mirrored the rage Li fought to control.

Chen had noticed the boat behind them. *Pono II* in green and gold letters—the name he saw painted on the side of the hull when they were leaving the yacht club. But later Chen had lost sight of the vessel in the darkness, until that same boat dropped anchor nearby.

Li visualized the face of the man behind the deception.

He knew it all too well.

All night he had given thought on how best to deal with the situation. Even now, he contemplated the success of his decision.

There was too much at stake for his plan to fail.

He met his cousin's gaze. "I'm trusting you with the most difficult part."

Resolve hardened Yong's expression. "You do not have to worry. What is it you want me to do?"

Li mentally laid out the details of his scheme.

Simple, really.

His cousin stared back at him. In Yong's eyes he saw the respect that bonded them together.

"It's the reason you're up so early." He laid his hand on the Glock sitting in front of him and slid the gun across the tabletop to his cousin. "We will be ready in plenty of time to put on the demonstration we promised."

Yong nodded comprehension. "And we will let the sharks do what they did to Matt Corvin."

"Precisely." Li grinned into the darkness beyond the salon door. Blood and piercing screams formed vivid in his mind. "And cousin, let's not forget about Simon Goddard."

It was Yong's turn to smile. "And those to come."

CHAPTER 65

Jack pried an eye open, followed by the other. He recalled rain had forced him inside. He sat up on the edge of his mattress and cracked the blinds covering his window. The sky had lightened some in the early morning and the rain had stopped, but a dark layer of puffy clouds remained. He noticed the change of tide had swung the boat around so that the bow faced inland.

"You're up," he heard Robert say none too cheerfully from the doorway.

"If you call this up." Jack checked his watch.

Robert stepped inside. "What time did you go to bed?"

"A few minutes before three; the rain drove me below. Since you're up, did you check on our friends this morning?"

"They're still there. What's your plan?"

"You're assuming I have one?'

"You always do."

Jack's intention had been to follow Li Fang and stop him from using the device. The staring contest with Oddjob hadn't changed a thing, but it did pose the question of how Fang would react knowing they had been followed.

He rose to his feet, ready to face whatever the day brought. "We'll see what Fang does. Early this morning, I saw his no-neck thug studying our boat through a pair of binoculars. It's possible they're on to us."

"As in, they know we tailed them here?"

"That's what I'm saying. Not that it matters, they must have taken notice of us when we left the yacht club a few minutes after they did. Then again here, last night. *Pono II* is not an easy boat to forget with her name painted on the sides of the hulls in three-foot-tall green letters with gold shadowing."

He saw Robert's lips crack as though he wanted to smile at finding humor in the comment about *Pono II* being east to spot.

Just as quickly, Robert's expression sobered. "So where does that leave us?"

"I guess it's time we come up with that plan you asked about."

"We didn't have one?"

Jack shrugged. "We were playing it by ear. We still are."

He followed Robert into the galley and found Kazuko there, cup in hand, dressed, and with her hair brushed. Looking none too worse for wear.

She motioned at the coffeemaker. "I brewed a fresh pot."

"Exactly what I need, thanks." He poured himself a mugful and filled one for Robert.

"Appreciate it." Robert picked up his cup, and said, "Did you know we have cell reception here?"

"You've been on the phone?"

"Noticed it when I checked the time."

Jack took a sip and peered at Robert over the rim of his mug as he lowered it. "Actually, I counted on it. I plan on calling Meg in a bit and fill her in on the latest development."

Robert said, "The only thing that has happened so far is a boat ride. Let's hope it stays that way."

"Speaking of Li Fang, let's see what he's up to."

They carried their coffee topside. It was six-fifteen by his watch. The sky was getting lighter by the minute. On the Bertram, half a football field away, Oddjob stood on the aft deck with binoculars pressed to his eyes. Had Jack not seen the thug duck inside out of the rain in the middle of the night, he would have sworn the man had never moved from that spot.

How long had he been there watching?

Asshole.

Jack didn't move, nor did he look away. He contemplated giving the big man the finger. Instead, he grinned and stared back.

"Our friend across the way is looking at us. You might want to wave to him and smile. I'm sure he'd appreciate it."

"I see the asshole," Robert said. "And I'm not smiling."

"Neither am I," Kazuko added.

Unlike a few hours before, it didn't turn out to be much of a staring contest. A couple of seconds later, Li Fang stepped onto the rear deck and Oddjob lowered his binoculars. Jack watched them converse and, in the gray dawn, saw Li Fang lift his phone, tap the screen, and raise it to his ear.

Interesting.

One thought came to mind, and then Jack's phone chortled.

He glanced at Robert and Kazuko and got a confused scowl back. He tapped on and put his cell on speaker, "Good of you to call, Mr. Fang."

"Your friends are listening. How nice, Doctor Ferrell."

Jack was in no mood to bandy about. "You didn't call to discuss the crappy weather. What's on your mind?"

"A man who likes to get to the point. Very well, I called to invite you over to my boat so we can talk."

"We can talk on the phone just fine."

"We could, but we won't."

The call disconnected. Jack tapped off. When he looked up, he noticed the smug bastard had already stepped inside the salon. Oddjob hadn't moved from where he had been standing with his binoculars raised. A rock-solid sentinel.

Li Fang's thug.

If there was going to be trouble, it would come from him.

He looked at his friends. They were staring back.

He said, "Help me with the dinghy."

Robert frowned. "You're not going over there?"

Jack didn't want to spend time debating his decision. Over, a quick chat with Fang to hear what he has to say, and back. Fifteen minutes, tops.

That was his plan.

"Fang wants to talk," he said. "I'll listen to what the man has to say."

CHAPTER 66

Jack could tell neither Robert nor Kazuko agreed with his decision.

But that wouldn't stop him.

He said, "I told you I'd listen to what Fang has to say. I'll do that first. Then I'll tell the asshole to buzz off."

Their response was a collective sigh.

The swell from overnight had settled with the passing of the storm. He pulled the cover from the twelve-foot dinghy and tossed it onto the bridge deck. He realized much of what he was doing had a lot to do with ego, but he intended to put an end to Li Fang's maniacal scheme and be done with the lunatic.

He pointed at the support straps. "I'll keep an eye on this end and you watch the other."

Reluctance showed in Robert's movements. "I still think this is a bad idea."

"It is what it is. Now do what I asked." Jack pressed the power button on the davit and watched the twelve-foot Boston Whaler descend.

Kazuko stood off to the side and asked Jack, "What do you suppose Fang wants to talk to you about?"

There was no question in his mind. "The man wants to talk about what we're doing here. What concerns me is he had my phone number. On speed dial, no less."

"I hadn't thought about that. Makes you wonder how he got it."

"There's a leak," he said. "And it's in the police department."

The dinghy settled on the water. The cable slacked and he killed the power. "I have my suspicions of who the mole is, but that will come later."

To Robert, he said, "Don't bother running the cable up. I doubt I'll be gone that long."

"Best not be. You going armed?"

"I'll take my forty-five."

Adrenalin pumped through his body, fueled by excitement and fear…a macabre curiosity about what waited for him across the water. He hurried below, grabbed his .45 semi-auto from the nightstand where he had left it, and met Robert and Kazuko on the aft deck. Robert stood holding the dinghy in place. Kazuko watched with her arms crossed. They clearly remained unconvinced he was doing the right thing.

Kazuko stopped him with a hand on his arm. "This is really a bad idea. You're sure we can't talk you out of it?"

He shook his head in response to her as much as to clear his thoughts. His mind flooded with images of Matt Corvin bitten in half, and the many needless deaths to follow; of a killer shark rising from the depths to attack fifteen-year-old Amy Watson; other sharks ripping a seventeen-year-old boy to pieces; the three triangular fins of fifteen-hundred-pound tigers closing on Charles Edwards in a horrific ordeal that cost him his legs. Nightmares that Jack knew would surface in his dreams of terror and blood.

He laid his hand reassuringly on hers. "Hold down the fort and I'll be back in a few minutes."

"If you're not?"

"Call in the cavalry."

She tightened her grip. "I'm begging you not to go over there alone."

"Alone," he said in an encouraging tone of voice. "That's a stretch. You and Robert will be here keeping watch over me; and Fang knows that."

A moment of silence. Then, "You're serious. You're really doing this?"

He kept his gaze steady. "Don't I look serious?"

"That's what worries me. I think you make a habit of taking chances you don't need to take."

"You're concerned I might get hurt. I get that. Robert obviously is, too. I love you both for it, but we came here to stop this madman from using the device. That's what I'm going to do. And if that means meeting the man face to face, so be it."

She let her hand slide from his arm, and he climbed into the Boston Whaler. To Robert, he said, "I'll keep my guard up."

* * *

Robert watched Jack skirt the sloop next to them by way of the stern, add power, and speed toward *China Doll*. The 25 HP Mercury outboard made short work of getting him there.

He said, "He'll be okay."

Kazuko fixed her gaze on him, fear widening her glassy eyes. "I'm not so sure about that. We shouldn't have let him go."

"You tried to talk him out of it. I did, too. Short of tying him up, there was nothing more we could do."

He saw her glance toward Jack's foamy trail, already shouldering the blame for whatever happened. Something he'd seen her do too many times.

"You're doing it again."

"Doing what?" she asked with her back to him.

He didn't answer. Instead, he took her by the shoulders and turned her so she faced him. Her eyes found his and he kissed her lightly on the lips. When he released her, she wrapped her arms around his middle and pressed the side of her head against his chest. He held her and glided his palm down the small of her back.

"I love you," she said.

He pulled her tight as a tear welled in her eye. "It's okay for you to feel the way you do about Jack. The thing is—you know this as well as I do—once his mind is made up there's no changing it. He does what he wants to do. He's been like that for as long as we have known the man. Now, let's go topside and keep an eye on him."

CHAPTER 67

Jack bumped the Whaler against the starboard side of the Bertram and tied the bowline to a chrome cleat a few inches forward of the transom. The dinghy drifted aft in the tide. Oddjob glared down from the gunwale and said nothing.

A man of few words.

Jack asked, "Where's your boss?"

"I am here, Mr. Ferrell." Li Fang stepped from the cabin and stood by the open door. "Please come aboard and join me inside."

Jack entered by way of a walk-through transom door and stepped into the salon. He noticed the scratches he had made on the door latch and wondered if they had as well. Two steps inside, he stopped to let his vision adjust.

"Nice boat," he said.

"Please sit down and make yourself comfortable. I insist."

Jack appreciated the man's pleasantries but did not believe for a second they were sincere. The man was as cold as Matt Corvin's remains inside the refrigerator at the Coroner's Office. He glanced behind him and saw Oddjob move into the hatchway. He felt he had been given no choice but to play out the hand.

"Since you insist."

He took a seat close to the door and stared across the Hi-Low table at Fang who sat, one leg propped on the other, at the opposite end of the U-shaped seating, fingers tented against his lips. The door clicked shut.

Here we go.

Jack didn't have to turn and look to know Oddjob had positioned his thick body to block the exit, ensuring no one left the cabin until Li Fang decided it was time.

A move Jack half anticipated.

Or was it for a reason far more sinister?

Refusing to back down, he kept his eyes focused on the man sitting across from him. "Your cousin's not here. What happened to him?"

Fang lowered his hands but didn't uncross his legs. "Yong had other business. I'm sure he would have enjoyed seeing you again."

Jack didn't like the sound of that.

He said, "No doubt once was enough."

Fang smiled. "I'm sorry I cannot offer you coffee. I only drink tea brewed from the tienchi flower."

"I've heard of it," Jack said. "Supposed to be some kind of cure-all. Sells for a couple hundred dollars a kilo; if I remember right."

"You know your teas."

"I knew a girl who drank it. But I didn't come here to talk about that."

"Then I will get to the point. You went to a lot of trouble following me here. What is it you plan to do?"

"First of all, I owe you for this." Jack pointed at the stitches in his scalp. "And for what you did to Detective Tokunaga."

The accusation seemed to have no effect on Fang's expression.

He said, "And the second?"

Jack settled into the cushion behind him, feeling the reassuring presence of the .45 stuck in the rear waistband concealed under his shirt. "I think the answer is obvious."

Fang's stoic expression slipped. "Humor me."

"Fine. I plan to stop you from using the device you took from Matt Corvin shortly before you dropped him into the ocean."

"What makes you think I had anything to do with that?"

"Enough games, Fang. You're finished."

"How so?"

Fang held onto his baffled look. Jack wasn't buying it.

"Have it your way," he said. "To begin with, a man named Devlin Maxwell developed a device that attracts sharks instead of repelling them. Matt Corvin, his coworker, was desperate for money and killed Maxwell to get his hands on the invention. Corvin then approached you wanting to make a deal. One-point-five million, to be exact. How am I doing so far?"

Fang's expression sobered. "An interesting story."

Jack pressed. "Now for the best part. You took Corvin out on this fancy boat of yours and he put on a demonstration that got a couple of people killed. You recognized the potential for big money, only you had no intention of going in as partners with him. You took the device and had Corvin dropped into the ocean from that helicopter I saw sitting on your lawn. My guess is big boy back here had everything to do with that. I do know Corvin hit the water alive, but he didn't survive the fall. Obviously, your plan was to have sharks dispose of the body. They did a good job on it but they didn't finish what they started. I know because I saw what they did to him."

Fang glared. "You think you have it all figured out."

Calm, cool, and collected, Jack thought. *Like in the TV commercial.* That's how Fang had appeared till now.

Only he had let the act slip.

And Jack had picked up on it.

Looking into the man's eyes, he caught a glimpse of the blackness behind them. Pure evil.

He said, "Maybe not all of it, but enough to know I'm not going to let you get away with this asinine scheme of yours."

Fang uncrossed his legs. "You should have minded your own business."

Jack heard the scuff of a shoe behind him.

He grabbed for his 1911 and got his hand on the grips.

Pulling the .45 from his pants, he turned at a rustle of fabric and saw the big man standing over him, arm raised.

Then…nothing.

CHAPTER 68

Robert had watched Jack climb aboard the Bertram and step inside the salon behind Li Fang, and the big man enter after them. For a full ten minutes he had waited for Jack to come out and get back into the dinghy.

Come on, Jack. Get your ass out of there.

Kazuko edged closer to his arm as though she read his thoughts. "Something's happened. He should be on his way back here by now."

Robert tried not to worry. Jack had his semi-automatic tucked beneath his shirt, and he knew how to use it.

Given the chance.

That's what concerned him.

He gripped her hand. "I know."

She continued to stare. "Isn't there something we can do?"

He hadn't been able to take his eyes off Li Fang's boat. Kazuko, he noticed, hadn't either.

"Maybe we—"

A man's voice from behind stopped him. "Face forward with your hands where I can see them, and keep them there."

The voice was clearly American with a distinct Asian accent. There was little doubt the man had a gun pointed at them.

Robert said, "Relax. There is no reason to get violent."

He was sure they had watched the man step aboard Li Fang's boat on Oahu, and that he hadn't seen the guy all morning. Now, distracted by their concern for Jack, he and Kazuko failed to hear him climb aboard and scale the ladder behind them.

The voice again. "Just do what I say."

Robert said, "You're Yong Fang, I presume?"

"You know who I am?"

"The police do, too."

"It makes no difference. What are your names?"

Robert turned his head enough to see Yong Fang, and know for a fact he held a gun on them. A semi-automatic pistol gripped tightly in his right hand. "Does it really matter?"

"This woman is your wife?"

"What if she is?"

"She's really quite lovely. Would you rather I make one up for her? You, I can call stupid."

Robert cringed at the thought of where this was headed. They would likely end up dead, but he could come up with no good reason to rush things.

Just play along.

"I'm Robert. My wife's name is Kazuko."

"Very well, Robert. You can operate this boat?"

Robert turned his head a few degrees, and out of the corner of his eye glared at Yong Fang. "What has your cousin done to Jack?"

"That is not your concern at the moment." The gun came up: a Glock. "Answer my question. Can you operate this boat?"

"I can."

"Then take a seat at the helm and start the engines. Do something stupid and your wife dies."

Robert considered making a try for the gun. Realizing how foolish it was to think he could do it without getting him or Kazuko or both of them shot dead in the process, he quickly abandoned the idea.

Until it became necessary.

He did as he was told. And in the process, watched Yong Fang, dressed in black, march Kazuko to the ladder leading to the lookout and electronics array overhead and lash her wrists to the rung above her. A complication he anticipated but could do nothing to change.

Under his breath he swore he would make the man pay.

Overhead the clouds began to separate with the passing of the storm. Bright blue sky filled the gaps. The rain was done for now.

He pulled the waterproof cover off the control panel and started the engines. They would need a minute to warm.

Fifty yards away, *China Doll* raised anchor. He saw the no-neck thug work the topside controls and heard the engines' RPMs increase. They were getting underway with Jack aboard and the dinghy towed behind. That could only mean one thing.

A sinking feeling hollowed his gut.

Yong Fang backed away from Kazuko and pointed the Glock at him. "Raise anchor and follow my cousin."

Robert realized he had no choice with Jack captive on the other boat.

And he and Kazuko held at gunpoint.

Once underway, she said, "At least let us know what you have planned. I would like to think my husband and I, and our friend over there, will come out of this alive. I think you owe us that much, don't you?"

Yong seemed to let the question rest. Just when it appeared he wasn't going to answer, he said, "I hear shark attack is a horrible death. Knowing you are next is surely almost as bad. My cousin has already taken care of your friend. In a little while, the two of you will go for a swim and I'll sink this fancy boat."

The sick scenario played out in Robert's mind.

He sucked in a breath.

Jack dead.

They were next.

Pono II would become one more relic on the bottom of the Pacific.

CHAPTER 69

Jack felt the roll of open water a lifetime before he could open his eyes.

His lids felt as though a heavy weight held them closed.

What seemed like a year later, and with much difficulty, he pried the lids apart.

First the right; then the left.

Two massive efforts, seemingly hours between each one.

The room came into view a piece at a time. Above him was a white paneled ceiling. A light fixture that wasn't turned on. He was on his back, gagged, his wrists bound behind him, his ankles tied. Something soft under him. A mattress.

Familiar.

The guest cabin.

Mirrors on the wall that made it appear larger.

He squeezed his eyes shut and opened them.

No help.

His skull felt as though his brain had come apart in a single massive explosion and been put back together with pieces of his memory missing. A lot can happen in a fraction of a second, or a minute or two…or five or ten. Like, how did he end up on a bed below deck? And what time was it now?

He imagined his unconscious body had been dragged into the cabin and flung onto the bunk by Oddjob, but that was only a guess.

And he still didn't know the time. His watch dug into his wrist underneath him, and there were no other clocks visible in the room.

He did know he was alive.

But for how long?

He searched out the door, open, and peered into the companionway. Sunlight filtered down from the salon.

Daytime. He knew that much.

But what day?

What mattered more was where they were taking him, and how the ride would end.

He thought about Matt Corvin's remains, and a similar fate awaiting him.

Only he'd be alive when the sharks attacked, just like the men from the *USS Indianapolis*.

The fog cleared, replaced by rational thought. *China Doll* was heading into deeper water, evident by the roll of the swells. There was still time to do something about his predicament. He went to work on the binding cutting into his wrists. To his surprise, the rope loosened.

But not enough.

Minutes later he heard a noise. He listened. Footfalls on the parquet flooring in the galley, and…closer. The companionway. Someone coming.

He stopped struggling and watched the entrance.

Li Fang stepped in and stood with his back to the doorway. Jack recognized the 1911 .45 in the man's hand.

Figures.

"I see you found my Colt."

Fang maintained a firm grip on the walnut stocks. "You have gone out of your way to cause me problems. Did you actually believe I would be stupid enough to give you the opportunity to use this?"

"You want me to say I'm sorry?"

"No. I want to watch you die."

Helpless to do much else, he hardened his gaze in a mental *fuck you*. "You didn't have to come down here to tell me that."

"I believed it best to deliver the news personally."

"It's mighty bold talk, I'll give you that much. But you're

forgetting about my friends. I'm certain they will make sure that doesn't happen. In the meantime, you might want to give some thought to what you're going to say to the Coast Guard when they put a shot across your bow."

"You are trying to be funny but I am not amused."

"Do you see me smiling?"

"You insist on irritating me. That is not wise. If you believe your friends are coming to your rescue, you are sadly mistaken."

"How so?"

"They are behind us, as you implied. Only Yong is aboard with them. He will not allow either of your friends to notify the authorities."

"Don't underestimate them."

"I assure you; it will be a mistake if they underestimate my cousin."

Jack clenched his jaw.

Asshole.

He wanted to say more, but his head ached, in back and in front where it had been struck—once by Fang's thick-chested bodyguard and once in the collision with the truck. The venomous banter didn't help.

"Let's stop playing games," he said. "What do you intend to do with us?"

Fang answered with a sad shake of his head. "Most unfortunate, I'm afraid. The network news will call the accident a terrible tragedy. That fancy boat of yours will sink quite unexpectedly, and you and your friends will be left floundering in the water, far from land with no flotation and no ability to swim to shore."

"You're delusional," Jack said. "You won't get away with it."

"Oh, but I will. You told me you saw what the sharks did to Matt Corvin. You can lie to yourself, but you know how this will turn out. The only question is, which one of you will be ripped to pieces first while the others watch?"

Fang jacked the slide on the .45 as though to add an exclamation point to what he had said.

It worked.

Jack glared.

Fang smirked, adding, "The best part is you—in spite of all your education and expertise in shark behavior—won't be able to do a thing to stop the inevitable from happening."

Jack continued to tug at the cordage around his wrists, gaining another inch of slack. "Don't be so sure."

"But I am." Fang removed a large folding knife from his pocket, flipped it open, and slashed the rope binding Jack's ankles. "Slide your feet off the side of the bed and keep in mind, I am a very good shot."

Jack did as he was told, his thoughts on the crew of the *USS Indianapolis*. Nine hundred men went into the water. Four-and-a-half days later, three hundred and sixteen came out of the sea alive.

The sharks took the rest.

CHAPTER 70

Robert needed to pee.

He glanced at his watch. Normally, he would have checked the time on his phone, but that had been tossed overboard. They had been heading in a westerly direction for over two hours. Molokai lay miles to the north. Oahu lay even farther to the north. By now, Lanai lay miles to the south.

Yong Fang stood over them with his nine millimeter pointed, a gut shot for the slightest wrong move. Li Fang on the boat a hundred feet ahead, led them out to sea.

It was clear how they intended this to end.

He didn't have to get Yong's attention. The man had his eyes fixed on him. He always had his eyes on him. Except when his leering gaze flashed to Kazuko.

Which soured Robert's stomach.

But he would have to tolerate the letch for now.

He said, "If you don't mind, I need to pee."

Yong smiled as though he found the request amusing, and motioned at the railing. "Be careful you don't fall overboard."

Robert had no intention of diving into the water leaving Yong alone on the boat with Kazuko.

Not ever.

He had promised himself he would make the guy pay. He reaffirmed that promise. If anyone was going over the side, it would be that asshole.

He stepped to the railing, positioning himself between Yong and Kazuko. He gave her a long look, winked, and did his business.

She was his best chance. He hoped she got the signal.

He zipped and Yong used his gun muzzle to motion him back to the helm. The timing had to be perfect in order for his plan to work. He positioned himself on the seat and looked at Kazuko. She gave him a slow nod in return.

Five seconds was all he needed.

She didn't hesitate. "He's not the only one who needed to pee. It's my turn."

Yong aimed a sick grin at her. "You can go where you stand."

"You're not serious?"

"Perfectly."

Robert hadn't expected this. He unloaded. "Show some class, asshole. You've got the gun. What are you afraid of? *Her?* Or do you just like humiliating women? Is that it? Is that what gets you off?"

"I will show you how I feel about women."

Yong turned and stepped toward Kazuko—a move difficult for Robert to watch, but necessary for the deception to work. He kept his seat in spite of his anguish, and put his faith in her having a plan.

She squirmed and yelled, "Stay away from me, you sick fuck."

Her plea seemed to make Yong even more determined to prove his point. He reached for the waistband of her shorts with his left hand and took another step. In his right, the muzzle of the semi-automatic lowered as he pressed forward. Clearly, he had become obsessed with his perverted game.

She flattened herself against the rungs of the ladder.

Robert could see at once she had lured Yong in closer. He noticed the muscles in her arms flex and, in the next second, saw her swing her legs up around Yong's middle and lock her ankles, pinning his arms to his sides before he could react.

Robert knew the power of her thighs, toned by years of Pilates.

He shoved aside the door to the storage cabinet under the helm and grabbed the flare gun from where Jack kept it.

Yong backpedaled but couldn't escape her hold on him, the ropes binding her wrists to the rung took the strain.

The man continued to struggle. Any second he could break free.

Robert didn't pause to think about his actions, or even to breathe. He raised the flare gun and yelled, "Now."

Kazuko unlocked her legs and Yong stumbled backward.

He pulled the trigger.

The red-hot flare burned a hole deep into Yong's chest. The man's eyes widened and his mouth opened in a millisecond of realization, followed by a banshee shriek of pain. His agonized screams continued as he flailed his arms like a wild man, pounding at the fire melting his flesh.

He staggered toward Kazuko. The muzzle of the 9mm came up.

She screamed and lashed out with both feet.

A final payback.

The kick to the face sent the man stumbling over the railing. The semi-automatic hit the deck, bounced, and slid. Robert lunged and caught the Glock with his outreached hand a fraction of a second before the semi-automatic followed Yong into the water.

Pumped on adrenalin, he hurried to free Kazuko. She had collapsed against the ladder, clearly exhausted from the effort. To her credit, she had acted without hesitation. And because of it, they were alive.

He was sure of it.

She straightened in front of him and he got busy with the knots in the rope. They had been pulled tight during the struggle. He looked into her eyes as he worked to free her wrists. And in that moment, he was consumed by those dark pools of oil.

"I love you," he said. "You know that?"

Her gaze held. "I was beginning to wonder."

He frowned. "You were?"

The bindings slid from her wrists and she collapsed into his arms. She smiled. "Not even."

He felt as though he could hold her in his arms forever. Never letting go. Ever.

But he knew that would have to wait.

He gave her a peck on the lips and eased her from his grasp. "We will continue this conversation later. Right now, we need to figure out a way to save Jack."

CHAPTER 71

Jack stood on rubbery legs, struggling to maintain his balance. The effort made more difficult by the pitch and roll of the Bertram's hull riding the swells.

He widened his stance and squeezed his eyes shut to calm the dizziness that threatened to take him down. His only concern at the moment was keeping his knees from buckling under him.

Not now.

His equilibrium settled, and he blinked away the last dregs of fog clouding his thinking. "Okay, I'm standing. You happy?"

Li Fang said nothing, nor did he crack a smile. His answer came when he raised the .45 and motioned him out of the guest stateroom. The large bore of the semi-automatic needed no words.

Jack gave in to the command. He had no choice but to bide his time.

The game is far from over.

Robert and Kazuko would find a way. He remained confident of that.

He took a chance, and said, "Think about what you're doing. There's still time to stop this madness."

Fang wagged the muzzle toward the doorway. "The desperate pleas of a man who is about to die. Move."

Jack realized the futility of making further attempts to sway the psychopath from his resolve to go through with his sinister plot.

Clearly, blind obsession and greed controlled the man's actions instead of common sense.

A lethal mistake.

Holding onto that belief, Jack stepped into the companionway. He didn't bother to look behind him. There was no reason to. Clearly, Li Fang followed close behind, the 1911 leveled for a gut shot—fatal but not immediate. The sicko would surely want him to bleed in order to draw the sharks.

The way the injured from the *USS Indianapolis* had.

A vision difficult to let go of.

"Onto the rear deck. Now." Fang accented the command with a jab of the gun muzzle in the back.

Jack stumbled forward.

* * *

Robert studied the Bertram a couple hundred feet ahead of them. The Boston Whaler continued to bob and weave on the swells in *China Doll*'s wake. Kazuko stood next to him; her gaze fixed on the boat. The success of what they planned hinged on what Jack did.

Providing he was alive to help.

Robert's gut told him his hunch had been correct. Simply killing Jack was not good enough for Li Fang. That the man had allowed Jack to live meant he wanted him to suffer the same fate he believed he and Kazuko were in for.

A slow death from drowning.

Or a quick one in the jaws of a shark.

But nothing was over until it was over.

The fat lady has yet to sing.

He had no way of knowing for sure his plan would work. But either way, Li Fang would not be allowed to escape.

Robert hardened his resolve.

And the only way to keep that from happening was to first remove the threat the man's oversized bodyguard posed.

He searched his memory for the old saying about Colt revolvers. There were several in history. One stuck out.

God made man. Sam Colt made all men equal.

He didn't have a Colt revolver, but Yong's Glock evened the playing field.

That coupled with the element of surprise.

So far Fang's bodyguard had given no indication he had heard the firing of the flare or the splash of Yong's smoking body hitting the water.

But how long will this continue?

Cat and mouse.

The game needed to end.

Kazuko said, "I don't think Fang's onto us."

Her comment pulled him from his thoughts. "Precisely what I've been thinking. Keep your eyes on the boat."

"Any ideas?"

He eased the throttle levers forward, increasing their speed by a couple of knots. He wanted to avoid being too obvious and chance exposing themselves too soon. "We'll creep up on their starboard side and be ready for whatever happens."

"I don't think that was part of their plan. Won't it draw attention?"

"If it does, I'll shoot Oddjob out of his seat."

"And Li Fang?"

"Him, too, if he shows his face."

She turned a furrowed brow on Robert. "Can you hit them with the boat bouncing around like this?"

He knew he could never hold the Glock steady. A wild shot at best, and a danger to Jack. One he would take only if he had no other choice.

Which seemed likely.

They were running out of options.

He said, "There's no reason for them to suspect Yong is no longer running the show here. I'm guessing they will stop to do their dirty work. At least, I hope they do. That's when I'll take the big son-of-a-bitch out."

She motioned him out of his seat. "You had better let me take the helm. Sounds like you'll be busy."

He smiled at her swashbuckling bravado. "When they stop, drift up alongside the boat and take cover."

"What about you?"

"I'll be the one shooting."

CHAPTER 72

Jack strained against the ropes with each step he took. The cord cut into his wrists, but his efforts gained him another inch of slack in his bindings. He heard a radio crackle behind him and Li Fang say, "It's time."

Time for what?

The answer became obvious the second Jack felt the boat slow. In the middle of the salon, he paused and faced the man who wanted him dead. A moment of reckoning…and another few seconds to work his hands free.

Fang jabbed the .45 at the air between them. "You heard me. Outside."

Jack felt he had to try one more time. Not to save his own life, but for the sake of the families around the globe who would fall victim to the man's lunacy. Those maimed or dead from shark attacks. And those poor people who would mourn the loss.

"Why?" He peered into Fang's eyes. "So you can kill again? Kill me…kill a bunch of vacationers who have done nothing to you?"

His plea got him a flinty stare back.

"Enough." He struggled to keep his tone soft the way a person does when trying to reason with someone. "You've taken your little game far enough. Let's bring an end to this madness before more innocent people die."

"Game?" Fang narrowed his eyes. "Is that what you think this is?"

Jack met the man's gaze. "Quite the contrary. You're absolutely serious. That's quite obvious. I'm also well aware it's all about money. But you have to see the insanity in putting this device in the hands of the world's crazies."

Fang didn't respond, and for a second Jack thought just maybe he had gotten through to the man.

But that belief was short-lived.

He worked on the rope, gaining another inch of slack.

Fang said, "Do you think I care what happens to people on some beach in the Mediterranean? Or the Caribbean...or any coast on the mainland, for that matter? What's to be gained? I'm an opportunist, not a social worker."

Jack nearly had enough slack to free his hands.

He said, "Money isn't everything."

"Wrong, Mr. Ferrell. Money is power." Fang stepped around Jack and opened the door. "For the last time, get outside."

Jack gritted his teeth. He was out of options.

For the moment.

He turned his head to buy himself another couple of seconds before stepping out, and through cracks in the blinds covering the starboard window, he saw *Pono II*'s bow approaching fifty feet away.

His only chance.

Be there, Robert.

* * *

Robert noticed the Bertram slowing.

He said, "Get ready."

Kazuko turned the wheel and faded starboard of *China Doll.*

"Take it slow," he said.

Pono II's bow rode the swells thirty yards off the other boat's transom.

He took a firm grip on the Glock.

He had no idea what Yong's instructions had been, and had zero way to find out. They were taking a risk, but short of a miracle, there was no other way to help Jack and stop Li Fang in the process.

Fang's bodyguard glanced toward the deck behind him but didn't react to their ruse.

Kazuko lowered her voice, "He hasn't figured it out yet."

Robert jabbed the flat of his palm at her. "Quiet."

He braced himself against the ladder leading to the electronics array and raised the 9mm. Kazuko throttled back, letting the momentum carry them forward. The engines gurgled softly on idle. In less than a minute both boats would be abreast of each other, dead in the water.

As if on cue, the salon door opened and Jack stepped onto the aft deck.

Robert stared, in awe of his friend's sudden appearance.

Alive. I knew it.

A surge of adrenalin gave him hope.

And then Li Fang stepped out behind Jack armed with a semi-automatic. The bodyguard was also on the move.

Robert kept the gun pointed, sweeping the muzzle from one target to the other.

An impossible choice even given sufficient time to react with deadly accuracy.

Time he didn't have.

He would be spotted any minute. And when that happened, he would have to choose which shot to take. Unless the decision was made for him. His gut told him Li Fang, first. The man appeared to be the greater threat at the moment. Second, the bodyguard.

He moved his index finger to the trigger, ready to squeeze.

Any second.

He drew in a breath and held it when Fang stepped into the open. He aimed, his finger on the trigger ready to pull, and sighed a millisecond later.

Not good.

His sight picture bounced around like a ping pong ball, making the shot too risky. Jack was right there, no more than a foot away.

An unimaginable situation.

His hesitation cost him when Fang moved, robbing him of the opportunity.

Damn.

He would not hesitate a second time.

He re-gripped for another shot, but the rollers lifting and dropping the hull under his feet made it near impossible to aim.

His hours at the shooting range offered little consolation.

Luck was his only ally.

CHAPTER 73

Jack yanked his hands free. In a heartbeat, he spun and batted the .45 aside a fraction of a second before Li Fang pulled the trigger. The heavy slug slammed into the gunwale.

The move left Fang stunned.

But only for a moment.

Jack didn't give him a chance to recover. He grabbed the semi-automatic's ejection slide with his left hand, twisted the 1911 sideways, breaking the man's hold on the grip safety, and hammered a right fist into Fang's face.

The punch knocked Fang backward and Jack went with him, refusing to let go of the Colt. The .45 came free in his hand, but Fang's index finger remained trapped in the trigger guard.

They slammed into the portside gunwale.

Jack didn't let up. He gripped Fang by the throat and wrenched the gun loose. The man's finger snapped.

Fang let out a gurgled scream.

The madman lashed out with a wild roundhouse left that connected with Jack's shoulder.

The blow, a frantic loose-fisted thump against muscle and bone as much as a solid punch, had little power in it.

Jack maintained his grip on Fang's throat.

The man slapped and tugged, and still Jack held on.

His heart pounded. Adrenalin surged into his muscles adding

strength he didn't know he had.

He stared into Fang's bulging eyes.

The man's mouth opened but only a gurgle of spittle came out.

Jack didn't let up. He couldn't stop thinking about the innocent young surfers killed by sharks, the swimmer who died, and the other victims seriously injured. Brian Tokunaga lying in a hospital bed, lucky to be alive.

And the one thought that haunted him.

How many more would be killed or injured because of this man?

Nothing would keep him from choking the life out of Li Fang.

Without warning, a swell rolled the boat from side to side. The port gunwale dipped low sending them tumbling into the sea.

The .45 splashed into the water with them.

* * *

Robert continued to sweep the Glock back and forth. The struggle on the other boat had lasted seconds. He saw the muzzle of the semi-automatic pistol in the bodyguard's hand come up and follow Jack's movement into the water.

His choice had been made for him.

Without hesitation, he brought the Glock to bear the best he could and fired three quick shots.

Two went wild. But he knew from the way the big man clutched his left arm, one had drawn blood.

The wound had been enough to get the bodyguard's attention but not enough to stop him. Oddjob returned fire with a three-shot volley of his own.

A bullet pinged off the ladder.

Robert ducked out of reflex and fired back at the same time. A wild shot that shattered the salon window on the other boat.

The bodyguard snapped off three more quick shots. One bullet slammed into the seat at the helm. Another cut a groove in the deck three feet away from Robert's feet. The other was a complete miss.

Again, Robert tried to hold his aim steady, but both boats continued to pitch and roll in the swells. All the time, they were drifting farther apart.

He feared it might already be too late to save Jack.

But he refused to believe that.

In seconds *Pono II* would drift too far from *China Doll* to have a chance of making a kill shot. He peered down the sights and chose the moment. He squeezed the trigger twice and saw the big man double over.

But how bad had he been hit?

Robert had no way of knowing. He steadied the Glock for another shot and saw the man raise his gun and topple into the water.

Dead or seriously wounded, the bodyguard was no longer a threat.

Robert's thoughts switched to the only person they needed to save.

Jack.

CHAPTER 74

Jack treaded water, searching the surface for Li Fang. The tide had separated them only seconds after tumbling overboard.

He rose on a swell and dropped into a trough between the upcoming waves.

All he saw in front of him was water.

But that didn't mean the man wasn't there.

He continued to ride the waves up and down. Each time he rose on a swell, he saw nothing but a vast expanse of ocean. It appeared Li Fang had gone under and not come up.

Drowned.

Fitting, Jack thought.

Until he saw Fang sputter to the surface thirty feet away.

He glared at the killer, and let the man flounder.

Fang deserved to die.

Jack's attention was on the struggling man when he heard water slapping against the hull of a boat. Closer than he realized.

He turned and raised a hand, but a fraction of a second too late.

China Doll's hull slammed into his head.

With a groan, he slid back into the sea.

His vision dimmed.

He fought the waves to remain on the surface, while desperately avoiding the deadly crush of *China Doll*'s fiberglass hull.

A struggle he couldn't win. The ocean pulled him down.

The sea reclaiming his body.

With one last flicker of consciousness, he saw something familiar bearing down on his head.

Then darkness swallowed him.

No tunnel. No white light.

More purple than black.

He swam in the murkiness, chasing a woman's familiar voice. Someone he was close to. He followed the vision into the sun on his face.

"Jack, come back to us. Goddammit, don't give up."

He opened his eyes but couldn't focus on the faces looking down at him.

"Jack, it's me, Kazuko. You're going to be all right."

"Kazuko?" He blinked, trying to make sense of his surroundings.

"You scared the hell out of us." Robert's voice. "Can you sit up?"

Jack wedged an arm under him, and with Robert's help worked his way into a sitting position. His eyes adjusted to the bright sunlight and everything came into view. He was on the lower deck of *Pono II*. He looked around, remembering.

"We thought we lost you, ol' buddy."

Jack fingered the lump on his head. The second one. Or was it the third? "You almost did."

"Too close, that's for sure."

Jack coughed up a wad of salty phlegm and spit it overboard.

Robert asked, "You okay?"

"Fine."

"I'll have to take your word on it."

Jack grabbed Robert's arm. "Fang's out there. Help me up."

Robert placed a hand on Jack's shoulder and eased him back down. "Take it easy, the asshole isn't going anywhere."

Jack struggled. "I told you I'm all right. Just help me to my feet."

Robert gave in and Jack stood for a moment finding his balance.

"Did you see him?"

"We were more concerned about you."

Jack heard his name called from the sea. Spectral? Poseidon summoning him to the depths. He looked at his friend. "Did you hear that?"

Kazuko said from the starboard rail, "Over here. It's Li Fang."

Jack let Robert help him to that side of the boat. He saw Fang waving at them fifty feet away.

Fang's words echoed in his ears.

The desperate plea from a dying man.

He said, "Jail is better than drowning, I guess."

Robert asked, "What do you think? Should we help him?"

Jack remembered having his hand on the guy's throat, and how much he wanted to choke the life out of him at the time. In that moment, it felt like it was something he had to do. Strictly a 'him-or-me' scenario. That wasn't the case now.

He said, "The asshole doesn't deserve it, but I guess we should."

Robert nodded. "I'll get the life ring."

He returned and tossed it to Fang.

"Like catching a fish," he said, and reeled him in.

Jack leaned over to give Fang a hand up. When he did, Fang grabbed hold, wedged his feet against the hull, and pulled Jack overboard.

Caught by surprise, he went in headfirst and came up sputtering.

He blinked to clear his vision, but not fast enough.

Li Fang was on him in a flash.

Through the saltwater haze stinging his eyes, Jack saw the four-inch folding knife open in the man's right hand in spite of the broken finger and got his arm up in time to keep the blade from slashing his face.

The calm Fang had exhibited a minute before, morphed into rage with the heat of hatred reddening his face and tightening the chords in his neck. He had become a madman yelling, "I'll kill you. I'll kill you."

Jack grabbed the guy's wrist in a life-and-death struggle to keep from getting stabbed.

The tide swept them away from the boat.

He heard a distant splash and knew Robert had jumped in to help in the struggle. His friend to the rescue.

Jack didn't wait. The fight was between him and Li Fang. He kept a death-grip on Fang's left wrist and hammered his right fist into the man's swollen face. And kept hitting him until Robert pulled him off.

Fang drifted away.

"Leave him," Robert said.

Jack didn't argue.

They made it back to the boat and watched from the railing. When they saw the massive dorsal fin surface and slice the water ten yards from Fang, the man was riding up on a swell, floundering in a futile attempt to stay afloat.

As quickly as the shark appeared, the dorsal fin slipped beneath the sea.

There was nothing they could do to save the doomed man.

In the next second, the twenty-foot great white struck Li Fang with enough power to carry the madman's ruined body fifteen feet in the air. Deep Blue—Fang protruding from each side of the massive fish's mouth; head, shoulders, and arms hanging limp on one side, lower legs and feet from the other—remained there as though suspended in a moment of time before she splashed back into the water with enough force to drench them in a surge of salty spray.

Jack recalled seeing the massive fish do the same thing to the tiger shark two days earlier. A thirty-five-mile-per-hour attack that started in the gloom a hundred and fifty feet or more beneath the surface of the ocean.

A five thousand pound cruise missile of teeth and cartilage.

For close to a minute, he and his friends said nothing.

Robert broke the silence when he muttered, "Damn."

Jack nodded. "No doubt about it now. The ancient Hawaiian's were correct in their belief in a good shark god."

Robert put his arm around Kazuko. "You can say that again."

CHAPTER 75

At four o'clock that afternoon, showered and wearing dry clothes, Jack greeted Cindy Adams with a passing smile and walked into Megan O'Connell's office unannounced. His mind focused on what he came to tell her, he pulled a chair to the front of his boss's desk and set the gym bag he brought with him on the floor next to it.

She peered across her desktop at him. "You look like hell."

"I've been to Hell," he said.

"Have you been checked out by a doctor?"

"I'm fine."

Her eyes said she didn't believe him. "Your face and head say otherwise."

He ran his fingers over the goose egg above his temple. "Just a couple of bumps and bruises from being hit on the head, and a black eye I got when I caught a knee from Li Fang during our tumble overboard. The stitches I already had."

"You're sure the doctor said you were okay? You could have a concussion…or worse."

"I could have a lot of things."

"I'm guessing sleep isn't one of them."

He could have laughed. "There will be time for that later."

She gave him a long look and an unconvincing smile. "There's coffee if you would like some."

He filled a cup from the carafe sitting on the table next to the wall across from the window, took a sip and winced. "Not very warm."

She laughed. "It's been sitting there a while. Now, I want you to sit down before you fall down."

He walked back to his chair. "I presume Cindy passed on my message that we are in the clear for now?"

"I notified Mayor Kobayashi immediately upon hearing it. As you can imagine, she was quite relieved. She said she would pass the good news on to the governor. I'm sure he is equally as grateful to have this mess over with."

"Just so it takes some pressure off of you. But I'm afraid it's a bit premature to break out the champagne."

"What are you getting at?"

He set his tepid coffee aside. "Like I said, the island is in the clear for now. But the shark threat is not over."

A deep furrow wrinkled her brow. "You're kidding."

"I truly wish I was."

She rocked back in her chair. "I'm listening."

He wanted to take his time and be perfectly clear in regard to what he was about to tell her. Reaching into his duffle, he removed a plastic baggie containing one of the two devices he found in the metal case on Li Fang's boat.

"This is what has been wreaking havoc on our beaches," he said. "There were two of them on the boat. I took the liberty of bringing one here to show you."

"And the other one?"

"I turned it over to the Coast Guard when they arrived to tow *China Doll* in. The police probably have it by now."

"You've told them everything?"

"Twice."

"Then once more won't hurt. Bring me up to date, starting with what happened after we talked last evening."

He told her the same story he told the Coast Guard and the two young police detectives that had taken over Tokunaga's case. They both knew and respected the detective and were happy to pass on the news; Tokunaga would require several months of physical therapy but would otherwise make a full recovery.

News that came as a relief to Jack.

Their respect for the work he and his friend had done on the case so far helped him get through the interview process more smoothly.

O'Connell rocked forward and picked up the Ziploc. Flattening the baggie against the plastic casing of the device, she turned the apparatus over in her hand, examining both sides. Her gaze met his. "People dead. Maimed. This simple looking gadget is responsible for everything that has happened over the past couple of weeks?"

He took a gulp from his cup and pointed. "Not that particular apparatus, but I'm guessing one just like it is responsible. Therein, lies the problem."

"I don't follow."

"You recall Matt Corvin murdered Devlin Maxwell for the device he then used to kill that man and boy the other day. The thing is, Corvin also stole the schematic to build more. Li Fang used those plans to make several duplicates. Truth be told, we don't know how many he had built. The two devices I recovered might be the only ones, but there could be a couple of dozen or more that we don't know about. The point is the schematic is still out there."

She sighed. "So we need to find it."

He nodded. "Before the shark attacks start up again."

"Do the police know this?"

"Not exactly. And before you ask, I have my reasons."

"Which you're not going to share with me."

He grinned.

She stared at him as though absorbing the full impact of his implication. Then, "I'll trust you on this. What is it you plan to do?"

He drained his cup and groaned to his feet. "When I leave here, I'm heading to the hospital to talk to Detective Tokunaga. From there…guess it'll depend a lot on what he has to say."

CHAPTER 76

On his way out of Director O'Connell's office, Jack stopped at her assistant's desk. Cindy, he took notice, wore a yellow hibiscus flower in her hair. Not the one he had given her a couple of days earlier but otherwise the same. It gave her a nice look. He asked, "Can I use your desk phone?"

Her brow furrowed. "Where is yours?"

Good question.

In spite of a thorough search, he hadn't been able to locate it on Fang's boat. He figured it had been tossed overboard while he was unconscious.

He grinned.

"Lost it." And with a nod, "I like the flower."

She handed him the receiver and winked. "You do know you don't have to call to ask me out to dinner."

She seemed to never tire of the game.

"Sorry," he said. "Unfortunately, I have other plans."

"I didn't mean tonight." She smiled in a way that left her lips full and kissable.

Another time, another place. Maybe.

"The phone." He pointed.

She angled it toward him. "Press zero for an outside line."

He pulled Tokunaga's cell number from memory and placed the call. The detective answered on the fourth ring.

"Brian, it's Jack. Sorry to bother you, but we need to talk."

"Aren't you going to ask how I'm doing?"

Ornery right off the get-go. It was good to hear his friend's voice.

"Okay," he said. "How are you feeling?"

"How do you think? I hurt like a sonofabitch. Now what's so important? You're interrupting my Jell-O."

"I take it you haven't heard the news?"

"What news?"

"Li Fang and his cousin Yong are dead as of this morning."

"Your doing?"

"Not just me. I had help."

"Robert?"

"And Deep Blue."

"Breaks my heart." A noticeable hitch in his voice. "Go ahead and tell me what happened. I'm not going anywhere for a day or two."

"Not over the phone. I'm on my way there."

"I'll be sure and hold off on the pain meds. Just don't make it too long."

The detective's tone had changed.

Focused. Professional, he thought.

Back in the saddle.

He said, "See you in driving time."

* * *

Jack knocked on the open door to Tokunaga's private room in the Med-Surg unit on the third floor. Tokunaga glanced at him before turning to his wife. Joan got up from a chair and stood at the side of the bed.

"Sorry to interrupt, Mrs. Tokunaga." He took a step inside. "It's important I talk to Brian."

She gripped her husband's hand. "I'll leave you two to talk."

He waited. When she walked out of the room, he took her place at the side of the bed. A gauze bandage partially covered Tokunaga's left eye. His left arm and leg were immobilized in fiberglass casts. It didn't look like he would be going anywhere *anytime* soon.

Tokunaga switched off the TV. "Talk to me, Jack. What's going on?"

The professional.

He said, "Aren't you going to ask how *I* am?"

"I can see how you are. Tell me what happened."

Jack had no reason to hold back. He'd given his statement twice already. A third time wouldn't change what happened. He took a seat in the visitor's chair Joan had been sitting in and filled the detective in on every detail.

Tokunaga winced and took a deep breath. "Ironic, don't you think? Mega shark eats loan shark. The psycho son-of-a-bitch certainly got what he deserved."

Jack couldn't resist grinning.

"My feeling exactly," he said. "Quite honestly, I'm surprised you hadn't been told before now."

"There's a lot going on. My sergeant probably hasn't had time."

"You know this isn't over with?"

Comprehension showed in the detective's eyes when he opened them. "There can be more devices out there."

Jack nodded. "And the plans to build even more."

Tokunaga adjusted his position on the mattress. "We have to find them."

"Me, maybe," Jack said. "You're not going anywhere."

"I was speaking figuratively. Did they tell you I have a closed head injury on top of everything else? There are more tests they want to do on me but my doctor says there is no obvious signs of brain trauma."

Jack knew what closed-head injury meant—medical speak for an injury that could be minor or leave a person a vegetable.

He had his own lumps.

"There's another problem. That's why I needed to talk to you in person."

"What problem is that?"

The detective's eyes were intense. His speech clear. Reassuring. Even after being rammed by a truck, his mind remained sharp.

The bulldog determination that Jack knew well.

And respected.

"The leak in your department."

CHAPTER 77

Jack gave Tokunaga time to let the accusation sink in.

After close to a minute of thought, the detective said, "Okay, run your theory past me. Who you think it is and why."

A nurse entered the room before Jack could explain. She inspected Tokunaga's IV and took his vitals. It gave Jack another couple of minutes to second-guess himself. He didn't need to. His suspicions hadn't changed.

The nurse left the room, and he asked, "How well do you know Detective Sergeant Edward Liu?"

"He's come up through the ranks. Took over the unit about five years ago. Has his way of doing things that I don't always agree with, but he and I get along for the most part. You suspect he's the leak?"

"Did you hear he ordered me off the case?"

"I hadn't heard. You sure the order came from him?"

"My boss delivered the bad news but Officer Williams told me the request came from Sergeant Liu."

"Can't imagine why he'd do that when you've been an important part of the investigation from the beginning."

"How about detective's Keala and Donohue? Tell me about them."

"They're both new to the unit. Only been there about a year. Other than lacking experience, they both appear to be solid detectives."

"Liu assigned them to take over the case. Does that sound like a smart move given their inexperience?"

It took a moment for Tokunaga to answer. "You think Sergeant Liu is purposely sabotaging the investigation?"

"Precisely."

"That's a stretch, Jack."

"I don't think so. Li Fang knew our every step. Someone fed him information. You kept Sergeant Liu updated on our progress and what we planned to do. Who in your department is in a better position to pass the information on to Fang?"

"A lot of the detectives knew what we were doing." Tokunaga let his head sink into his pillow. "Let's say he is the mole, though. It changes nothing. If there are more of these devices out there, we need to stay focused on recovering them and the schematic to make more. Then we can talk about Sergeant Liu."

Before anyone else dies.

Jack couldn't argue with that.

The sun shining through Tokunaga's window slipped behind a solid bank of dark clouds, bathing the room in shadow. He grasped the arms of his chair and made a move to get up. "I'll turn the lights on."

"Leave them off."

Jack settled back into his seat. "By now word of Li Fang's death, as well as his cousin's, has surely gotten back to his people at the house. They are no doubt scrambling to figure out what will happen next. Rest assured, there will be a power vacuum and someone will step in to take over the operation."

"Any idea who's at Li Fang's place now?"

"His staff, I imagine. Beyond that, I don't know."

Tokunaga stared unblinking at the ceiling as though seeing beyond the confines of his hospital bed. "I doubt Fang made the devices he planned on selling. Wouldn't want to get his hands dirty, even if he could. Which means he used someone to assemble them for him. We need to find out who did the work and if they have more. And we need to find out what's going on inside the walls of that big-ass estate of his."

Jack smiled to himself. His thoughts exactly. It felt reassuring to know the detective's brain functioned just fine in spite of a very close call.

He said, "The white-collar detectives who did the work-up on Fang's financials should be able to provide a list of people who might want to take over where he left off. Also, you told me Keala and Donohue are solid. After what happened this morning, there is plenty of probable cause to get a search warrant for the residence and seize whatever evidence is found there."

Tokunaga's gaze fixed on the ceiling. "We still have to worry that Fang's people at the house will be tipped off that the detectives are coming."

"I have an idea about that, too." Jack checked his watch. "Is there any way Keala and Donohue can get a search warrant tonight?"

Tokunaga's attention refocused on him. "They can go to the judge who gave us the warrant for the helicopter. What is it you have in mind?"

He grinned. "A way to smoke out your leak."

"Let's hear it."

"Talk to Keala and Donohue but don't tell them we suspect Sergeant Liu has been leaking information. They look up to you. Advise them to get a warrant for Fang's house and be ready to serve it first thing in the morning, and instruct them to make sure Sergeant Liu knows what they have planned. I'll keep an eye on the house and see what shakes out."

"A mighty big gamble."

Jack nodded. "With nothing to lose."

CHAPTER 78

The sun had gone down by the time Jack parked at Robert's house. The lights were on inside. He walked around to the lanai in back and found his buddy stretched out on a lounge drinking a beer. Rebel and Swagger lay sacked out next to each other on the tiled deck under the chaise. Neither animal bothered to lift their head.

A good sign the cat had settled into his new home.

Robert raised his bottle. "Care for one?"

Jack shook his head. "Not tonight. Where is Kazuko?"

"She helped me hose down the deck of your boat, and crashed early."

"And you didn't join her?"

"Too wound up, I guess."

"Makes two of us."

"It's not like you to pass up a free beer. I assume all went well in the meeting with your boss?"

"I told her we still have a shark problem and she agreed. Then I stopped at the hospital and talked with Tokunaga. I think finding out Li Fang died a horrible death cheered him up."

"He hadn't heard?"

"You sound surprised."

"Weren't you?"

"Totally. I couldn't believe someone from the department hadn't called to give him the news. Especially his sergeant. But nobody had."

"What did Tokunaga think?"

"He basically shrugged it off."

"Sure you don't want a beer?"

"Positive. But I will help myself to a cup of coffee here in a minute. Remember me saying there had to be a leak in his department? We talked about that too, and a plan on how to expose the mole."

"Who do you think it is?"

"His sergeant, Edward Liu."

"Any particular reason?"

"Mainly my gut. If things go the way I hope, I'll find out tonight."

That made Robert sit up, his legs and feet over the sides of the chaise. "Really? What do you have planned?"

Jack took a minute to explain.

Robert gave his head a slow shake. "I would have thought you had enough excitement for one day."

Jack did not feel he had a choice in the matter. He had to play the hand he had been dealt. "Not until I see this through."

Robert set his bottle aside and got up. "Then count me in. I won't let you do this alone."

Jack shook his head. "Sorry, bud. Not this time. Kazuko would skin me alive."

"What in the hell do you mean?"

"I mean I won't endanger anyone else. You two came close to buying it out there today. Too dammed close for my liking."

"You did too, more so than us."

"I was at Hell's door when you pulled me out of the water, no doubt about it. But it's my life I'm risking. I'll not endanger yours. Not anymore...at least today. But I would like to borrow your camera and night lens. While you're at it, let me borrow that .38 Chief's Special you keep in your desk."

"Ah, here we go again. I supply the equipment and you run off to have all the fun."

"What fun?"

* * *

Jack drove past Li Fang's estate an hour later dressed in a deep blue t-shirt, black cargo pants with extra-large Velcro pockets, and dark canvas deck shoes. Through gaps in the gate, he saw the lights were on, both in the house and on the grounds.

A lot of lights.

He made another pass, parked in a darkened area on the side of the road a hundred yards away from the gate, and watched. Ten minutes later, he got a call on the burner phone he'd purchased on his way to Robert's house. Only two people had the number.

He tapped on. "This is Jack."

Tokunaga's voice came across in a whisper. "The bait has been set. Keala and Donohue will serve the warrant at eight o'clock in the morning."

"Thanks, Brian. I'm at the house now. I'll be in touch."

He disconnected the call, and for a moment he sat in his seat feeling uneasy. The plan was a gamble. But it had to work. Otherwise, he and Tokunaga might lose their best chance to find out if he was right about Sergeant Liu.

The compound was right there, he told himself.

You're wasting time.

He grabbed the camera off the seat next to him and got out. The corner where the north and east rock walls connected loomed in shadow thirty yards away. Areca palms swayed above the rockwork in a perfect blind spot to avoid possible detection by camera surveillance. He jogged the ninety feet, climbed the rough stone, and dropped into a dark shadow on the other side.

When he and Tokunaga were at the residence to serve the search warrant on the chopper, he couldn't see this end of the property. Which he now saw held a tennis court. A dozen yards beyond it sat a small building—guest quarters or perhaps housing for the help. The windows were dark, no sounds of lovemaking or snoring or movement of any kind could be heard, which he took to mean the place was unoccupied at the moment.

Guard dogs remained a real threat.

He kept to a crouch and moved along the plantings to the far end of the building. Peering through gaps in the leaves of a heliconia, he could see the glow of the lights in and around the main house. A lone sentry stood outside the front entrance a hundred and fifty feet away.

A white BMW sedan sat at the end of the drive.

Through the telephoto lens, he had a clearer view of the man—unmistakably Asian—and saw some sort of submachine pistol supported by a sling hanging over his right shoulder.

He panned to the car. A new BMW M5 super-sedan. Expensive.

He snapped a couple of pictures and turned his attention on the house.

Movement on the other side of a second-floor window caught his eye. A back-lit shadow, nothing more. Sheer curtains made identification impossible.

He took a photo.

The guard out front presented a problem, but not at the moment. And certainly, Jack thought, not from his hiding spot behind the heliconia. He decided it was as good a spot as any to wait.

Which didn't turn out to be that long.

He had sat on his heels for ten minutes when he saw headlights appear in the driveway.

The gate had obviously been opened from inside the residence.

But no golf cart this time. And certainly no Yong Fang.

Robert had seen to that.

Now came the moment of truth.

Had his gamble paid off? Or was it another dead end?

He found himself holding his breath.

CHAPTER 79

The visitor's arrival had clearly been expected. Perhaps that explained the absence of a mean-tempered guard dog roaming the grounds.

Jack let himself breathe.

Show yourself, asshole.

He backed into the shadow of the heliconia and waited for the headlights to pass. As soon as the vehicle rolled by, he eased out and snapped two photos of a black Charger with dark-tinted side windows, and one of the rear license plate.

He'd seen the car before at Devlin Maxwell's house.

Or one like it. New additions to the police fleet.

In a few seconds he would find out if his hunch had been correct.

He peered through the lens of the camera, his left eye squeezed shut like a sniper sighting through a rifle scope, and followed the Charger until it stopped at the front of the house. The driver exited the vehicle with his back turned. He wore a flowered aloha shirt and khaki pants. At this distance, and with the man's back to him, Jack couldn't tell if this was the same man he had seen at Maxwell's residence or not.

Turn around asshole.

He snapped a photo anyway.

The guard stepped out and greeted the unidentified driver. They talked a moment and the guard motioned the man inside.

Jack snapped a photo of the driver's profile but he needed a closer look.

He had two choices—one being marginally better than the other. He could wait for the mystery man to leave, or take his chances crossing the well-lit driveway in a hundred feet of open space.

Every second was a second closer to being discovered.

A risk he didn't want to take.

Not knowing how long the mole would be inside, he selected a dimly lit area halfway between the lights at the main house and those shining down on the front gate.

A straight dash to the plantings on the other side.

His best chance.

As he saw it, there were two ways this could turn out. One, he would be riddled with a magazine full of 9mm bullets. The other, he would make the sprint across the drive undetected. No in-between.

Timing was everything.

He picked his spot and tensed his muscles for the moment when the guard had his attention focused elsewhere.

That opportunity came a minute later when he noticed the flare of a cigarette lighter in the guard's hand and saw him walk in the direction of the beach access gate at the rear of the property.

Jack knew where it led. There would be the sound of breaking surf coming from the other side providing even more distraction.

Perfect.

He bent low at the waist and made a run for a cluster of plantings at the corner of the house nearest to him. Peering over the top of a split-leaf philodendron, he saw the guard turn and head back. A slow walk with the cherry on the end of the cigarette glowing reddish orange with each draw he took.

Jack melted into the bush.

The guard continued on to the front gate before crushing out the cigarette butt with his shoe and heading back to his post at the front door. Three- or four-minutes tops. A lifetime on Jack's nerves.

But he hadn't been seen.

His destination was an arched ground-floor lanai between him and the guard. A muted light seeping through a set of curtained

French doors leading into a room at the far end left the patio bathed in shadow. Directly above it sat the second-floor lanai, where Li Fang had stood when he stared down at him and Tokunaga. Beyond that, the window where he had seen movement on the other side of the curtains.

He scanned the grounds, half-expecting to see one of Fang's thugs pointing an automatic weapon at him.

Machine guns…

The .38 caliber model 36 Smith and Wesson concealed in his pants pocket seemed pitifully inadequate. Two-inch barrel, five shots in the cylinder, with lady-sized rounded, walnut grips.

A snub-nosed belly gun.

He missed his .45 caliber 1911, but the ocean wouldn't be giving that up anytime soon.

A shadow signaled movement in the room at the end of the lanai in front of him. Ten feet lay between him and the dimly lit alcove. Three long strides. His opportunity came when the guard turned his attention away from him. Moving fast, he bounded over a raised planter lush with flowers and melted into the darkness beyond.

Keeping down, he crept to the French doors and listened to muted talking.

He put his eye to a gap in the curtains and peeked inside. A hospital bed sat directly in front of him six to eight feet away. The foot of the bed faced the door. The driver of the Charger stood next to it with his back turned. The head of the bed had been cranked up. The elderly man lying in it looked Asian.

They were engaged in a conversation, the guy in the garish aloha shirt doing most of the talking in English. At times, lifting his palms as though pleading a point he was making.

Jack raised the camera, adjusted the lens, and snapped a photo.

A pretty, thirty-something Asian woman stepped into the frame and joined in the conversation.

The elder Asian listened and said nothing.

Jack kept the camera pointed.

Aloha shirt turned to the woman and snapped verbal outrage at her.

Jack snapped a photo.

Donohue….

CHAPTER 80

Jack crouched in shock that he had so misjudged Sergeant Liu.

All the markers were there, or so he'd thought.

He wanted to hear what was being said inside the room, but felt he had spent too much time at the window already. And even though he hadn't gotten all the evidence he would have liked, he had the photos of Donohue and that would be enough.

Time to go.

He mentally retraced the route he had taken to get to the spot by the door. The plantings at the corner of the main house, a dash across a hundred feet of open space to the corner of the guest quarters. Another sprint along the backside and over the wall next to the Areca palms in the far corner of the compound.

Easy enough, provided he remained unseen.

Or he could make a run for the front wall with the house between him and the guard at the front door.

Either way he had to make it to the split-leaf, twenty or so feet in shadow and three long strides in the open.

He crept to the opposite end of the lanai, picked his opportunity, and bounded over the planter and back to the philodendron. Concealed in the darkness beneath the plant's broad leaves, he studied the front wall no more than fifty feet away.

A better choice.

His plan changed when he heard a guttural snarl. Blood-chilling in the dark of night. So close he expected to turn his head and be eye-to-eye with the animal. But to his relief, the Doberman stood ten feet away, straining at the end of its leash, baring his teeth in a vicious fit of frenzied barking. There had been a watch dog after all, and a second guard, apparently patrolling the south end of the grounds.

The sentry wore a holstered sidearm but he made no move to draw it. Instead, both hands were on the leash. The man's smirk suggested a sick enjoyment of watching the beast tear into someone.

Jack had no intention of letting that happen.

The barking had sounded the alarm. There was no doubt about that. The guard with the machine gun would be running to do his part.

Game over.

Jack's choices flashed through his mind with no more than a millisecond of thought. Pulling the short-barreled .38 and shooting the murderous creature would only waste precious seconds, with no guarantee he could draw the gun in time or that the bullet would stop the crazed animal before it sunk its teeth into his flesh. The other option: run and not look back.

The gamble seemed worth it.

He sprinted toward the wall.

He'd always considered himself a fast runner.

The dog was faster.

When he realized he would never make it, he turned.

The black shape launched at his throat.

Jack got his hands up, and with no idea how he managed it, he grabbed the dog by its outstretched forearms as the animal was about to sink his teeth into him, and stumbled backward. Combining the Doberman's forward momentum and his rearward movement, he heaved as hard as he could. A second later he heard a meaty thud as the killer slammed into the wall.

There was no time to examine the animal, or care how badly it was hurt. Only to know that his quick reaction to the charging beast saved his life.

But he needed to move.

Powered by a surge of adrenalin, he scaled the stones and

jumped down on the opposite side a split-second before a bullet pinged off the rock above his head. He managed to land on his feet but lost his balance and fell forward onto his hands and knees. The camera he had slung around his neck slammed into the sand.

He got his feet under him and took off on a dead run for his Jeep.

It began to rain. And when it rains in Hawaii, it pours.

Usain Bolt from Jamaica held the world record for the one-hundred-meter dash. Nine-point-five-eight seconds. Jack figured he had that beat.

Only Usain Bolt didn't have someone shooting at him.

There had only been the one shot, but that had been enough.

Jack gripped the camera in his left hand and the keys to his Jeep in the other. Pointing the key fob, he unlocked the driver's door on the run with twenty feet to go. After skidding to a stop, he jerked the door open, tossed the camera onto the passenger seat, and jumped in soaking wet. Fumbling the key in the ignition took another couple of seconds.

Fuck...

The engine started on the first crank. He jammed the transmission in reverse, made a K-turn and sped away northbound toward Kaneohe Bay.

No other shots had been fired. He guessed their desire to avoid drawing attention from the other residents in the area had something to do with that. Possibly even Donohue's presence at the house, and not wanting to attract the police.

The last thing the detective would want.

He checked the rearview mirror and saw a vehicle's headlights exiting the estate. What he expected. But the car turned southward, which came as no real surprise. It was the quickest way for someone in a hurry to get to town.

Donohue's attempt to cover his butt.

The only explanation that made sense.

Not going to work, asshole.

Jack switched on his headlights and dug the burner phone from his pocket.

Now maybe I'll be able to sleep.

He placed a call to Tokunaga.

CHAPTER 81

Jack fell into bed on his boat knowing all hell was about to break loose. Tokunaga, it turned out, had been equally surprised to discover they had been wrong about Sergeant Liu. And even more surprised he had been duped by Detective Donohue.

Tokunaga insisted he, alone, had to take the hit on that.

Jack tried to dispute the issue but couldn't.

The point was immaterial.

Tokunaga viewed the photos, seized the SD card from the camera, and said he would make sure they got to the right person.

Jack had a feeling that by the time the dust settled, Tokunaga wouldn't be the only one feeling foolish about Donohue.

The detective's parting words to him had been to not worry.

Easy to say.

Jack closed his eyes, confident he had done all he could to fulfill his obligation and, more importantly, his promise to Megan O'Connell.

And the innocent lives he'd saved.

* * *

At eight o'clock the next morning, Jack walked into HPD headquarters in downtown Honolulu. Five minutes later, he took a seat in a straight-backed chair across from two Internal Affairs investigators: a stone-faced man named Edward Tanaka; and a humorless woman named Sarah Bowman—both in their late thirties.

Enlargements of the photos he had taken the night before were spread out on the tabletop between him and the officers. He scanned the pictures and said nothing. This was their show. He'd leave it up to them to begin the interview.

"Doctor Ferrell," Tanaka said. "We'd like you to start at the beginning and tell us everything that has happened."

Jack eyed the stack of documents sitting in front of the investigator. "From the beginning? Is that really necessary? Can't you read Tokunaga's reports and jump to last night?"

"You have to understand it's our job to find out when and how Detective Donohue got involved with Li Fang."

Jack was in no mood to play. "It's my understanding Donohue is in custody and no longer a detective for your department."

"True. We arrested him last night. Now please tell us what happened…from the beginning, if you would."

Jack looked at the deadpan expression on Bowman's face. She appeared content to let Tanaka ask the questions. Not that it mattered who took the lead. The interview wasn't supposed to be a good-cop, bad-cop confrontation and there was no reason for him to give them any reason to think he had done something wrong.

Unless they'd already decided he had.

"I'll make you both a deal," he said to Tanaka. "I'm not trying to derail your investigation in any way, but I'd rather not rehash everything that is written in those reports. So go ahead and ask specific questions you want answered and I will decide whether or not I'll answer them."

Tanaka gave it a moment. "Truthfully?"

"To the best of my ability. Providing, that is, you don't consider me a suspect in some heinous crime I'm not aware of. If that's the case, you can get my attorney in here right now and talk to her."

"No tricks." This time, humorless Bowman spoke up. "We all want the same thing. Donohue is in custody and we want the charges against him to stick."

Jack couldn't disagree, but there was more to his reason for wanting to keep the interview brief.

Way more.

He said, "Mostly I want to put this all behind me and take my boat on a nice, long, leisurely cruise."

Bowman cracked a smile for the first time. "How about we start with what happened last night, and then we'll go from there."

It turned out they didn't have a lot of questions. He answered the ones they did have and walked out of the department not more than an hour after first sitting down.

He had a phone call and two more stops to make.

Standing in the shade of a kukui nut tree, he used his burner phone and placed a call to Robert. The pavement on the street in front of him glistened with the prior night's rain. The sky had been scrubbed clean.

A new day.

"I'm out of there," he said when Robert answered. "How is Kazuko? Did she talk to Kiana and Jeffrey?"

"Kazuko is fine. I'm treating her to a late breakfast. She told Kiana it would be best if she returned to the mainland to start over. Jeffrey got off with a stern warning to never let something like that happen again."

"Hopefully, she learned her lesson. Jeffrey, too."

"Kazuko and I are in agreement on that. Where are you off to?"

"I'm going to drop by the hospital and talk to Detective Tokunaga. When I'm done there, Meg wants to meet with me."

"Try to stay out of trouble."

Jack had his fill of trouble. "I'll see you back at the house."

He let the events of the past week roll through his mind while he drove the few short blocks to the hospital. His thoughts didn't stop there. Tucked into those memories were faces he recognized. A stream of them. The beautiful women he had known. Men he had killed. Mistakes he had made.

Blunders he could not undo.

There was no way he would try to kid himself that they would be his last, but he could do his best to not let them happen again.

And he would.

He took advantage of valet parking and hurried past the gift shop without glancing inside and up the stairs to the third floor. He entered Tokunaga's room and found the detective awake, with his back propped up against the pillow, the light on, and a novel open in front of him. Color had returned to his face.

Jack passed on sitting down. "Where is your wife?"

"Stepped out for a while. She'll be back soon enough, I suspect. How'd things go with Tanaka and Bowman?"

Jack thought he detected a smirk. "We reached an understanding. You heard they arrested Donohue?"

"Tanaka called and told me. Apparently, Donohue is talking." Tokunaga set the book aside. "Think you will be able to put this case to rest now?"

"It's all yours, Detective."

"Technically, it's the departments. I won't be doing any case work for a month or two." Tokunaga let a smile creep in. "You did a good job, you know that?"

Jack smiled back. "A lot of it was pure luck. And you were right there in the middle of it with me."

"Until I ended up here. Can't even wipe my own ass."

"Maybe so, but you never stopped doing your part. Even laid up in bed. Not many men would do that."

"It all worked out. That's what's important."

Jack felt finality in the detective's words. The world was back in order…at least for the time being. In a matter of weeks, Tokunaga would be back to his old self. A reassuring thought.

One Jack would take with him.

He said, "On that note. I need to get going. I have a meeting with my boss."

"Best not keep her waiting."

Jack started to leave and stopped. He met the detective's gaze and held it. He was sure there was more he should probably say to this man, but was it necessary? Some things between two friends don't need to be said.

He gave a slight nod. "Brian, take care of yourself."

With that, he turned and walked out. A lot of questions remained, but Li Fang's house of cards had begun to tumble. The answers would come with its collapse.

Some of them no longer seemed that important.

Perhaps in time that would change.

He descended the stairs feeling rejuvenated. And this time he drove to Ford Island thinking about his future.

For now, it was here.

Megan O'Connell stood when he walked into her office.

"I'm glad you're here. I just got off the phone with the mayor. She talked to the police chief. Apparently, detectives recovered several of those damn devices. They think they got them all. The schematic, too."

To hear her swear took him aback. Even the use of a word as mundane as *damn* was unusual for her.

"I hadn't heard," he said. "If that's the case, we can all relax."

"She mentioned nominating you for the Meritorious Civilian Service Award. I told her I felt you deserved it."

Jack helped himself to a cup of coffee. He hated the thought of a dog and pony show with Mayor Kobayashi.

"Knowing we can put this problem behind us is enough reward."

"You're too modest, Jack."

He grinned. "For my own good?"

She let the comment go. "What are your plans? Back to your research in the Philippine Sea? I think a first-class ticket is in order this time."

He sipped his coffee; lukewarm again. "Good question. That's certainly a nice offer."

She stepped around her desk and extended her hand. "I can't tell you how much I appreciate everything you did."

He reached to take her hand, and she put her arms around him instead. The first time she had given him a hug.

Ever.

Better than any award he could receive.

When it seemed she was ready, she eased out of his arms.

"Glad I could help," he said.

She smiled. "Get some rest."

CHAPTER 82

Jack stopped at Cindy's desk on his way out of the building and pecked her on the cheek. She reddened, and raised her fingertips to the side of her face.

"One of these days," he said, "we'll make that dinner date."

The red faded from her cheeks. "Promise?"

He winked, and after a moment, "The flower looks nice."

"You're leaving?" she asked; a hint of crimson returned to her cheeks.

He smiled, knowing they'd both miss the game. But they would see each other again, he could just about guarantee it, and he just might buy her that dinner.

An evening shared by two friends.

"Until next time," he said.

She stood and looked at him. "Take care of yourself, Jack."

Her eyes betrayed genuine concern when he turned to leave.

He pushed through the exit door and raised his face to a bright, blue sky and took a breath of warm air. The palm trees swayed lazily in the breeze, and he realized what he had found in the islands. It was the kind of day he could build a future on.

"Headed somewhere, sailor?"

He lowered his gaze and saw Cherise standing at the bottom of the steps, leaning against the hand railing. He grinned like a fool.

"I have research work to finish up in the Philippine Sea."

"Sounds interesting." Her brow arched. "No hunt for rare and unusual treasure this time?"

"There's always riches to be found," he said. "It's just a matter of recognizing them for what they are when you find them. I found wealth beyond any I could have imagined in the unique privilege of having been allowed a close-up view of the remains of the WWII cruiser *USS Indianapolis* resting in peace in perpetual darkness three and a half miles beneath the surface of the ocean."

"I take it Admiral Casey came through for you?"

"More than I could have envisioned."

"Not surprising. So, when you wrap up your research in the Philippine Sea, what's your next grand adventure?"

"Good question. At the moment, I'm thinking a leisurely cruise to Tahiti on *Pono II* sounds good."

She smiled up at him, her stare soft and pensive. "Want some company?"

The eyes. Always the eyes.

"Love some."

*

AUTHOR'S DISCLAIMER

Deadly Tide contains the actual names of people and places. The same is true for certain businesses and bars frequented by Jack Ferrell and other characters in the story. In all other respects, this novel is a work of fiction. Names (unless used by permission), characters, places, and incidents in the story are either the product of the author's imagination or are used fictitiously. Any resemblance to actual persons, events, or locals is unintentional and coincidental.

ABOUT THE AUTHOR

William Nikkel is the author of ten *Jack Ferrell* novels and two steampunk westerns featuring his latest hero Max Traver. A former homicide detective and S.W.A.T. team member for the Kern County Sheriff's Department in Bakersfield, California, William is an amateur scuba enthusiast, gold prospector, and wildlife artist who can be found just about anywhere. He and his wife Karen divide their time between Northern California and Maui, Hawaii.

www.williamnikkel.com

Lightning Source UK Ltd.
Milton Keynes UK
UKHW020627250821
389444UK00012B/811